little black dress

· IT'S A GI...

Dear Little Black Dress Reader,

Thanks for picking up this Little Black Dress book, one of the great new titles from our series of fun, page-turning romance novels. Lucky you – you're about to have a fantastic romantic read that we know you won't be able to put down!

Why don't you make your Little Black Dress experience even better by logging on to

www.littleblackdressbooks.com

where you can:

Enter our **monthly competitions** to win **gorgeous** prizes

Get **hot-off-the-press** news about our latest titles

Read **exclusive** preview chapters both from your **favourite** authors and from brilliant new writing talent

Buy **up-and-coming** books online

Sign up for an essential slice of romance via our **fortnightly email** newsletter

We love nothing more than to curl up and indulge in an addictive romance, and so we're delighted to welcome you into the Little Black Dress club!

With love from,

The *little black dress* team

Five interesting things about Jessica Fox:

1. I can't resist stopping to look at newly married couples emerging from churches.

2. My palm-reader told me I have a lifeline that is shorter than my heart line. I assume this means I will be with my husband Rob in this life and the next. I just hope he will have learned to pick up his socks by then.

3. I have a phobia of elevators. On our honeymoon, the Eiffel Tower was definitely worth it. Until I realised I'd left my camera at the top.

4. I was once on a hen night where the groom appeared in the early hours and started chatting me up!

5. If my house was on fire, and I could only rescue one thing, it would be my antique tarot cards. Sorry, Rob.

By Jessica Fox

The Hen Night Prophecies: The One That Got Away
The Hen Night Prophecies: Eastern Promise

The
Hen Night Prophecies:
Eastern Promise

Jessica Fox

little
black
dress

First published in 2009 by
LITTLE BLACK DRESS
An imprint of HEADLINE PUBLISHING GROUP

A LITTLE BLACK DRESS paperback

1

Cataloguing in Publication Data is available from the British Library

ISBN 978 0 7553 4958 6

Typeset in Transit511BT by Avon DataSet Ltd,
Bidford-on-Avon, Warwickshire

Printed and bound in Great Britain by
Clays Ltd, St Ives plc

Acknowledgements

With special thanks to Ruth Saberton

Priya Gupta didn't believe in Fate or destiny or soulmates.

Definitely not!

At school, while the other girls sobbed their way through the final scenes of *Romeo and Juliet*, Priya had simply made neat notes in the margin of her set text and wrinkled her nose with scorn. Star-crossed lovers? Fortune written in the heavens? What a load of old nonsense! Everyone knew that the only luck was the luck you made yourself and the only way to shape your future was to go out and grab it with both hands. Sitting and waiting for things to happen to you was just ridiculous! If Priya's grandfather had thought that way the Guptas would still be living in the Punjab eking a living from the land and her father would never have become a respected academic. So when her classmates had crowded round the latest copy of *Just 17* clamouring to hear their stars Priya had simply ignored them and buried her nose in her text books. She didn't need Mystic Meg to tell her that if she studied hard she'd pass her exams with flying colours and win her longed-for place at Oxford.

No, as far as Priya was concerned the only future was the future you made yourself. Anything else was just nonsense, a way of getting the gullible to part with their cash, which was why she couldn't understand why the other girls at her friend Zoe's hen night were all so excited at the idea of having their fortunes told. Personally Priya hated the idea of Fate; she much preferred surprises and choices. She also hated superstition and spooky stuff, preferring to anchor herself with facts and figures. Some people might have described Priya as a control freak but that, as far as she was concerned, was their problem. She preferred the description *well organised*.

Priya hadn't needed psychic skills to know she'd graduate from Magdalen with a first class degree. Just like she knew getting her job at the BBC was the result of her hard work and planning rather than some vague celestial design. She'd ignored all the voices saying it was impossible for a woman, especially a young British Asian woman, to succeed as a journalist and document-ary maker, knowing hard work and a good dollop of talent were all it took and that she had plenty to offer of both. If she'd believed for a second that Fate existed and her path was already mapped out she'd have given in, concentrated instead on the law degree that her parents had set their hearts on, and not have had a shelf crammed with awards for her documentaries.

No, Priya Gupta was living proof that people made their own futures. Fate, fortune and psychics with crystal balls were only there to hoodwink the credulous and make money. There was no such thing as Fate. She'd proved that already.

'It's all a con anyway,' she said firmly as Zoe's sister, Libby, sloshed more Chardonnay into her glass. 'Honestly, girls, I bet I'm as psychic as she is.'

'She's supposed to be really good,' said Libby, busily topping up more glasses. 'That's why I booked her. My friend, Rachel, had a reading last week and apparently this woman knew everything about her. Rachel said it was incredible.'

'It's called cold reading,' said Priya, tossing her razor-sharp bob and raising her neat eyebrows. 'One of my colleagues did a documentary about psychics and apparently they all do it. They analyse body language and clothing and then make really vague comments which could apply to anyone. It's all total hokum but it really convinces a lot of people.'

'God, it must be hard work being so cynical,' sighed Libby.

Priya wasn't cynical, she just liked to get to the bottom of things and ensure that the truth was told – qualities that made her remarkably successful as a documentary maker – but she understood that, to Libby, she must seem like a real killjoy.

'I'm realistic, that's all,' she shrugged. 'Maybe it's the journalist in me.'

'Well, put your journalistic instincts into gear now,' said Fern, a small slim college friend of Zoe's, whose merry, freckled face and tumbling golden curls made her look like a blonde imp. 'It's your turn.'

Sure enough Zoe was stumbling into the room, looking rather perturbed.

'Oh no, did she get it all wrong?' wailed Libby.

Zoe sank into a chair and curled her slender hands

around her wine glass. 'Actually she was spookily accurate about most things. I've never known anything like it.'

'See!' Libby cried, turning triumphantly to Priya. 'I told you she was good. Now it's your turn. Try to have an open mind.'

'I do have an open mind!' Priya protested, setting down her glass and tucking her dark hair behind her ears. 'I'm just a bit sceptical about psychic stuff, that's all.'

But, as she left the cosy sitting room, where the other hens were settling back down to the serious business of emptying wine bottles as fast as possible, Priya felt a little tingle of anticipation run down her spine. Was it her or did Zoe's kitchen suddenly feel cooler than usual? And was the atmosphere really super-still, as though unseen ears were straining to hear what might be said?

'For God's sake!' she said sternly to herself. 'You're being ridiculous! You don't even believe in this stuff, remember?'

So why did it feel as though a school of piranha fish were chomping away in her stomach? She couldn't be nervous at the idea of seeing some phoney psychic? It was only a bit of a giggle for the hen night. With the exception of Zoe's gloomy future sister-in-law, all the other girls were up for it.

Maybe working so hard lately has robbed me of what remained of my sense of humour, thought Priya. Not that she'd felt like laughing much lately, not since Vikram had—

Stop right there!

She shook her head as though shaking away all thoughts of Vik. She wasn't going to think about him right now or at all if she could help it. He was best left in the past, or as much in the past as he could be seeing as he was still her boss. Priya didn't need this psychic to foresee that having to take orders from her ex wouldn't make for happy working relations. To say that things were strained between them was putting it mildly.

Priya paused at the heavy curtains that divided Zoe's restored Victorian conservatory from the kitchen. Her mouth was dry. This was ridiculous! She *never* got nervous of the dark. As a kid she used to lie in bed with the curtains open and fix her eyes on the blackness of the world outside. The dark didn't frighten her the way it did her sister Neeshali. Instead Priya had longed to leap into it and find out what lay beyond. She wasn't any different now. Her documentary on immigration had won three awards and the one about people trafficking had earned a BAFTA nomination; gruelling topics that had kept her awake at night long after the film was in the can, so why was she feeling so on edge about seeing this so-called psychic?

It wasn't as if any of it was true.

So, not wanting to be a party pooper, Priya took a deep breath and stepped forward through the curtains. She just wanted this ordeal to be over as quickly as possible.

'Hello, love. I'm Angela.' A woman seated at the table beamed up at her. With her greying curls, sweater and slacks she would have looked like an ordinary mum if it hadn't been for the crystal ball and tarot deck laid out before her. 'You must be Priya? Come and sit down and we'll begin.'

Priya took the Lloyd Loom chair set opposite Angela and folded her hands into her lap. There was no way she was going to give anything away, like a lack of engagement ring for example.

'My, you're a beautiful girl,' said Angela, with a gentle smile.

Priya mentally rolled her eyes. So Angela was going to go down the flattery route, was she? 'Thanks, but I think you'll find the dim light helps.'

The fact was that Priya was exceptionally pretty, with perfect *café au lait* skin, shoulder-length glossy black hair, high cheekbones and, most unusually for an Asian girl, eyes of hazel flecked with green. But Priya came from a background where family honour was prized far more highly than looks and worked in a male-dominated world where appearing feminine set her at a distinct disadvantage. So most of the time she just pinned her hair up, disguised her curves with well-cut suits and hid her eyes behind brainy-looking plain-glass specs. Beauty wasn't an attribute she'd ever associated with herself.

Angela shook her head. 'There's nothing wrong with being beautiful, Priya. Now, my love, you often distrust people because you feel they keep secrets, don't you?'

Here we go, thought Priya. She'll wait to see if I agree and then she'll pick up on it.

'But never mind that now,' continued Angela. 'Taking things at face value and trusting people is not a lesson that I can teach you.' She looked at Priya through thoughtful eyes. 'In fact, lovey, I don't think there's a lot anyone can teach you. You're a young woman who likes to find things out for herself, aren't you?'

'Mmm,' said Priya.

Angela sighed. 'Sweetheart, I can sense you've closed your mind to anything I might say tonight. But would you do me a favour? Just listen to what I tell you and think about it. Sometimes what Spirit tells me makes more sense later on.'

'Okay,' Priya agreed. Whatever. The sooner this was over the sooner she could get another drink.

Angela pushed her tarot cards aside and peered deeply into the crystal ball. It was opaque and milky, the glass appearing to glow in the reflected lamplight. In spite of herself Priya felt a prickle of unease.

'You work too hard,' Angela said, her eyes not leaving the crystal ball, 'but I can see that's the way you like it. It's how you define yourself. And you're successful, too.' Then she frowned. 'There's someone at work who's upset you, isn't there?'

That's a lucky guess, thought Priya. There was no way that Angela could possibly know about Vik and what he'd done. Only one person knew, her friend and colleague Ray, and she'd sworn him to secrecy.

'Your love life is a bit quiet, isn't it, my love, after a bit of a roller coaster? He really let you down, didn't he? And now, well, now you think there's no time for love.'

'I'm busy,' said Priya quickly. And I've also got my mum and three aunties on my back about finding a good Hindu boy, she added silently. Thank God that Neesh had recently got engaged and taken the heat off her for a bit. If Priya had discovered any more eligible young Indian guys 'accidentally' turning up at the Gupta family home she thought she'd scream. Her mother couldn't have been any more obvious if she'd walked round Kingston-on-Thames wearing a sandwich board declaring *I have a single daughter in her late twenties (the shame!). Please marry her!*

Angela smiled. 'I'm sure you are, love, but some things are more important than work and sometimes work is a way of hiding from what's really important.'

Priya snorted. Angela sounded just like her mum. *Chi, chi, Priya! This work is all very well but will it find you a husband, hmm?*

But Angela was serious. 'Please take notice of what I'm saying, sweetheart. My guides have a message for you and they're insisting that I pass it on.'

Suddenly the atmosphere seemed to grow heavy and Priya found she was holding her breath. It was easy to scoff at psychic stuff in broad daylight, but now that the shadows seemed to be closing in and the darkness pressing against the glass roof Priya wasn't so certain.

'What is it?' she whispered. 'What do you see?'

The psychic ripped her gaze from the crystal ball. Was it Priya's imagination or were her pupils suddenly darker than the night sky? 'My guides want you to know this, and they're telling you to heed it well: *in matters of love, mother knows best.*'

'What?' Priya stared at her in disbelief. 'That's it? That's my important message?'

'So it would seem, love.' Abruptly, Angela appeared to sag and her face looked haggard. 'That's it. There's nothing more, I'm afraid. I can't see anything else.'

'In matters of love, mother knows best?' Priya

echoed. 'You clearly never met my mother.' She shook her head, furious with herself for being suckered in even for a minute. How easy had she been for Angela to cold read? Take one young unmarried Asian girl, add a few cultural stereotypes and bingo! The pushy Asian mother desperate to marry off her daughter scenario. The fact that in her case this just happened to be true was totally irrelevant. Angela had just made a lucky guess.

Mother knows best, thought Priya as she headed back through the kitchen, pausing at the fridge to collect a well-deserved bottle of wine, I don't think so! As far as she was concerned that reading just confirmed all her worst suspicions about the unscrupulous ways of so-called psychics.

Besides, her mother had adored Vik, which just showed how much she really knew about matters of love!

No, Priya decided firmly as she rejoined the hens, Angela's spirit guides could take a hike. In matters of love *she* knew best, which was just the way she liked it.

And that was the way it was going to stay.

One month later
July 2009

'No! No! No!'

Priya shot across the sitting room in a blur of crimson silk and glittery slippers and just managed to bar the way in the nick of time. One second later and Steve would have trampled his size tens right across her brand-new cream rug. Unthinkable!

'Sorry, Steve,' she said breathlessly, 'but would you mind leaving your shoes at the front door? It's just that the carpets are really delicate and—'

'And she doesn't want your dirty great clodhoppers wrecking them,' finished Zoe as she dropped a kiss on Priya's cheek and shooed her new husband back towards the front door. 'Honestly, Priya, and there was I thinking he was nearly house trained. Will I do, though?' She held up one elegant stockinged foot and rotated it slowly. 'Or should I wrap my feet in giant fluffy slippers as well?'

Priya laughed. 'Am I really that much of a nightmare neat freak?'

'The worst,' said Steve, rejoining them, minus Timberlands and sporting a fetching pair of Bart Simpson socks. 'But we love you anyway,' he added, pressing a bottle of Chardonnay into her hands. 'Thanks for inviting us to the housewarming. We'll try hard not to wreck the joint, won't we, Zo?'

Zoe punched him playfully on the arm before turning back to Priya. 'This place looks absolutely amazing. I can't believe it's the same flat. You've worked wonders.'

Priya followed Zoe's gaze around the flat and felt a warm glow of pride. Finally, after weeks of living and breathing DIY and decorating, the apartment in Spitalfields looked exactly as she'd dreamed it would. Talk about a labour of love, though. When the estate agent had first shown her round Priya had almost turned tail and run away as fast as her boots could carry her. The estate agent's details had brimmed with breathless prose about how quirky, trendsetting and smart Spitalfields was and how this conversion was a prime investment opportunity. What they had failed to mention was that the converted warehouse had walls running with damp, plaster more pitted than teenaged skin, windows boarded up and floors strewn with chunks of masonry and rubbish. It had looked like a squat.

'Actually, I think it was,' the estate agent had said apologetically. 'But imagine the potential!'

'For what?' Priya had wondered, pulling her pashmina around her shoulders and shivering. 'Consumption? A head injury from falling plaster? Asbestosis?'

'But it's such a wonderful investment opportunity.'

So, five months later, as she looked around at her guests chatting in the minimalistic open plan space, all wood floors, glass walls and shiny chrome fittings, Priya felt very proud. She loved the funky fire bowl, the vast white leather sofas and the thick rugs that swallowed her feet right up to the ankles; relished coming home, flicking on the lamps and kicking back with a cold glass of wine. Her flat was uncluttered, ordered and pristine, which was just the way that she liked things to be.

But best of all, the flat was hers: bought and paid for by countless hours cloistered in dark rooms and edit suites or out filming with only Ray and his camera for company. It was Priya's space, with no squabbling siblings or bossy female family members to hassle her, and she loved every clean and tidy inch of it.

And if that made her a sad neat freak then she was guilty as charged.

'Thanks for your wedding present, by the way,' Steve was saying, his gentle tones plucking Priya away from thoughts of renovations and back to her party. 'I'm not sure what *I'm* supposed to do with a year's pass to The Sanctuary Ladies' Day Spa, though.'

Zoe laughed. 'That's Priya's clever way of buying you some time on the golf course without me moaning.'

'Then I'm very grateful,' Steve said, grinning at Priya. 'I can improve my handicap while my wife improves her body. Genius!'

'Hey, what do you mean *improves* her body?' Zoe echoed, pulling a face at Priya. 'This is what happens once you marry them, babes! They reveal their true colours. Remember that when it's your turn.'

'I think I'll leave the getting married stuff to my sister,' said Priya, who felt that she was more likely to visit Mars than to get married any time soon. As far as her aunts were concerned Priya was well and truly stuffed when it came to husband hunting. She was destined to sit on her shelf and gather dust – or as much dust as a girl who owned the latest turbo-charged Dyson could gather – and, after Vikram, it actually didn't feel like too bad an option to her. There was a lot to be said for the single life, like being able to eat garlicky food whenever you wanted and getting reacquainted with the remote control.

'Ignore my wife,' Steve said, winding his arms around Zoe and dropping his chin on to her blond head. 'She loves every minute of married life really.'

As Zoe and Steve shared a tender kiss Priya sighed wistfully. Perhaps her mother was right and she was being too picky? But surely a girl was entitled to be picky when it came to choosing the man she was going to spend the rest of her life with? It wasn't like going to DFS and choosing a sofa.

Although, thinking about it, most of the guys that her mother kept 'accidentally' inviting over for dinner certainly had the desperate whiff of the bargain bucket about them . . .

In matters of love, mother knows best. Yeah, right! If that phoney psychic had known that Priya's mum thought that moustached men who could double as draught excluders were suitable husband material she might have changed her tune. Besides, Priya thought, her mother hadn't a clue about relationships. 'Love comes with time' was her mother's motto, and it had been true in her experience. She and Priya's father had had an arranged marriage which had worked out beautifully, luckily for them, but privately Priya thought this was down to the fact that her father was probably the easiest going man on the planet. As long as Ashwani Gupta was left in peace to his studies he was happy for Divya to make all the decisions, an arrangement which suited them both perfectly but was down more to luck than to design.

Priya thanked God every day that there was no chance of her parents ever arranging a marriage for her. The thought of the bridegroom her mother would produce was too awful to contemplate. After all, she'd thought Vikram was perfect.

Saved by the bell from maudlin thoughts, Priya excused herself, and wove her way through her guests to answer the door. She immediately wished she hadn't because five feet six of trouble was standing on the doorstep.

Her sister Neesh had decided to join the party.

'About time!' shrilled Neesh, barging past her sister and dragging an apologetic Sanjeev in her wake. 'I thought you'd never answer! I'm bloody frozen out here.'

Even though it was midsummer Priya wasn't surprised to hear this. Her younger sister was poured into a tiny skirt and tight red corset above which her goosepimpled breasts were making a valiant break for freedom. With her naked shoulders rising up like two scoops of coffee ice cream, smoky eye makeup and mane of tumbling ebony hair extensions she looked more like an Asian exile from the Playboy Mansion than a respectable lawyer's fiancée.

'Maybe you should put some more clothes on next time?' Priya suggested, resisting the impulse to chuck one of the sofa throws over her sister. The jaws of some of the male guests were on the reclaimed floorboards and drooling surely wouldn't do the wood any favours. 'And take those bloody stilettos off. You're wrecking my floor.'

Neesh rolled her false-lashed eyes. 'Chillax, sis! You sound like Mum.' Her gaze swept Priya up and down, taking in the floaty sari, strappy sandals and distinct lack of cleavage. 'Come to think of it you dress like her too. You need to come out shopping with me, I'll sort you out.'

Since Neesh favoured the kind of outfit that even Jordan would baulk at, Priya felt she could be forgiven for not jumping with joy at the suggestion. Not that Neesh was bothered. She was far too busy adjusting her corset and tugging her tiny skirt over her perfect peach of a backside.

'How did you get past Mum anyway, dressed like that?' Priya wondered, half horrified and half in awe. Neesh might be twenty-four but she still lived at home where her mother's word was law. 'Don't tell me you're still sneaking your clubbing gear out under your jeans?'

'Like duh!' Neesh checked her scarlet lipstick in the mirror and pouted. 'I got dressed at Sanjeev's. Not that Mum would notice if I went out stark naked these days. She's far too busy trying to keep the aunties under control.'

The aunties were bad enough separately but together they were a force of nature. Last month her father had suffered a nasty bout of pneumonia and his three sisters had moved in uninvited to help care for their brother, the precious only son of the Gupta family. Four weeks on they showed no inclination to move out, content to bicker, watch endless repeats of their favourite Indian soaps, eat lorry loads of Bombay Mix and generally send her mother crazy but, because family honour and hospitality was so important to the Guptas, Divya had no choice but to grit her teeth and put up with them.

Which was easier said than done.

'They must be driving her mad,' Priya said. She needed a big swig of her wine just at the thought of life with the terrible trio.

'God, yeah, and not just her either!' Neesh pulled a face. 'I can't wait to get married and move in with Sanj, if not for the red-hot sex, then for the peace. If it isn't Mum nagging me about the wedding, it's bloody Auntie Bhavani moaning to Mum about how she spoils us.' She put on a nasal voice, puffed out her cheeks and wagged a finger at her sister. '*It is not right to squander your husband's money for which he works so hard, Divya!*'

'Bhavani's a menace,' Priya agreed.

Neesh beamed at her reflection in the hall mirror and scraped a smear of scarlet lipstick from her front teeth before turning her attention back to Priya, regarding her sister critically through narrowed eyes. 'Since you don't live at home and have to do daily battle with the auntie fashion police you've no excuse for dressing like that, sis. You've got a gorgeous figure under all that flipping cloth. God, if I had boobs like yours I'd wear a bikini all year round.'

Priya flushed. Although a slender size ten she was

blessed – or cursed depending upon which way you chose to look at it – with full C-cup breasts which she hid under baggy tops and shapeless shirts. Unlike Neesh, Priya didn't like to flaunt her body, preferring to look like one of the boys when filming and editing. Life was simpler that way.

'You look great in a bikini, babe,' Sanjeev chipped in, dropping an adoring kiss on Neesh's naked shoulder. 'But you'd look great in anything.'

'Don't encourage her,' Priya warned him. 'She's practically naked as it is.'

'Priya, you know as well as I do there's no point trying to tell Neesh what to do,' said Sanjeev.

'Glad you realise it already. Now be a sweetie and get me a drink, Sanj,' Neesh ordered. 'And get one for Kettan, yeah? But you'd better make his a juice or something. Kettan's driven us over,' she explained, turning back to Priya but in actuality checking her reflection again in the glass of the door behind her. 'He's parking. Did I tell you he's just got a brand-new Mercedes?'

'You brought Kettan?' Priya exclaimed.

What was it with couples that they suddenly had to try pairing everyone else off? From the second Sanj placed the enormous square-cut diamond on his fiancée's finger, Neesh had taken on the zeal of a religious fanatic in the cause of finding Priya a man. She meant well, but Neesh was to subtlety what John Sergeant was to ballroom dancing: more than a little embarrassing. God only knew what poor Kettan thought if he'd been on the receiving end of similar treatment.

Apart from being the latest hapless object of Neesh's matchmaking plans Kettan Adani was also Sanjeev's elder brother. Priya had met him on several family occasions and he seemed pleasant enough, but she didn't know him and she certainly hadn't invited him to her housewarming. Actually she hadn't invited Neesh and Sanjeev either. She'd specifically arranged a separate gathering the following day for her family, all part of Project Keep the Boundaries Clear. But of course Neesh had ignored this, just as she'd ignored everything else Priya had said to her over the past twenty-four years, from not stealing her makeup to not borrowing her newest clothes.

While Sanjeev trotted off to fetch the drinks, his trendy Mohawk bobbing above the partygoers, Priya gave her sister a steely look. 'Anyone else coming I should know about? Mum? Dad? The aunties?'

'No, just a handsome, single bachelor armed with a bottle of champagne,' grinned Neesh. 'Oh, don't be such a miserable old cow, Pri! Let him in and give him a chance. You might even find you like him! I'm off to dance. Laters!'

And off she sashayed, slim arms held high and snaky hips swivelling in time with Beyoncé, leaving Priya fuming. Gritting her teeth so hard that she thought they'd shatter, Priya opened the door and pasted a smile to her face.

Actually, it wasn't that much of an effort to smile at Kettan. With his high cheekbones, Malteser-brown eyes and mole's pelt short hair hugging his well-shaped head, he was certainly a good-looking guy. Maybe if Neesh wasn't so pushy she might be more inclined to spend some time with him. He certainly had great taste in champagne, she decided, as he pressed a chilled bottle of vintage Krug into her hands.

'Kettan! This is far too much. You shouldn't have.'

Kettan smiled shyly. 'Of course I should. It's the least I can do after gatecrashing your party.'

'You're not gatecrashing,' Priya said quickly, crossing her fingers behind her back. After all, it wasn't Kettan's fault her sister knocked Machiavelli into cotton socks when it came to being manipulative. 'You're very welcome. Besides, we're practically family now.'

'I guess you're right,' Kettan agreed, following her into the kitchen area and accepting a drink. 'I can't believe there are only a few weeks to go before the big day. We seem to have been planning it for ever.'

'Tell me about it!' Priya sighed. 'Neesh has been wedding obsessed for months and Mum isn't much better. And don't even get me started on the aunties. I don't know what they'll do with themselves when it's all over.'

'Plan one for the next victim, I expect.' He laughed ruefully and she found herself thinking she liked how his eyes crinkled at the corners and the way the strong muscles in his throat contracted as he sipped his champagne. Sensing her gaze, Kettan met Priya's eyes questioningly and she looked away, heat flooding her cheeks. Thank goodness Neesh hadn't said mind reading was on his list of talents!

'So, are you all set for the big day?' he was asking, breaking the awkward moment. 'Bags all packed and passport at the ready?'

Priya gulped. The honest answer was a resounding

no. She'd not even bought her ticket yet. Renovating the flat had cleared out her savings and since she was almost up to the limit on her plastic she was waiting until pay day to book. The same went for buying her wedding outfit and the Dualit toaster Neesh was convinced she couldn't live without. Things would have been a lot simpler, not to mention cheaper, if the happy couple had decided to get married in London. But Neesh had her heart set on getting married in India, and what Neesh wanted she generally got. Priya sighed. She adored her little sister and was the first to admit that she was equally responsible for spoiling her rotten, but she really could have done without the extra expense of an enforced holiday. The thought of being squeezed into Economy with her squabbling aunts brought her out in a cold sweat, as did the knowledge that for a fortnight everyone would be speculating about her own marital status.

It must be so much easier to be a man.

But there was no point in dumping all these woes on Kettan, especially since it was his family who had suggested having the wedding in India and kindly offered to play host to the Guptas. He probably couldn't wait to jump on board the Air India jumbo and zoom back to see the folks. Maybe he even had a potential fiancée tucked away in the wings.

'I'm as ready as I'll ever be,' she said diplomatically. 'Now, can we forget weddings for a while? I have a feeling there'll be plenty of time to think about those in the next few weeks.' She set her glass down as an idea occurred that would change the subject nicely. 'Since this is a housewarming, would you like a quick tour?'

For the next hour or so Priya mingled happily with her guests. Aware that Kettan only knew Neesh and Sanj, who, oblivious of anyone else, were grinding away to R&B in a manner that would have outraged the aunties, Priya did her best to make sure that he didn't feel left out. Not that Kettan seemed concerned; he had a warm and easy manner that enabled him to chat happily to everyone he met, and as the evening wore on Priya found him more and more appealing. Could there be something there or was the champagne blurring the edges of her judgement? A little knot of delicious tension tightened in her stomach and the air suddenly seemed rich with possibilities.

Maybe it was just as well that the doorbell shrilled at this point, pulling her out of these rather dangerous thoughts, Priya decided.

Murmuring her excuses and leaving Kettan deep in discussion with Zoe, Priya went to answer the door for the umpteenth time. Who on earth had decided to arrive so late? She hoped it wasn't the neighbours coming to complain about the noise. Why Neesh insisted on having it up at eardrum-blasting levels she'd never know. Perhaps this was where the three-year age gap between them really started to show.

'Bloody hell, pet! I thought I'd break my knuckles hammering on the door, the music's that loud!' complained the tall man who was standing on the doorstep and nursing his hand. 'I tried to phone but no one answered.' He peered over her shoulder into the crowded apartment. 'Ah! Now it all makes sense. You're having a party. No wonder you didn't hear the phone. I've been to quieter Metallica gigs!'

'Ray, what are you doing here? What happened to the Gorbals shoot?' Priya was taken aback. Her staunch ally and cameraman had been shooting in Scotland for a gritty piece on social deprivation, which was one of the reasons she hadn't invited him to her housewarming.

One of the reasons.

There was no way she could invite Ray in. He knew far too much about what had really happened between her and Vikram, and after a few drinks he was incapable of being discreet. If he blabbed to her friends it would be bad enough, if he said anything to Neesh and she told their mother all hell would break loose. Much as she loved him and hated to hurt him she just couldn't take the risk.

Ray cracked first. 'Anyways, you're busy here so I'll be on my way. I'll catch up with you at work. It can wait.'

'Ray, what is it you needed to tell me? It must be important if you've driven all the way from Southall.'

'You're busy, Priya. It'll keep. I'm sorry for intruding.' Ray began to turn away, his long craggy face looking so downcast that Priya was mortified.

'You could never intrude,' she told him, slipping her slender arm through his burly one and guiding him into the throng. 'I'm so sorry, Ray. Please come on in. I must be losing the plot in my old age. You're really welcome, honestly.'

'You sure?' Ray didn't look convinced and Priya didn't blame him. The apartment was heaving with her friends and the empty plates and glasses practically screamed preparation and planning.

'Of course I'm sure.' For the second time that

evening Priya found herself crossing her fingers. 'Come on, I'll get you a drink.'

'You'll need one yourself when you hear my news! We got the commission!' Ray said, following her through the dancing and into the kitchen area where he dwarfed the counters and made the six-ring gas range look like something out of a dolls' house.

Priya gaped at him. 'You're kidding! We've got the commission? Seriously?'

For the last four weeks Priya's team had been planning a documentary about a long-running ashram in India which had recently come under the management of a new swami. Nothing unusual in that, of course, but what was rather out of the ordinary were the reports of the miracles that had occurred since she had taken over.

'Seriously,' laughed Ray. 'It's going to be made official tomorrow.'

'I don't believe it! I honestly thought Ajay's team had it sewn up.'

'Aye, so did they, and their pitch was bloody good, but not as good as yours.' Ray beamed. 'Vikram's signing the project over to you. For a total twat he's actually made a decent decision for once. Not that this means I'll ever forgive him for—'

'Never mind all that right now,' Priya interrupted quickly, before Ray could get back on his (very) high horse and start ranting about Vik. The last thing she needed was Neesh overhearing and repeating the whole sorry tale to Divya. Sweat prickled between her shoulder blades at the very thought. 'The main thing is we won the pitch. That's fantastic!'

'Bloody right it is, Priya! Now do you understand why I had to tell you straight away? You could look a bit more excited.' Ray looked disappointed. 'I thought you'd be turning cartwheels.'

Priya bit her lip. She wasn't sure about cartwheels but there was certainly a Ferris wheel set to full speed in her stomach. By signing over this project Vik was doing her a major favour. At the stroke of his Mont Blanc pen all her worries about financing the flights and a month in India were quelled, only to be replaced by a new host of more shadowy concerns. Was she really the best person to direct this documentary or did he have an ulterior motive? Was he trying to buy her off, or had she really got the job for the right reasons?

'Of course I'm excited,' she told Ray, not wanting to take the gloss off his happiness. 'I'm just surprised, that's all.'

'What are you surprised about, babes?' Zoe said over Priya's shoulder, as she and Steve helped themselves to more wine. Explaining quickly, Priya left Ray with Zoe and Steve, whom she would trust with her life to keep any secrets that he might blurt out, and made her way towards Neesh. If she stayed with her little sister she might just manage to keep her and Ray apart. Damage limitation was the name of the game.

3

Departure day and the Gupta household was a buzzing hive of busy-bee activity as the entire family tore around cramming clothes into suitcases and doing emergency last-minute shopping. Directing proceedings with an iron fist was Bhavani, driving Neesh crazy by raiding her suitcases to get rid of any flesh-baring clothing and make certain only modest saris were packed.

'I'm going to bloody kill her!' Neesh was screeching now, rummaging through yet another suitcase only to discover that her aunt had struck again. 'She's gone and swiped my Seven jeans and my Vivienne Westwood corset! She's a bloody liability!'

'You won't catch me arguing with that,' Priya agreed with feeling. She'd spent the last few days frantically trying to keep the peace between her aunt and her mother and was feeling more beaten than a bowl of scrambled eggs. Over breakfast the two women had almost come to blows when Neesh asked for her bikini back only for her aunt to begin berating their mother for allowing her daughters to run wild. From the fuss Bhavani made over the admittedly skimpy swimwear you'd think Neesh had planned to sunbathe in a G-string and nipple tassels.

Not that Priya would put it past her.

'You had better contain those girls before it is too late and they do something really scandalous, or God forbid blacken the family name!' Bhavani had wheezed, chins wobbling with indignation. 'At least Neeshali will soon have a husband to guide her, but Priya is always mixing with young men unchaperoned. She lives alone without a husband! What about the family honour, hmm? What about her virtue?'

Priya had almost choked on her toast. Her aunt need have no fears on that score; the state her love life was in lately, her virtue was perfectly safe.

Unfortunately.

'Bloody woman!' Neesh was ranting now as she plucked yards of cat-puke-yellow sari fabric from her suitcase. 'I swear to God I'm going to ram this crap so far up her fat backside she'll be blowing it out her nose!'

Moving across the bedroom, which was so strewn with suitcases, clothes and boxes that it could double as an assault course, Priya put an arm round her sister.

'Come on, you know what Auntie Bhav's like. Just humour her.'

'Me humour her?' shrieked Neesh, who could give Etna a run for its money when it came to erupting. 'I'm the bloody bride and they're *my* clothes! She should bloody well humour me!'

Priya knew from experience that when Neesh got started on her precious clothes there was no stopping her. She also knew that if her sister threw a major tantrum yet another row would blow up and Ashwani, who was supposed to be resting, would have to get out of bed to referee. Another female squabble was the last thing her father needed. Luckily, years of managing Ray and the rest of her crew had taught Priya negotiating skills that a UN Peace Envoy would covet, and she said quickly, 'I've heard that the shopping in Mumbai is amazing. Apparently they've got all the labels and at half the price. If you left some of your stuff here you could get Sanj to take you there on a major spree. If you haven't got many clothes he'll have to buy you some, won't he?'

Priya could practically hear the cogs grinding in the materialistic depths of her little sister's brain. Fortunately the promise of more shopping was more attractive than another spat with Bhavani and before long Neesh was more than happy to abandon half her wardrobe. Thank God for that, thought Priya, as she returned to her own packing.

'My God!' shrieked Neesh as the taxi pulled away from the house, causing the driver to swerve across the road. 'I'm going to get married! Can you believe it! I'm bloody well getting married! How mad is that?'

She bounced up and down on her seat, long coal-black hair flying and her dark eyes shining with excitement. Priya felt exhausted just looking at her, but then Neesh hadn't just lugged twelve suitcases down the stairs and along the garden path, nor had to run back at least four times to fetch items that the aunties suddenly realised they couldn't live without. Neesh had suddenly vanished, leaving everyone else to do the hard work, only to reappear at the eleventh hour with freshly applied makeup and newly manicured nails. If only Priya had had the chance to remove her chipped nail varnish, or even to drag a brush through her tangled hair. In between all the frenetic activity she'd been on the phone to Ray in order to make sure that all their expensive equipment had been checked and packed properly.

Talk about multi-tasking. No wonder she was shattered! All Priya wanted to do now was close her eyes and rest. Not that there was much hope of that with her mother and her aunts around. The taxi hadn't even left Wimbledon yet and they were already bickering. Delving into her Chloe Paddington (a cast-off from Neesh as apparently it was *so* last season) she fished out her iPod, and tutted in frustration when she realised the battery was flat. Now she'd have to listen to squabbling all the way to the airport.

'I do think you're being a little selfish having this wedding in India.' Auntie Chandani was needling Neesh now. 'It's too far for dear Ashwani to have to travel. You should have got married in London. Then all the family could have come.'

'God forbid,' shuddered Neesh. 'I'll leave the big family do to Priya when she finally gets round to tying the knot.'

Bhavani snorted rudely. 'We won't hold our breath there, dear. We all know that Priya doesn't recognise a good thing when she sees it. That boy Vikram was lovely.'

'That's what you think,' muttered Priya under her breath. Great, now it would only be a matter of nanoseconds before her mother joined in. She was a fully paid up member of the Priya Should Have Grabbed Perfect Vikram When She Had the Chance club.

'There's nothing wrong with being picky,' she said aloud.

'There is when you're turning a perfectly good man down for no reason,' snapped Divya. 'That's always been your problem, Priya: you're far too quick to dismiss men. Take Kettan, for example. He's perfectly lovely, an eligible bachelor ripe for the picking. And he likes you too, I can tell. He's definitely interested.'

'He is nice,' piped up Neesh. 'And he's almost as fit as Sanj.'

'He's single and he's got a wonderful job,' added Divya, getting into her stride now. 'Why won't you give him a chance, Priya?'

Priya blushed scarlet, her thoughts rushing back to the evening of her housewarming. There she'd been, concentrating on keeping Ray and Neesh apart, only to be blindsided by Kettan.

'Hey, there you are,' Kettan had said, looking genuinely delighted to see her. 'This is a fantastic party.' Then his dark brows had drawn together in a concerned frown. 'Are you okay? You look a little fraught.'

Priya had sighed and pushed her hair behind her ears. Her face felt flushed and her pulse was racing. Just the mention of Vik's name could do this to her. Kettan's eyes had been full of sympathy and for a split second she had been seriously tempted to tell him everything. Why not? He was a sensitive guy, he was a good listener and he was practically family.

Ah yes, there was the sticking point, that nearly

family thing. This perpetual trying to remember who knew what and who might give something crucial away was just so complicated, a bit like holding all the plots of her favourite soaps in her head without getting them confused. That was why she always tried to keep the different areas of her life carefully compartmentalised. Things were simpler that way.

So rather than spilling the beans Priya had just shrugged. 'It's personal stuff, Kettan. I won't bore you with it. I'm even starting to bore myself.'

'You mean you don't think you can tell me because you don't know whether you can trust me,' Kettan had said, leaning in so close to Priya that his thick dark eyelashes had practically brushed her cheek. His lips by her ear and his breath warm against her skin, he had whispered, 'How about I trust you with my secret first? Then we'll have to trust each other.'

Goosepimples had rippled across Priya's body. He smelled nice, she found herself thinking, a sharp lemony spicy scent that was masculine and distinctive. And he really was attractive . . . Maybe it was time to put Vik behind her. This union would make everyone happy.

'Go on then,' she had whispered, swayed by the air of conspiracy between them. 'What's your dark, terrible secret?'

'I've been seeing a girl,' Kettan had said softly. 'My parents have no idea. In fact, nobody has.'

Priya had downed her glass in one. So much for pleasing the family, then. Swearing her to secrecy, Kettan had gone on to explain how he'd been secretly dating a white British girl.

But, of course, sitting in the taxi, Priya could only shrug. 'He's not really my type.'

'Ai!' wailed Divya, raising her eyes to heaven. 'See what I'm up against? What's wrong with you, Priya? Why won't you give anyone a chance?'

'I will if I meet the right guy. I've got to love someone if I'm going to marry them,' Priya protested. They hadn't even got to Heathrow and everyone was already having a go. How would she cope with weeks of this?

'Love?' scoffed Bhavani. 'A successful marriage is based on mutual respect and family background. Not love! Marrying for love is a western idea.'

'Love comes later,' added Darsani. 'As it did for me and your Uncle Ajay. You need to be more realistic, Priya Gupta. Marriage isn't about romance.'

'Of course it isn't! You need to stop being so selfish, young lady. Your father needs to know that you are settled; it would be a great relief to him,' was Chandani's opinion. 'Wouldn't it, Divya?'

'Indeed it would,' agreed Divya. 'Once Neeshali and Sanjeev are married, Priya, you really must start to concentrate on your own future. After all, you're nearly thirty!'

And all four of them fixed her with bright beady eyes, nodding manically and in total harmony for once. Priya sighed. Her unfortunate unmarried state was the only thing they ever agreed on.

She supposed every cloud had a silver lining.

Just at the point when Priya was considering flinging open the taxi door and making a break for freedom her mobile rang. Her heart plummeted about twenty storeys when she saw that the caller was Ray. Oh, God, she thought as she flipped the phone open, what's gone wrong?

Priya's gut reaction was spot on. Ray was calling to tell her that there was a slight hiccup in their plans. The sound engineer had just phoned to say he'd lost his passport.

'You've got to be joking!' Priya raked a hand through her hair, stress fizzing through her nervous system like sherbet. 'It'll take weeks to get a replacement!'

'I know. It's a disaster.' Ray sounded equally fed up. 'Vikram wants you to phone him asap.'

'I've got to phone Vikram?' Priya echoed, then seeing Divya's ears prick up she lowered her voice and hurried to get Ray off the line. Conscious that her mother was dying to overhear, she switched the phone to her other ear and turned away from the others. 'Oh that's great, Ray. What the hell for?'

'Presumably so he can find a replacement and probably to tell us off for hiring such a flake in the first place,' sighed Ray. 'Bollocks. I really wanted Dave to do the sound. He's great.'

Personally Priya felt like wringing Dave's neck. He might be a brilliant sound engineer but right now he'd sent her pulse racing so fast she felt giddy. At least this sudden adrenaline took her mind off the awkwardness of speaking to Vikram; facing her ex was the least of her problems.

Priya took a deep breath and called Vik, trying to ignore the five sets of eyes trained on her. Moments later he answered, his voice meltingly rich and warm, like hot chocolate sauce on profiteroles.

'It's a pain about Dave but it isn't the end of the world,' he assured Priya. 'I've got some contacts out there so I'll see what I can do. I'm pretty confident I can sort it.'

'Thanks,' Priya muttered. God, she really was an ungrateful cow but she hated the fact he'd come charging in like a Prada-clad Sir Lancelot. Given a bit more time she was sure she too could have found a solution.

'No problem,' he said airily. 'Anything for you, Pri, you know that.'

Priya said nothing but the words *yeah right* reverberated through the ether and eventually Vik cleared his throat and continued rather awkwardly. 'Anyway, I'll call you once you've landed and let you know what I've sorted. I'm really excited about this project; I think there's a really good story underneath all the crap about miracles.'

'I don't doubt it for a minute.' As a sceptic Priya was deeply suspicious about the reports of 'miracles'. Everyone knew there was no such thing and she fully expected to find the ashram under the control of some dodgy guru who raked money in from the gullible and banked it all in Switzerland. Nothing remarkable there except that the new swami was a woman, and one who'd lived in England for most of her adult life. Priya supposed it was a whole new slant on girl power.

'Was that Vikram?' Divya asked, as Priya snapped the phone shut and started chewing her thumb nail, an old nervous habit that had seen her through GCSEs, A Levels and a degree. Whether it would see her through Vikram was anyone's guess, but she had yet to find an alternative form of therapy since sadly shooting him was illegal.

'Fit Vik with the lovely car and even fitter bum,' said Neesh with a cheeky wink. 'Mmm, yummy scrummy. Is it back on with him?'

'No it bloody well isn't, that was just work stuff.' Priya shoved the phone into her bag. 'He's very definitely an ex.'

'I really liked him,' sighed Divya. 'He had lovely manners.'

'He was good husband material,' added Chandani, while her sisters nodded wisely, even though they'd never even met Vikram and, if Priya had anything to do with it, never would.

'She's too picky,' sighed Bhavani. 'You're far too picky, young lady. Tick tock, tick tock! Time isn't going to stand still, you know.'

And on and on and on she went, her monologue only interrupted by similar comments from her sisters and Divya. Priya sighed and buried her face in her hands.

Something told her this was going to be a very long journey.

'My God,' she groaned, dumping her bag on the
pavement outside Heathrow and joining Neesh
who was hauling their bags out of the boot. 'If that's a
taster of what the next two weeks are going to be like I
think I'll hop back in and ask the cabbie to take me
home again. And you weren't much help, either,' she
added, giving her sister a poke in the ribs. 'Couldn't you
have distracted them or something? Was it really
necessary to talk to Sanj all the way to Heathrow when
you're about to spend hours on a plane with him?'

Neesh grinned. 'I couldn't interrupt my elders, could
I? Especially when they've got your best interests at
heart. I'd never forgive myself if you died a spinster!'

'I almost did. I was only a heartbeat away from
flinging open the car door and making a jump for it.
Getting flattened by a juggernaut would have been less
painful than listening to Bhavani witter on.'

'That would have made her day,' giggled Neesh.
'She could have accompanied you to Casualty where
she'd have been guaranteed to find you a nice Indian
doctor!'

Priya grimaced. 'I'd rather be locked in a broom

cupboard with Bernard Manning than let Bhavani loose on my love life.'

'Isn't he dead?'

'Dead, alive, mouldering; it's still a preferable option.'

'Thank God I found Sanjeev,' said Neesh with relief. 'Apart from the fact that he's got an enormous knob and is a red-hot shag, he's saved me from the Auntie Inquisition.'

'Too much information,' muttered Priya, but Neesh wasn't listening, being far too busy running in the direction of the terminal where Sanjeev and Kettan were waiting for them and waving cheerfully.

'Sanj!' screeched Neesh, hurling herself into her fiancé's arms and nearly knocking him to the ground. 'Oh my God! We're going to get married! Can you believe it!

'It's mental,' laughed Sanjeev, winding his fingers into her glossy black hair and smiling down into her eyes so tenderly that Priya found a big lump filling her throat.

Maybe Vikram hadn't left her quite as bitter and as cynical as she'd thought. That could only be a good thing.

'Isn't young love grand?' murmured Kettan, his eyes sherry warm as he followed her gaze.

'Mmm,' said Priya, unable to speak. Had Vikram ever looked at her like that, as though she were the most precious, delicious thing he'd ever seen in his life? Somehow she didn't think so. The lump in her throat was more like a football now.

Get a grip, she told herself sternly. It's better to have loved and lost than be stuck with a git like him.

'We'll have to stick together if we're going to survive

this wedding without getting too green and hairy,' Kettan was saying, pulling a rueful face as Neesh and Sanj went for the full smooch. 'Thank God you're here to keep me sane, Priya.'

She smiled up at him. 'Things may get tricky, though. I think I should warn you that my mum's already lined you up as a potential suitor.'

'And if I were single I'd be delighted to oblige her,' he said chivalrously. Then his brow crinkled thoughtfully. 'Perhaps it would take the heat off us both if everyone thought there *was* something going on?'

For a second Priya was seriously tempted. If her mother and the aunties thought she was with Kettan it would put paid to all the matchmaking and snide comments about her single state. Then her habitual good sense kicked in. Lies, even the whitest of white ones, had a nasty habit of coming back to bite you on the bum. She shook her head.

'Thanks for the offer, Kettan, but I think my aunties would just explode with joy, and seeing as they've just eaten enough Bombay Mix to sustain a small country it wouldn't be a pretty sight!'

Right on cue the aunties came lumbering towards them, chins wobbling and sausagey fingers gripping their wheelie bags for dear life as they elbowed their way through the crowd. Scuttling behind was her mother, looking stressed as she tried to locate the right check-in desk, manoeuvre her luggage and shove her purse back into her bag. Kettan twinkled down at Priya. 'It might not be a pretty sight but I bet it would clear the crowds and get us right to the front. I don't think I've ever seen the terminal this busy.'

She laughed.

'Welcome to travelling the Air India way!'

Kettan certainly had a point. The terminal was jam-packed with people trundling suitcases and chattering excitedly as they waited in long queues that snaked across the concourse. The check-in desk was manic and the airport personnel looked very close to tearing their hair out or quitting on the spot. It was a case of people pile-up and boxes overload; the whole of the Air India check-in section was close to bursting point.

As the Guptas inched their way forward it was almost impossible to distinguish between who was leaving and those who'd simply come to see their nearest and dearest off. Whole families were huddled together. Overexcited children were running around maniacally in what was now their makeshift playground area while elderly people made just as much noise complaining about everything. Parents were looking close to having a nervous breakdown as they tried to manhandle their families towards the check-in, counting and recounting heads and then checking and rechecking each passport and boarding pass. They looked even more harassed than the airport personnel.

Then, casting her gaze a little further, Priya saw something which instantly made her feel twice as harassed as any other traveller and caused her heart to accelerate with a speed that would put Jenson Button to shame.

Three queues away, designer shades dangling from his fingers and watching the entertaining scene with growing amazement, was Ray. He should have flown ages ago. He shouldn't be here!

She had to do something. She couldn't let her

mother spot him. If Divya found out why Priya had broken up with Vik she'd be lectured all the way to Jaipur and back again.

No. Way.

Priya pushed her hair behind her ears and rummaged through her bag, pulling out a wad of passports and airline tickets. Tucking her own back inside, she explained the situation to an intrigued Kettan. Even leaving out the personal details Priya still managed to convince him that she absolutely had to keep Ray and Divya apart, and Kettan quickly agreed to take charge of the Guptas.

'Go on, it's fine,' he assured her, placing his hand fleetingly on her shoulder. 'I'll take care of getting everyone through passport control. I'll tell them you've had to deal with some work stuff.'

That was true, anyway, thought Priya as she wove her way towards Ray's lanky frame. Slipping away from her family was a lot easier than she'd thought; Sanjeev and Neesh only had eyes for each other. Divya was on the phone to Ashwani and the aunties were tearing round the shops in a valiant attempt to spend Britain's way out of financial disaster. The crowds were so thick that it was easy to melt into the throng and away from beady family eyes.

'All right, Priya,' Ray said, looking delighted to see her when she materialised at his side. 'What on earth's going on here? Are you sure we're in the right place, pet? This looks more like a market than an airport. What's with all the boxes and the TVs and the electronic stuff? And why is that bloke carrying a carpet? Don't they have any shops in India?'

In spite of her surging adrenaline levels Priya chuckled. 'All this lot is presents for the rellies back home. Indians are a very generous bunch, Ray. You should see how much we've packed for the Adanis. I think Mum may even have squeezed the kitchen sink in.'

'I feel like I'm travelling far too light in that case,' said Ray, glancing down at his small case and camera bag. 'I just hope they don't give all our kit to someone else by mistake. It's bad enough that my plane's been delayed. Can you believe we only started checking in forty minutes ago?'

Forty minutes ago? Crap! That meant he'd be in Departures at exactly the same time as her family. Priya felt the colour drain from her face and her legs turn to boiled string. Keeping them apart would be impossible.

'Don't look so worried,' said Ray cheerfully, mistaking the look of horror that flitted across her face. 'We'll still get there, right? Maybe we'll even have time for a few pints first in Departures? It'll be great to see your mam again too.'

Ray could swig beer like it was squash, and real ale was his greatest passion. The thought of him coming across her mother when he was half cut and chisel blunt was not a happy one. Fighting the impulse to scream, Priya smiled weakly while her brain worked overtime on a plan to keep him and her family apart. She'd have to be really careful, because Ray was still sensitive about not being invited to her housewarming and she hated the thought of hurting him further. There was no point in making him swear not to mention Vik, either, because Ray just didn't work like that. He suffered badly from foot in mouth disease and there was no known cure.

For the next hour she was run ragged trying to keep her mother and Ray apart in the departure lounge. Luckily Divya vanished into the depths of Duty Free with the aunties while Neesh dragged a white-faced Sanj and his credit cards into every designer shop she could find. Parking Ray in the bar with a pint Priya dashed between him and her family, with the odd circuit of Duty Free thrown in for good measure. Luckily Ray hated shopping as much as any other man and was content to leave her to it, and apart from a rather hairy moment when Neesh suggested having a quick drink away from the disapproving gaze of the aunties Priya's heart rate gradually returned to a less cardiac-arrest-inducing rhythm. Once she'd waved Ray through to the gate for his flight she soothed her frayed nerves with a large glass of white wine and rested her hot forehead on the sticky bar table. They hadn't even left Britain yet and she was already shattered. How on earth was she going to keep this up, make a documentary and help to arrange a wedding? She'd need to clone herself!

5

Priya hadn't really given much thought to what Jaipur itself would be like – surviving the long journey without strangling her nearest and dearest had been her main concern – but once she stepped out of the air-conditioned depths of the airport she gasped with amazement.

Never mind arriving on a different continent; this was more like arriving on another planet! Gone were the pewter clouds of Heathrow and in their place a gold sovereign sun beamed scorching rays from a cobalt sky. The tarmac shimmered with the fearsome heat, giving the hills and buildings beyond a dreamlike quality, and for a second Priya swayed on her feet before Kettan took hold of her elbow.

'Okay?' he asked. 'The heat comes as something of a shock, doesn't it?'

The last thing Priya felt like was a long sticky car journey. At least, she hoped it was a car journey they were about to undertake; she didn't fancy one of the odd moped rickshaws that were putt-putting their way past the terminal. Neither did she fancy taking her chances in the ox cart that lumbered by, so it was with great relief that she heard Kettan explain to Divya that they were only twenty minutes away from long cold drinks at his Aunt Akhila's and would be riding in a couple of the yellow and black taxis that swarmed around Arrivals.

'I've asked our drivers to take us through Sanganer rather than on the ring road because it's the real India,' Kettan said to Priya as they heaved their cases into the taxi. 'It won't add too much time to the journey, I promise.'

But ten minutes later Priya had lost all desire to reach the Adanis' house as soon as possible. All thoughts of feeling tired and thirsty flew from her mind the second her taxi passed through the arched gateway into the old town, because she was instantly spell-bound.

It felt to Priya like she had been transported right on to the set of one of her favourite Bollywood movies – everything was so bright and busy. It was like peering into a treasure chest brimming with precious stones; women in jewel-hued saris strolled through the streets, jostling with men in crimson turbans and flowing white dhotis, pausing to admire glittering rows of slippers or to finger the endless rolls of fabric that gleamed with gold and silver embroidery and shimmered like a heat haze. In spite of the burning sunshine Priya rolled the window down and inhaled the heady aroma of spices and hot earth, and the undertone of something more pungent, probably the dung from the skinny cows that seemed to wander at will through the streets. The chatter of countless dialects mingled with the tooting of horns and the buzz of the mopeds that wove through the traffic.

The whole town was a masala, Priya thought, slipping on her shades as the harsh sun glanced off the corrugated iron rooftops, a heady spicy mixture of colours and cultures. Huge posters for Coke jostled with billboards for Bollywood films; ox carts lumbered beside shiny new cars and a cross-legged snake charmer plied his trade beside a young man in a cream suit and Ray-Bans who was speaking rapidly into his mobile. She felt giddy just looking at it all, from the confusing flow of vehicles and the throbbing crimsons, burnt siennas and acid greens of pedestrians' clothing to the sandalwood idols, drifts of textiles and oceans of ceramic beads laid out for sale in an eye-popping display. Everywhere was flooded with life and colour and her head spun with the intensity of it all.

India was so alive!

'Wow,' breathed Neesh, peeking out from under her Oakleys. 'It's like Southall meets Bollywood!'

Priya nodded. She almost expected the townsfolk to break into an elaborate song and dance routine. She had never seen such teeming streets and such vibrant life. How she wished Ray were travelling with them so that he could capture the scene on film. It would make the most spectacular introduction to their documentary.

'Pleased we came this way?' Kettan asked, smiling at her reaction.

'Very,' Priya said, returning his smile and settling back into her seat. She wound the window up and removed her sunglasses. 'It's amazing!'

But amazing seemed too trite a word for all this colour and vitality. As the taxi crawled through the busy streets towards the second gate Priya feasted her eyes like a glutton at an all-you-can-eat buffet, drinking in everything from the gaunt beggar children to the swaying people balancing precariously on the roofs of buses. Her skin prickled with excitement and suddenly she felt more alive than she had for months.

'And I thought it was bad driving through London,' said Neesh. 'This traffic's mental, isn't it, Mum?'

Their taxi driver certainly had a kamikaze style all of his own, narrowly avoiding buzzing swarms of scooters on which entire families seemed to balance, children sitting precariously on the handlebars and mothers riding pillion with babies on their backs. There were rickshaws too, both pedal-powered and motorised, as well as crazy yellow taxis that cut them up constantly, and every model of Nissan under the sun.

'Mmm,' murmured Divya. She'd been unusually quiet during the journey. Every now and then Priya caught her staring with narrowed eyes, but when she tried to make eye contact Divya had looked pointedly away, pretending to be fascinated by the tips of her sandals. She was clearly sulking about something and nothing Priya said or pointed out could tempt her to engage in conversation. It wasn't until they pulled up outside a modest-looking apartment block, and the others were out of the taxi, that Divya hissed into Priya's ear how disappointed she was that her elder daughter hadn't seen fit to introduce her *male* friend to her family.

'Sneaking off to meet him like you're ashamed of us,' she added, her slight figure puffed up with indignation. 'What is going on, Priya? I thought I could trust you and now I find you're meeting men in secret!'

'One man, Mum, and I wasn't meeting him in secret, as you put it! It was work stuff. That was my cameraman, Ray. You know Ray. He's been over for dinner. He's my friend.'

But even as she spoke Priya knew it was pointless. Divya had no concept of friendships between men and women and was suspicious of any young man she saw talking to her daughters, from college mates to the pizza delivery man. The more Priya protested that Ray was just a friend, the more convinced her mother would be that she was seeing him romantically and trying to keep it secret. This idea was laughable to Priya. She loved Ray as a friend, but romantically? Nothing could have been further from her mind.

Priya watched her mother scuttle out of the cab and towards the apartment where a crowd of people had gathered, their voices raised excitedly as they greeted their guests. At least Divya wouldn't cause a scene in front of the future in-laws. No, she'd save the lecture for later on, and what a lecture it would be.

Swallowing back a growing sense of frustration, Priya picked up her bags and followed. Her mother already had her eye on Kettan as a nice suitable Indian alternative to Ray, and it would be easier to stop the tide coming in than to halt Divya in full matchmaking mode.

'Hurry up, Priya,' Divya called. 'No, leave the bags. Kettan will get them. Such a good boy! So helpful!'

Priya rolled her eyes but did as she was told. Sometimes it was just easier that way.

She could hardly wait for the morning to come so she could escape to the ashram. Some tranquillity and head space were exactly what she needed. She'd only been with her mother for twenty-four hours; what was she going to be like after three weeks? Suddenly, Priya felt very, very tired.

From the moment Priya arrived at the Adanis' apartment, however, it was clear that slipping away to bed and drifting into sleep was not an option.

The Guptas were guests of honour and it seemed that weeks of planning and endless hours of preparation had gone into making their reception perfect. Priya guessed she really shouldn't have been surprised: Indians were very hospitable people and it was a point of pride that any guests should be well treated and crammed full to bursting point with food and drink. As soon as the front door of the Adanis' town apartment opened, the hot air was filled with the most delicious aromas, and in spite of her exhaustion Priya's mouth watered.

'Welcome! Come in! Come in!' A short woman in a crimson sari and with iron-grey hair pulled back from a round smiling face stood in the open doorway, her chubby arms open wide in greeting and her chins wobbling in time with her words. 'Welcome to Jaipur!'

'Everyone, this is my Aunt Akhila,' Sanjeev said, hugging his aunt – no mean feat seeing as she was as wide as she was tall – 'the best cook in all of Rajasthan!'

'Chi, chi!' Akhila chided, black boot button eyes bright with mock indignation as she kissed her nephew soundly on the cheek. 'Just Rajasthan?'

'Okay then, the whole of India,' laughed Sanj. 'Seriously, you guys are in for a treat. We'll eat so much that the plane will never take off when we leave.'

Akhila tutted as her bright gaze swept over Neesh and Priya. 'These English girls are far too skinny. They need to put some weight on.'

Priya caught Kettan's eye. During the long plane journey he had told her all about the India branch of his family and according to him his Aunt Akhila ruled over them all. Her word was law in the Adani clan, and it seemed that she was already asserting her authority over the Guptas. Following her broad beam up the stairs Priya recalled how Kettan had said that everyone in the family, from the numerous chubby-cheeked children to the adults, treated her with the utmost respect and did her bidding without question. She hoped Bhavani wouldn't be getting any ideas about this matriarchal system. She'd be even more unbearable.

The Adanis' second floor apartment was situated right in the heart of Jaipur and even though the windows were shut and an ancient fan stirred the soupy air in whirring circles the noise from the bustling street below still seeped inside. Ringing bicycle bells competed with honking car horns, while the shrill cries of a street vendor wrestled with the tinny wail of a transistor radio. A blind shielded the room from the harsh sun and Priya could only glimpse slices of the swarming world outside, but she shivered with delicious anticipation. She could hardly wait to explore what looked just like a scene from *Bride and Prejudice*. Maybe her very own Mr Darcy was just round the corner, all Bournville-dark eyes, honey-smooth skin and flowing ebony hair. Or maybe she was getting a bit carried away thanks to all those giant boards plastered with huge images of smouldering Bollywood heroes.

Oh well, it was nice to dream of being swept away by a handsome prince, even if most of hers seemed to have a nasty habit of reverting to frogs.

'Sit down, sit down,' Akhila insisted, gesturing for her guests to take their places at the large Formica-topped table which dominated the kitchen. 'You must be hungry after such a long journey.'

Priya hadn't thought she was hungry, but when a bevy of Akhila's female relatives started to carry in dishes piled high with fragrant rice, fluffy naan breads and vegetable curry her stomach growled. The air was suddenly rich with spices and she realised that she wanted nothing more than to dig in. Moments later her taste buds were having a party as delicious flavours exploded across her tongue. The vegetables were chunky and fresh, the sauce was hot and just the right side of oily, and the rice tasted of jasmine and herbs. If this went on she'd never fit into the new size eight Earl Jeans she'd bought at Heathrow. But if it was a competition between her figure and Indian cooking then the food was definitely winning, and she mopped up every last drop of sauce with the naan before placing her hands on her stomach and thanking her hostess.

An hour later, her ears buzzing from listening to at least ten simultaneous conversations and her eyes heavy, Priya really was ready for her bed. Never one for crowds and attention, she was feeling rather like a goldfish in a bowl as all the family members introduced themselves and welcomed her to Jaipur. And since the Adanis were a huge extended family, this took quite some time. Priya counted over fifteen people all poured into a small town apartment that wasn't much larger than her flat. Shoes, toys and assorted clutter spilled from room to room and Priya's neat streak itched to tidy it all up.

Priya had met countless relatives and neighbours, all of whom cooed over her pale complexion and button nose, making her feel more like a visiting supermodel than just an ordinary girl from London. She tried to explain that her pale skin was the result of the miserable English weather but the female Adanis clicked their tongues in disbelief and envy. It seemed they bleached their skin with special products, pale being the Indian ideal of beauty.

Looking at their glowing bronze complexions Priya shook her head in amazement. Vanity and fashion it seemed were universally crazy.

Hmm . . . she felt another documentary coming on. If only she had her laptop.

No one seemed at all fazed that another eight people had just descended on them. Priya wondered how they could bear the lack of peace and privacy. She was only here for a few weeks and already she was wondering how she'd cope with being at such close quarters with so many people. She was dreading sharing a room with Neesh and Divya. Neesh's room normally resembled the Steptoes' yard and Divya's snores were the stuff of family legend. As Priya unpacked her bag and checked out her narrow pallet bed she realised dismally that she'd get less sleep than Macbeth. Ray would be able to stow all his camera kit in the bags under her eyes. Maybe she ought to book another holiday to get over this one. Was it too late to phone the ashram and plead with them to let her stay?

'So, Priya, your mother tells me that I simply must find you a husband,' Akhila said the next morning, looking up from her dish of sweet semolina and fixing Priya with Mrs Tiggywinkle eyes.

Priya nearly choked on her breakfast. If it hadn't already been hard enough to force down the oily pancakes and chickpea curry that the Adanis had proudly served up she certainly couldn't manage now. Family members were crammed into the kitchen like human cannelloni and instantly every pair of eyes in the place swivelled to rest on her, some tongues clicking their displeasure while others murmured agreement. She felt like a specimen in the lab; any second now someone would start prodding her with a scalpel.

She'd not been in Jaipur for even twenty-four hours but already Priya had come to realise that privacy in the Adani household was an alien concept. With smaller family cousins watching her get dressed and having to share a tiny room with Neesh and Divya Priya was starting to feel like Marie Antoinette must have done at Versailles. All areas of her life were public property, including her shameful single state, already up for discussion before they'd even finished their cornflakes.

She sighed and set down her spoon. How long before they went home?

'This is exactly what I keep telling her,' agreed Divya swiftly, her cheeks red with embarrassment. 'But she is so picky. There's not one young man she'll agree to. And it's such a worry to her father and me. He's been ill and I'm sure worrying about who will provide for Priya hasn't helped. Stress does strange things.'

Priya's mouth swung open on its hinges. Ashwani was suffering from pneumonia, brought on by a nasty chest infection. The only stresses in his life came from his squabbling womenfolk and the increasing cost of Neesh's wedding. To suddenly find herself blamed for his ill health was an unfairness too far.

'Dad knows I'm more than capable of taking care of myself.'

'He knows you're not getting any younger and he feels he's let you down as a father if you're not settled soon. Let me tell you, my girl, it worries him a lot even though he won't say anything to you.' Divya laid a theatrical hand on her heart. 'Why don't you listen to me? Do you want to worry him when he's so frail?'

Priya shot her mother a look that in a just world should have laid her out face first in her breakfast. Making an early night of it the evening before had been a huge mistake. By the time she'd woken to the warm slices of buttery sunshine falling through the blinds the damage had already been done and Divya had spent a busy evening bringing Akhila and probably all the Adanis up to speed on her marital status. From the way they were all now staring at her with accusing eyes it looked as though everyone had been drafted into Divya's husband hunt.

Bloody marvellous. If Priya escaped back home without some weedy third cousin in tow it would be a miracle.

'These young girls today don't understand the importance of marriage and family. Not like when we were young,' Bhavani said thickly, through a mouthful of chickpeas. She swallowed, wiped her greasy lips with the back of her hand and added, 'She puts her career first. That's the problem. No man likes to come second. No man should come second.'

All the women at the table nodded vigorously and murmured their agreement, while the men looked smug.

Priya rolled her eyes. Whatever happened to feminism? Germaine Greer needed to spend less time in the Big Brother house and a bit more in India. An entire continent needed her!

'Don't pull faces, your aunt is right,' Divya agreed, conveniently forgetting that she spent most of her time bossing Ashwani about like she was running a boot camp. 'It's time to think about your future, Priya. We only want the best for you and we really do know what that is. Why won't you listen to us? Don't you trust us?'

Priya pushed her plate away. 'Mum, please! Do we really have to have this conversation now?'

'Why won't you just accept that your mother knows best?' added Chandani, happily jumping on the bandwagon. 'I arranged all my daughters' marriages and not one word of an argument.'

Since Chandani's daughters had all the personality

of single cell amoebas this was hardly surprising. What had really amazed Priya and Neesh was that Chandani had managed to find not one but three men who were willing to marry them.

She supposed there was a lot to be said for dowry.

'Don't fret, Divya,' said Akhila calmly, pouring a cup of wickedly strong coffee. 'I know most of the eligible Hindu bachelors in Jaipur and one of them is bound to suit Priya. There's my friend Sonal's son Haleem, who's a civil engineer, and his two brothers Taber and Baba. All lovely boys. Taber's a doctor and Baba works in investment.'

Divya's eyes lit up like Oxford Street in December. 'They sound perfect!'

'And if they don't suit,' continued Akhila calmly, in a voice that wouldn't be argued with, 'there are many others, all of whom would be delighted to meet your daughter.' She narrowed her eyes and considered Priya carefully. 'She's a pretty girl, a little on the skinny side maybe, but she has lovely skin and nice shiny hair.' Any minute now she'll leap the table and check my teeth, thought Priya.

'She's got a lovely singing voice, and she can sew,' added Divya proudly.

'She can't cook, though. Her chapattis are a disgrace,' pointed out Bhavani, unable to resist the role of downpour on her sister-in-law's parade.

'And I have a degree and a successful career,' muttered Priya, but none of the aunties were listening to her, so she gave up and let them get on with it. She sipped her scalding coffee and wished Neesh was there for back-up, but since she'd already dragged Sanjeev off to one of the bazaars and Kettan was busy doing jobs for Akhila she was on her own. She checked her watch and her heart plummeted like an express lift when she saw there was still an hour before Ray collected her for work. She'd go nuts.

By the time Kettan finally arrived at the breakfast table she had given up the will to live and was trying to drown herself in the coffee pot. The conversation had moved back to Vikram and what a wonderful catch he'd been. Yeah, right, Priya thought, stabbing a slice of mango with her knife. Herpes was a catch too, wasn't it? And nits. And lots of things equally nasty. Mashing some melon to a pulp, wishing it was voodoo melon and that Vik was clutching his guts somewhere, Priya tried to swallow her building annoyance. Much more of this and she was going to say bollocks to respect and honour and tell Divya exactly where she could stick her matchmaking.

Well, either that or ruin the entire plate of fruit.

'Stressed?' Kettan asked, sliding into the seat next to her and helping himself to a piece of splatted melon. 'Or is there a problem with your teeth I don't know about?'

'I'm grinding them so hard that there soon will be,' she told him grimly. 'Apparently your aunt's taken it upon herself to join matchmaking forces with my mother.'

'Oh, dear. Inevitable but not good,' Kettan said sympathetically. 'Still, I'm here now, which should take the pressure off a bit. Safety in numbers, Priya. Let's be two hopeless singletons together.'

'Did you manage to fix that broken tap, Kettan?' asked Akhila, temporarily distracted from Priya's hopeless love life by the arrival of her nephew. As far as the Adanis were concerned the sun shone out of his every orifice and the womenfolk couldn't do enough for him. Priya wondered what his English girlfriend would make of it.

'I certainly did.' Coffee poured and a plate piled high with pancakes served by another adoring Adani female, Kettan smiled broadly at his aunt. 'It was only a washer. I fixed that wonky bathroom shelf too.'

'You're such a good boy,' Akhila said proudly. 'So kind and so helpful.'

Bhavani, busy cramming as much food into her face as was possible without the aid of a forklift truck, paused with her spoon halfway between her plate and her mouth as though something had just occurred to her. 'Oh! Divya! Kettan will make some lucky girl a wonderful husband. Don't you think?'

The other aunties were nodding madly like the dog in the insurance adverts and Divya looked as though she'd just won the Euro Millions. Priya sighed. Her family were so predictable. She should have opened a book at William Hill.

'Are you seeing anyone at the moment, Kettan?' Divya asked brightly.

Kettan looked up from his breakfast, fixing her with wide honest melting chocolate button eyes. 'Absolutely not, Divya. I'm totally single.'

Wow. He was a cool customer, that was for sure. Priya wasn't sure she could have lied so calmly. In fact she knew she couldn't. She'd have gone all pink-faced and twitchy and couldn't have looked guiltier if she'd had *I'm secretly dating someone* written in scarlet across her forehead.

'What's wrong with all the young women these days?' exclaimed Bhavani, spraying chickpeas across the table. 'Such a catch! Don't you think, Priya?'

'Mmm.' As Kettan shot her an imploring glance, Priya realised that suddenly she wasn't so sure. He was a pretty accomplished liar which was hardly the most desirable quality in a potential husband. Suddenly the gym-toned body, full cupid bow lips and smooth shaved hair didn't seem quite as appealing.

But the oblivious Divya gave Priya a look which sent her newly plucked brows – courtesy of Neesh – arching into her hairline, while the aunties were practically drooling into their breakfast. Akhila, however, fixed Priya with a gaze cooler than the Arctic blast from the air conditioning, no doubt trying to decide if she was good enough for her nephew.

Priya looked down at her plate, biting back a scream. What was it with the women in her family? Why did they feel qualified to comment on her love life? Now she'd hear nothing but how marvellous Kettan was while his family sized her up as a potential wife, only to feel insulted when it was clear she didn't reciprocate.

The situation did not bode well.

'You look troubled,' remarked Akhila, serenely accepting a cup of chai from one of her daughters-in-law. 'What's wrong?'

Apart from you and my mother trying to run my love life, thought Priya drily. Still, not wanting to open that particular can of worms again, she plumped for a simpler answer.

'I'm a bit stressed about work stuff,' she fibbed. 'I'm making a documentary about the Vedanta ashram. You know, where they've supposed to have had miracles happen?'

Akhila looked blank so Priya decided to spare her the details and just sketched out the problems, not expecting any sympathy from this quarter. In fact she was bracing herself for another lecture on a woman's place being in the home only to be taken aback when Akhila calmly informed her, 'My youngest daughter has a first-class education. Ishani graduated with full honours from the University of Rajasthan.'

'Oh?' Priya exclaimed, wondering where this was going. Never trust an Indian mother when she casually tried to drop something into the conversation. There was always something more going on.

'In fact, she's a sound engineer.'

Priya looked up sharply to catch a look passing between her mother and Akhila. Bloody hell, her mother really had been blabbing this morning. She should have known better than to have a work conversation in earshot of Divya. And she could already guess what was coming. She was going to be lumbered with some inexperienced sound engineer.

Akhila laughed. 'Don't look so surprised! A little bird mentioned your spot of trouble. Aren't you glad we mothers share such things? Ishani'd be delighted to help out. I'm sure she'll be an asset to you.'

'Akhila, that's really kind but I couldn't possibly

expect her to give up her time to do that. I'll find someone.'

'Nonsense! I won't hear of it. You're family now and she'll be delighted to have something to do besides chores. Ishani!' she barked at a tall, bespectacled girl who was up to her elbows in washing-up suds. 'Leave that for a moment and come here!'

Ishani dutifully abandoned her chores and pulled off her rubber gloves, dripping soapy water all over the floor and causing her mother to tut at her in annoyance.

'Priya here is making a film about the Vedanta ashram and she needs a sound engineer for a few days. I've told her you'll do it.'

'You don't have to,' said Priya hastily. Ishani, ridiculously young looking and trembling under her mother's gimlet gaze, would never cope with Ray's banter and jokes. She didn't even look strong enough to lug the equipment about; those little spaghetti arms would never lift a boom mike. 'Honestly, it's fine,' she insisted.

'She wants to,' insisted Akhila, prodding her daughter in the ribs. 'Don't you, Ishani?'

Neither girl had any say in the matter because Akhila had already made her mind up and in this house her word was law. Realising that it was impossible to refuse, Priya had no choice but to agree and ignore a niggling sense of unease. She just hoped Ishani wouldn't prove to be an extra complication.

7

'Are you sure this bus will make it to the ashram?' Ray asked doubtfully as the ancient vehicle creaked its way out of Jaipur. 'I know we've only got fifteen kilometres to go but those hills look bloody steep!'

Priya couldn't help agreeing with him. When the elderly bus had pulled up outside the Sheraton she'd done a double take because it had looked more like a museum piece than a viable means of transportation. Whatever the swami did with the money raised by the ashram it certainly wasn't going into luxury transport for her guests. As the bus jolted its way through the city Priya made a mental note to try to find out exactly where the cash *did* end up.

'Don't look so worried,' said Ishani, folding her long slender body into the seat beside Ray. 'This bus is years younger than most of the others on the road. We'll be fine. Trust me.'

'I trust you, pet,' Ray muttered, casting a nervous eye over the psychedelic Bedford trucks and ancient Nissans trundling by. 'I'm just not sure I trust this bloody heap. Where's the seatbelt?'

'You poor old fogey,' Ishani said pityingly. 'We don't

have seatbelts here. Just close your eyes and have a snooze. I'll tell you when we get there.'

Ray closed his eyes and tipped his baseball cap down over his eyes. 'Okay, young whippersnapper, I might just do that. Maybe you should get some rest too. Because believe me, once we start shooting I'll really crack the whip.'

'I think I'll cope,' Ishani told him kindly.

Sitting down behind them Priya smiled to herself. In spite of her initial misgivings Ishani wasn't going to have any trouble holding her own with Ray. The two of them had hit it off as soon as she'd introduced them outside the hotel. In fact, Priya reflected, from the second Ishani had left the Adanis' house she'd proved to be something of a revelation.

'I owe you one,' she'd breathed, collapsing into the seat of the taxi. 'I thought I'd be stuck there for days having to do the whole dutiful daughter thing and much as I love my mother that would seriously drive me crazy!' The eyes behind the glasses were a sparkling mosaic of excitement and her serious face was wreathed in smiles. 'I've been meaning to go freelance since I quit my job with the Moving Picture Company, so this will give me a real taster.'

'You've worked with Ramesh Sharma?' Priya was taken aback and impressed. To work for Moving Pictures you had to be among the best in the industry.

'Don't look so surprised,' Ishani said, twisting her long hair into a knot and securing it with a clip. 'There is life beyond the BBC, you know!'

'I didn't mean that. I was just a bit surprised. You're so young.'

'I'm twenty-six,' Ishani told her.

'Wow! Do you bathe in Oil of Olay or something?'

'No, I have a mother who won't let me out for any sex, drugs and rock and roll. You've seen how it is at our place,' she said with a shrug. 'Still, one advantage of a demanding mother is that I've been able to totally focus on my career until she marries me off. You know how it is.'

'Don't I just,' sighed Priya. 'Demanding mothers seem to be my speciality these days. Breakfast wasn't my finest hour.'

There was an awkward pause as both girls recalled the earlier conversation.

'Look, I'm really sorry about that,' said Ishani finally. 'Mum doesn't mean to offend. It's just her way to always want to be in charge of everything. I'm sorry I've been foisted on you.'

'You haven't been foisted on me. It sounds like I'm pretty damn lucky to have got you on board.'

'You were totally bulldozed into it. Your face was a picture earlier and I don't blame you. But, seeing as you're stuck with me, we may as well make the best of it. I haven't got a copy of my CV but I promise I have got loads of experience.' Ishani then reeled off an impressive list of all the projects she'd worked on. By the time she'd finished Priya was ready to hire her on the spot.

So now, as the bus chugged its way out of the crowded city, Priya was really starting to feel that with the talented Ishani on board her luck had taken a turn for the better. The tensions of the morning were slipping away with each twist and turn of the road.

While Ishani and Ray chatted and bantered Priya pulled some of the ashram's brochures from her bag and, settling back into her seat, began reading about how she would soon find serenity, bliss, wisdom and life enrichment. Bring it on, she thought, flicking through the glossy pages. Especially the serenity bit.

'Excuse me, but is it your first time to the ashram?'

This question came from the woman sitting directly behind them. Dressed in a plain brown trouser suit, with her mousy hair in a bun and wire-rimmed spectacles balanced precariously on her shiny nose, she looked more like a genteel librarian on a day trip than someone in Asia on the search for spiritual enlightenment.

'I'm Maggie,' she continued, holding out her hand. 'I live in Cowes. Do you know it?'

'In Cowes?' echoed Ishani, looking confused while Priya dutifully shook hands with Maggie. 'How can you live in cows?'

'It's a town on the Isle of Wight,' Ray explained. 'A beautiful spot,' he added to Maggie. 'Fantastic sailing.'

Maggie blushed as though personally responsible for Regatta Week. 'Thank you. I'm the organist at St Mary's. Have you visited?'

'Er, I'm afraid not,' said Ray.

'It has some lovely brasses, twelfth century,' Maggie told him. 'Lots of holidaymakers like to come and do rubbings. And now I'm a holidaymaker too. I love to visit India.'

'You've been here before?' Priya asked.

'Oh, yes!' Maggie's face lit up. 'This is my third visit to the ashram. I absolutely love it here. Swami

Attuttama is the most amazing woman. Have you been before?'

Priya shook her head. 'It's our first visit. We're actually here to make a documentary for the BBC.'

'My goodness! How exciting! Well, you're all in for a treat. The ashram's the most fantastic place. I'm sure you'll soon love it every bit as much as I do!'

Priya seized her chance. 'Maggie, would you mind telling us a little bit about the ashram for our documentary? It would be great to have your perspective to put things into context, especially seeing as you've witnessed the changes since Swami Attuttama took over.'

'Oh!' Maggie patted her hair self-consciously. 'Me? Go on the telly? I'm not sure about that.'

'Just a quick sound bite,' Priya said quickly, not wanting to panic her but at the same time signalling for Ray to get his camera out. 'Nothing much, just like you're chatting to me now.'

'Hey, l'il missy! We'll go on your film,' bellowed a rotund man three seats further down the bus. His round crimson face, topped with the kind of Stetson last seen on JR Ewing, clashed vividly with his Hawaiian shirt, and massive thighs like Canadian redwoods strained the fabric of his board shorts. 'I'm Clay West senior and this is my wife Clara.' He pointed to a moon-faced lady wearing a tight floral frock and an even tighter perm. 'We're happy to be in your movie!'

'Hello,' wheezed Clara, waving a pudgy hand and trying to peer round her husband, no mean feat even if she hadn't been wedged in her seat. 'It's just great to meet y'all.'

'It's our first time,' boomed Clay, whose voice was as

loud as his shirt. 'We've come to have our medical problems healed. They do miracles at this place.'

'You might be disappointed,' said Maggie gently. 'I've been coming here for three years and I've yet to see any miracles.'

Ray, already sensing TV gold, had his camera on his shoulder and was busy filming. He gave Priya a quick thumbs up before turning his attention back to the discussion, zooming in on Clara who was speaking now, a long and breathless monologue about how her sister, apparently a virtual cripple, had arrived at the ashram with chronic arthritis and left six weeks later a new woman.

'Ah declare, that swami is a miracle worker,' Clara concluded. 'Isn't she, Clay? Isn't Avril like the Bionic Woman now?'

Priya was suddenly struck by an image of Clara's double, clad in a tight red track suit, jogging in slow motion like a running strawberry jelly, and had to swallow the urge to laugh.

'She sure is,' Clay agreed heartily. He glanced fleetingly at his crotch, adding, 'Ah'm sure hoping I can have a miracle for my problems. Little Clay could do with being bionic too.'

Priya avoided Ishani's eyes.

Maggie was still pooh-poohing the idea of miracles, saying that as far as she was concerned the ashram was all about manual work and selfless service to others. Clay looked rather alarmed at this, especially when Maggie described how digging the gardens and preparing the simple meals were all part of the swami's philosophy and the daily routine of the place.

'The ashram's all about work, yoga and meditation, not quick fixes,' Maggie finished firmly. 'Anyone who thinks otherwise is in for a shock.'

Clara crossed her arms defensively. 'Well, ah only know what ah've seen. And Avril was a new woman.'

Priya was about to ask Clara a little more about her sister's miracle cure when the bus passed through elegant wrought iron gates into a secluded flower-filled grove.

'We're here!' Maggie cried, bouncing up and down with excitement. 'Isn't it beautiful?'

The ashram comprised a series of small white-washed low-rise buildings in a serene setting. Odd-looking pyramidal structures were dotted around, wild flowers nodded and swayed on the hillsides, and closer to the buildings a small group of people clad in white practised their sun salutations.

'Look at all the flowers, Priya. They're everywhere!' Ishani exclaimed in delight, as they stepped off the bus into the golden sunshine. 'Aren't they stunning?'

Priya couldn't disagree. The gardens looked as though they'd been liberally sprinkled with pink and white confetti as flowers stretched as far as the eye could see. She didn't have a clue what they were but they were certainly plentiful and made a beautiful backdrop to the ashram. The warm air was heady with their rich scent and she felt both soothed and invigorated by every deep breath she took.

Maybe Maggie was right and there was something really special about this place.

Or perhaps, said the cynical part of Priya, it was just such a huge relief to be away from Divya that even the

M25 on a Friday afternoon would seem relaxing in comparison.

'Isn't it wonderful?' Maggie gushed, her pale skin already turning milkshake pink in the heat. 'Isn't it the most serene and spiritual place? I knew you'd love it!'

'You were absolutely right,' Priya agreed, smiling at the older woman's exuberance. Ten years seemed to have slipped from Maggie's skinny shoulders faster than you could say yoga and as her faded blue eyes twinkled behind her glasses Priya caught a glimpse of the girl she must have been.

Rejuvenation while you wait? Wow, a miracle already! Making a mental note to interview Maggie as soon as possible she motioned for Ray to get his camera out and began mentally composing her introduction.

Clay and Clara were less enthusiastic, already complaining about the heat and the lack of facilities. What were they expecting, wondered Priya, sliding on her Ray-Bans and gazing around her. A pool maybe or perhaps a gourmet restaurant? As far as she could see there was nothing but miles and miles of desert and hills beyond this oasis.

'Talk about the middle of nowhere,' she said.

'There's no bloody pub for miles and I'm gagging for a cold beer. I bet it's all carrot juice here,' sighed Ray, who was setting up his equipment and checking the light. He screwed his eyes up against the glare. 'Christ, that sun's fierce. I'll need filters.'

Priya laughed. 'We're supposed to be here for our souls, remember? Meditation and yoga and chakra cleansing! Not getting tanked up in a bar.'

'Drinking's great for the soul. I always bare mine

after a few drinks,' Ray argued, as he squinted into the lens. 'Anyway, don't you start going all New Age on me, Priya Gupta! We all know if you're not within five minutes of a Starbucks you get twitchy.'

She held up her hands. 'Okay. Guilty as charged. And what I wouldn't give for a Frappuccino right now. Still, it'll probably only be holy water for the next few hours which is just as well seeing as we're actually here to work rather than socialise. And on that note, Ray, can you get the desert in the establishing shots? We really need to set the place in context. Or maybe create a contrast.'

'Can ah be in the movie?' squealed Clara, parking herself slap in front of the lens. 'Ah've always wanted to be in the movies.'

'Me too,' boomed Clay, fanning a shiny head with his Stetson. 'What d'ya want us to say, honey? Ah must admit ah'm a bit disappointed. This isn't a patch on Sandals!'

'There's no pool,' Clara said to the camera. 'Ah do love to swim. How can they have a health spa without a pool?'

'We'd love to talk to you both,' said Priya smoothly, gently manoeuvring them out of Ray's way – which was rather like having to shift two hot sweaty Sherman tanks – 'and once Ishani has set up our sound equipment you'll be first on the list.'

'You'll need to settle in first, and there might not be time to be interviewed. It's a spiritual retreat, not a holiday camp,' Maggie pointed out. 'Normally we're met by someone and given a tour before we have to begin the first meditation. In fact there's someone coming now,' she added, her lined face creasing into a huge smile of joy. 'Oh, it's Noah! How lovely to see him again!'

Priya recognised the name. Noah was her contact at the ashram and for the last three weeks her point of email reference. Looking up and shading her eyes against the glaring sun she peered around for the ancient monk she'd pictured, all wrinkled raisin face, wispy candyfloss hair and Gandhi-style nappy, but saw no sign of him. Instead a tall lean handsome man, stripped to the waist, with ebony gypsy curls brushing his muscled shoulders, was striding towards her holding out his hand. He was wearing only a loose pair of combats, and a faded friendship bracelet on his wrist.

'Hi,' he said with a smile that crinkled wide-spaced grey eyes set above slanting cheekbones. 'I'm Noah. I'm guessing you must be the film crew. Priya, right?'

As anyone who knew her would testify, it wasn't often that Priya Gupta was lost for words, but as Noah held out his hand in greeting her tongue seemed to forget what it was for. So not a monk then, she registered swiftly as she returned the gesture.

'I'm so sorry I'm late meeting you,' Noah apologised, his smile wide and welcoming. 'I've been working in the vegetable garden all morning and I totally lost track of time. It's like that when you're gardening, isn't it?'

'Absolutely!' Priya agreed with gusto, although the closest she ever got to vegetables was meandering down the fruit and veg aisle in Tesco's. So why was she acting like she had a subscription to *Allotment Weekly*? And was it her imagination or was Ray looking at her oddly? Colouring, she stiffened. This would not do. So Noah looked good, amazing actually, so what? Priya gave herself a mental shake. He was probably some student on his gap year doing his bit for the world before getting a law degree and buying a Jag. Some middle-class do-gooder trying to find himself.

Recovering her cool, she introduced herself and her

crew, now mildly put out that she was going to be saddled with some head-in-the-clouds tree hugger as her guide. She'd met Noah's type before: *Guardian*-reading Greens abounded at the BBC.

'We grow all our own food here,' Noah was explaining. 'It's part of our philosophy that everything we put into the body is as pure and natural as possible. It's a sound green ethos, isn't it?'

The rest of the group were nodding. Now Priya was all for recycling and switching off the standby button on her telly, but who in the real world actually had time to grow their own vegetables? Only people who had the luxury of not working for a living. If she'd had a million pounds to bet instead of a terrifying and rapidly increasing overdraft, Priya would have wagered every penny that this Noah was one such person. Probably a Trustafarian who'd never had to do a day's work in his life. It was easy to be green when the daily grind didn't get in the way.

'Why doncha just buy 'em, son? Save yourself some work?' Clay wondered, looking genuinely perplexed.

Maggie rolled her eyes and Ishani smothered a giggle but Noah just looked thoughtful before saying gently, 'Well, you see, we would. But they closed the local Tesco Metro only last month. It's a nightmare. First Woolworth pick-and-mix. And now this.'

Priya couldn't resist laughing, liking his light-hearted attitude. She hadn't been expecting Noah to have a sense of humour, especially an irreverent one. The Americans still seemed perplexed though, Clay wondering what pick-and-mix was, and Clara asking where the nearest shops were. Noah's humour it seemed didn't quite translate.

'Anyway, that's quite enough of me rattling on,' Noah said with a self-deprecating shake of his head. 'I expect you're all very thirsty?'

There was a chorus of agreement at this and a cheer when Noah suggested that everyone followed him to the dining room where they'd be able to enjoy some refreshments before having a tour of the ashram. As the group trekked after his lithe form to the largest of the low whitewashed buildings Priya noticed that one couple peeled away, choosing to enter one of the smaller dwellings instead. Nothing sinister in that, of course; they might have been tired after the journey or such regular visitors that they didn't feel Noah's tour was necessary, but what did strike Priya as odd was that they were dressed in smart business suits and were carrying briefcases.

Her hazel eyes narrowed thoughtfully. Hardly the average ashram clientele. The other guests, with the psychedelic exception of Clara and Clay, were mostly clad in ethnic gear: long beaded skirts, kaftans and loose white cotton trousers; but these two looked as though they were about to meet Sir Alan Sugar in the boardroom. Her journalistic antennae were instantly alerted and, shouldering her bag, she decided to try to find out more about the odd couple. They could offer a very different perspective on the place.

Lunch was served in the ashram's dining room, a grand name for what was really a simple shed with six trestle tables flanked by roughly hewn wooden benches. Inside it was dark and cool after the brightness of the midday sun and it was a relief to all the new arrivals to be out of the burning rays. Priya sat down gratefully and rested her elbows on the rough tabletop. Would she ever grow accustomed to the relentless heat of India? After the incessant rain of the English summer it was something of a shock and already her forearms were looking pink.

'Here, you must have something to drink or you'll dehydrate very quickly,' Noah said, sliding on to the bench next to her and pouring a large glass of iced water. 'The heat is fierce this time of day, which is why we use the afternoons for meditation. Well, either that or a welcome nap for the lazier among us!'

He smiled as he said this and Priya found her lips curling upwards too. Accepting the glass she drained it gratefully, her parched throat welcoming the cool liquid, while Noah filled tumblers for Ray and Ishani.

'Thanks, I needed that,' she said, setting the glass down.

'A cold beer would be nicer,' grumbled Ray. 'But I don't expect you spiritual lot drink, do you?'

Priya sincerely doubted it. Noah was probably a teetotal vegan. Not that there was anything wrong with that, of course. It kind of went with the territory, along with dreadlocks, sandals and not washing very much. Mind you, Noah didn't smell unwashed and she should know seeing as he was sitting right beside her. In fact he smelled of a rather nice sharp citrusy scent.

'Don't mention cold beer!' groaned Noah, pulling a face. 'What I wouldn't give for one of those right now! But I'm afraid the ashram's dry. The swami's very strict about that.'

'You drink alcohol?' Priya was taken aback.

'Don't look so surprised,' Noah said, fixing those huge grey eyes on her and raising an eyebrow. 'I have been known to have a drink or two and once . . .' he paused dramatically, 'I even smoked a cigarette!'

Ray hooted with laughter and Priya flushed. She supposed that was what she got for trying to pigeonhole people too quickly. In her mind's eye Noah shifted from a *Guardian*-reading left-winger to some wild party boy who'd blown his inheritance on drink and drugs and was now finding himself in India while he dried out and went cold turkey. Sneaking a look at him from beneath her lashes, as he and Ray discussed the benefits of real ale as opposed to the bottled variety, she decided that Noah was a perfect cliché. Good looking, privileged and with the money to indulge himself. According to Kettan India was full of such folk. They peddled cod philosophy, followed wacky gurus and wouldn't know a hard day's work if it bit them on the bum.

Over lunch, a plain but tasty meal of brown rice and vegetable dhal, Priya listened as Noah chatted to Maggie and some of the other guests and explained the philosophies of the ashram and gently suggested classes or activities. Maggie seemed to hang on his every word and even the Americans appeared enthused by the prospect of sunset yoga. Was the image of the rotund Clay in the cobra pose another example of Noah's quirky sense of humour or did he genuinely think it would be a good idea? Priya stabbed a lump of okra thoughtfully. Time would tell.

'So,' Noah turned from Clay to Priya, 'what kind of films do you make, Priya? Would I know any of them?'

She put down her knife and fork with a clatter. 'I doubt it. You probably don't have telly here, do you?'

'No, Sky Plus has yet to make it this far,' Noah sighed, 'which is hard when a guy needs his *Simpsons* fix, but I'm slowly coming to terms with it. But in my other life I do have a television and once or twice I did watch it and I love documentaries so I may well have seen something you made.'

'We've done quite a few together,' chipped in Ray. 'Did you see *Dying to be Thin*? That was about anorexia. Or there was the one on domestic violence, *Home Sweet Home*. We got a BAFTA nomination for that.'

Noah looked thoughtful. 'That one rings a bell.'

'What did you think of it?' Priya had to ask when no following comment was forthcoming. *Home Sweet Home* was one of her proudest achievements. She'd sweated blood in the editing room over every frame. 'Hard hitting and emotionally devastating' was how the *Sunday Times* had described it, so why she was waiting for – or even interested in – the opinion of some hippy dropout was anyone's guess.

Noah frowned. 'Parts of it were very moving, especially the case of the woman whose teenaged son ended up stabbing her ex-partner when he attacked her.'

'Cally Thomas,' Priya recalled.

'Her story was very powerful and I can totally understand why you included it,' Noah agreed. 'But on the whole I'm afraid I found the documentary rather unbalanced, gender biased if you like.'

Priya didn't like. She goggled at Noah, hardly able to believe what she was hearing. 'Excuse me? How the hell can you possibly say that? Unless you side with the perpetrators?'

'Of course not. I was just rather surprised you didn't feature any male victims. A significant proportion of men are victims of domestic violence too, aren't they? And in some ways it's even harder to deal with because for a man to admit that his female partner hits him is socially and ideologically very difficult. It undermines conventional notions of masculinity, doesn't it?'

'Good point, mate. Can't believe we didn't think of it,' agreed Ray, and Priya felt like thumping *him* except that would probably prove Noah's case.

'We did think of it,' she said, 'but we were dealing with female victims.'

'Thus sweeping the problem even further under the carpet and reinforcing the idea that only women – or, putting it another way, weak girly men – suffer from domestic abuse,' Noah pointed out.

Priya glowered at him, lost for words for the second time in an hour. Her scalp prickled with irritation. Not because she was annoyed – although she was – but because he'd made a valid point and one she wished she'd thought of.

'Noah's right. We ought to plan a documentary on the issue,' ploughed on the enthusiastic Ray, oblivious of Priya's annoyance. 'It's a good idea, don't you think?'

'Mmm,' Priya murmured, pretending to be lost in thought. It *was* a good idea, but she'd no intention of admitting this to Noah. She wasn't about to tell him how to plant his vegetable garden, so who did he think he was criticising her BAFTA-nominated documentary?

'Wouldn't it be hard to get guys who'd been hit by

their partners to go on film if they're embarrassed?' Ishani wondered. 'How on earth would the researchers find them?'

'I've got a friend I met when I was inside who I'm sure would help,' Noah said. 'He'd been beaten for years by his wife and finally retaliated when she went for him with a knife. He was cleared on appeal eventually and it's kind of his life's mission to raise awareness of all faces of domestic violence.'

'Inside? You mean you've been in prison?' Priya blurted, taken aback. Somehow she couldn't imagine Noah, whom she'd now pegged as a wealthy guy indulging his spiritual side for a bit, in prison. He was hardly Wentworth Miller.

'Yes, I've been in prison,' Noah said calmly. He smiled at Priya, his grey eyes crinkling at the corners. 'Don't look so worried. I wasn't in for murder. I got away with that, as it happened.'

For a moment they all stared at him, chins nearly on the trestle table. Then Noah shook his head and laughed.

'Not really. Don't look so alarmed. It wasn't anything nearly so exciting. I got involved with some stupid stuff when I was a lot younger, the police decided to take a hard line, and to cut a long story short I did twelve weeks in an open prison. That was where I got into gardening, actually, and first really thought about the environment.'

'Blimey,' said Ray, looking relieved. 'You had us going there, you bugger. So you've been into green issues for a while then?'

Noah nodded. 'My parents brought me up to really think about conservation; I guess they were ahead of their time in that respect. But when you think about it, what could be more important than protecting the earth for the next generation?'

Everyone looked suitably impressed and murmured their agreement except Priya who, knowing for a fact that Ray drove a big gas-guzzling four-by-four and not doubting for a minute that the Americans did the same, pulled a face.

Catching her expression Noah said, 'Sorry, Priya. I'm getting preachy, aren't I? Time to jump off my high horse. Forget my shady past; tell me a bit about you. When you're not making award-winning document-aries what do you get up to?'

'Who's the interviewer here?' Priya joked, wrong-footed because actually these days she didn't get up to much apart from work. God, how boring was she?

Note to self: get a life when she returned to England.

'Priya's a workaholic,' said Ray. 'She lives in the office, don't you, pet?'

'I do not!' Priya snapped, shooting him a look which in a just universe should have laid him out at her trainers. 'I'm pretty busy at work, it's true, but I do other things as well. Lots of other things.'

'Such as?' Noah asked. His grey gaze was candid, just as it had been when he told them about his back-ground, and in spite of resenting being interviewed Priya found herself telling him about her flat and her demanding mother. By the time they'd finished their fruit dessert she'd given away far more information than she'd intended and was surprised and annoyed in equal measure.

Exactly what was in that dhal? Truth serum? Or was Noah just very skilled at wheedling information out of people? She'd have to keep a careful eye on him, she decided. Something told her there was more to him than met the eye. She'd never in her life encountered anyone so hard to put in a box. And if there was one thing Priya liked to do it was label and order everything, from her collection of shoes to the people she knew.

But Noah defied all straightforward definitions. What was he doing at a remote ashram in Rajasthan? Was he running away from something? Unlike the stereotype she'd imagined of the average ashram guide, who wouldn't have a clue about the real world or an ounce of common sense, Noah had experienced life in the raw and was passionate about many issues. He wasn't smelly or beardy and he didn't even have the obligatory dreadlocks.

He even liked *The Simpsons*!

Noah was a puzzle.

L unch over, the new arrivals were feeling refreshed and ready for their guided tour.

'Is it okay with you if we film as we go along?' she asked Noah, as they trailed out of the dining room and back into the hot sunshine. 'It'd really help to be able to set the ashram in context. It'd be great to get you in the shots too, explaining about the place.'

Noah looked down at her, his wide grey eyes thoughtful. 'Me? I'm hardly a television presenter. I'm just a gardener. Who wants to watch a gardener on the television?'

Lots of people if they look like you, Priya thought. With his tall sculpted body, chiselled face and voice as warm and rich as chocolate pudding Noah would be TV gold.

'You're approachable and knowledgeable,' she said, 'and you obviously feel passionate about this place. Besides, I want to give a balanced view of what happens at the ashram and who better to do that than someone who works here?'

'So what angle are you coming from, then?'

Priya felt herself flush to the cynical roots of her

hair. Those eyes, grey as an English sea, had a way of looking right into her soul and seeing all the murky bits.

'I'm just more scientifically minded, I guess. All those potions and stretches are all very well, I suppose, if you believe in them.'

'And you don't, I take it?'

'Only the gullible believe all that New Age claptrap,' said Priya as they entered a cool shady courtyard flanked by three plain white buildings, 'people who are looking for something, anything, to give meaning to their lives.'

Noah looked at her thoughtfully. 'You really believe that, don't you? Wow. It must be amazing to have all the answers so early on in life. Congratulations!'

'I'm not saying that I have all the answers. It's just that I suppose I'm more logically minded than some people.' Priya paused, suddenly aware that her voice had risen an octave. More gently she added, 'But it's great that you believe it. Your passion and enthusiasm probably inspire the visitors.'

'So what balances out my passion and enthusiasm? Cynicism?'

'I'm not cynical,' she said indignantly. 'I'm here to make a documentary about spiritual India and I'm more than prepared to be open-minded.'

He looked doubtful. 'Really?'

'Yes, really.'

She was starting to feel rather irritated by his doubt of her ability to be unbiased. As a documentary maker she'd always prided herself on that aspect of her work and wasn't about to change now.

She sighed. 'Look, Noah, I promise that while I'm

here, a guest of the swami, I'll listen to what you guys have to say and then I'll make up my mind. Okay?'

Noah nodded. Then he stretched out and took her hand in his. 'May I?'

Surprised at the unexpected contact she nodded mutely. Perhaps this was some strange custom at the ashram? Only skim-reading the brochure might have been a mistake.

Noah's tanned hand was large, and calloused from manual work, but his grip was warm and firm and very different from that of Vikram's slender, soft fingers. In spite of the warmth Priya shivered at his touch. It was only a handshake but it felt oddly intimate, especially when he turned her hand over and grazed the palm with his thumb. She swallowed.

'According to Ayurveda everyone has a mixture of mind/body principles, or doshas, which create our unique mental and physical characteristics,' Noah said quietly. His eyes left her hand and swept up to meet hers. 'Some of us are dominated by one dosha. In your case, vata dominates you. Slim and creative but also driven and restless. Sound familiar? Your doshas need rebalancing before your drive burns you out and leaves no space for the other areas of your life, especially the personal areas, which you've neglected for too long.'

Priya stared at him. How the hell did he know all that?

Then Noah winked. 'If you believe me, of course. It could just be a really cunning chat-up line!'

She laughed. She had a camera crew in tow, had travelled thousands of miles to make a film, and was an unmarried Asian girl of a certain age. It didn't take a genius.

'God, you're good! You almost had me going for a minute,' she said, sliding back her hand. 'What shall I do to rebalance these doshas? Buy a course of treatment? Or maybe take some yoga classes? Or shall I give my savings to the swami?'

Noah's generous curly mouth lifted into a rueful smile. 'We're not a profit-making venture, but I'm not going to convince you, am I? Perhaps I shouldn't even try. Why don't you just look round, ask as many questions as you like and make up your own mind?'

She crossed her arms. 'That's exactly what I intend to do.'

'So let's make a start,' said Noah, clapping his hands for attention. Although his tone was crisp Priya had the distinct impression that he was enjoying their difference of opinion. So he liked a challenge? Just as well, because she had lots of questions, starting with why the gate to the small herb garden they were passing was padlocked.

'The herbs in there are very rare,' Noah explained when she asked him. 'We're growing some of the most highly valued and delicate medicinal plants in India and can't risk their being damaged.'

'Can't you trust people to look and not touch?' she countered.

'It's not about trust. Nobody would intentionally harm the plants, but even so, to lose them would be devastating because they're vital to so many of the herbal cures we make. We simply can't take the risk.'

Priya nodded. 'I understand.' Or at least she thought she did.

They passed a group of white-robed people performing their yoga under the banyan trees, and another well-tended herb garden. The gate to this one was open and people wandered at will. Amongst the herbs were swathes of flowers, jasmine, hibiscus and lilac, which blew in the warm breeze and filled the air with delicious fragrance.

'What are the flowers for?' Ishani asked, her nose crinkling as she inhaled the fragrance. 'Are they cures too?'

Noah smiled at her. 'They can be but they're also more than that. We like to think of them as balm for the soul. Nature's beauty can often be the most effective cure of all when it comes to helping us find relaxation.'

'Like magic?' asked Clara, blushing to the roots of her bubble perm when Noah picked a jasmine sprig and offered it to her.

'If you like,' he agreed.

'Magic plants?' scoffed Ray, lowering his camera. 'The only magic plants I've ever come across were mushroom-shaped. Maybe you should grow some of those?'

Noah laughed. 'I think the swami might have something to say about that. Besides, we get our highs from fresh air and meditation here.'

'If you say so,' said Ray doubtfully, looking at a group of people toiling on the land.

'I do, but don't take my word for it. Come and talk to some of the others.'

Leading them across a neat, gravelled path, Noah

joined a squat, Italian-looking man who was hoeing a tract of soil with great concentration.

'Luigi, these are our new arrivals,' Noah said. 'I've been giving them the grand tour.'

Luigi straightened up. One hand in the small of his back, the other taking Priya's and raising it to his lips, he beamed. 'Luigi Marconi, head gardener and herbologist. It is a pleasure. Welcome!'

'Luigi's being far too modest,' Noah said warmly. 'He's actually Dr Marconi and head of our sustainability project. He's working on a new way of recycling plant waste to make energy. It's a really revolutionary concept and very exciting.'

Luigi Marconi spread his hands. 'Is all true! My aim is to create a sustainable herb garden which can be harnessed as a renewable source of energy at this *bella* place. Over there,' he added, pointing to a small concrete building, 'is my lab and also the renewable energy plant.'

Everyone looked impressed.

'Wow,' said Ray. 'That could have amazing implications for more than just this ashram.'

Dr Marconi nodded. 'It certainly could. This is a very, very exciting time!'

'Can we see inside?' Priya asked. 'It sounds really fascinating.'

Luigi Marconi and Noah exchanged a swift glance, then Noah shook his head.

'I'm afraid that's not possible. We're still developing the processes and patents are pending so for the foreseeable future that area's out of bounds.'

'We're tourists, not industrial spies,' Priya said.

But Noah was adamant. 'Sorry, but the answer's still no. This is a working ashram, not a theme park. There are plenty of unrestricted areas that you can explore and film to your heart's content.'

'But surely you want people to see what you're about here? This would amaze them.'

'The answer is no,' Noah said firmly, and for the first time she sensed the steel beneath the gentle voice, steel which was echoed in the hardening of those grey eyes. 'Priya, I want to help you and your crew, I really do, but I must ask you to be respectful of other people's space and free movement. Certain areas here are out of bounds – for good reasons – and I must insist that you respect their privacy.'

Priya hated being kept out of things and instantly felt on the defensive. What were they hiding in there, she wondered? She'd find out if it was the last thing she did, although judging by the expression on Noah's face it probably would be if he caught her trying to sneak a look inside.

Deciding to leave the matter for now so as to not raise his suspicions, she changed the subject.

'What about all these so-called miracles?' she asked. 'Arthritis cured, cancers healed? Is it true?'

'If you believe in miracles, then of course,' Noah replied. 'Every day is a miracle, isn't it, if you really think about it?' He looked at her, a long intense look. 'Do you believe in miracles, Priya?'

Er . . . could she ask the audience? Phone a friend? Priya stared at Noah for a moment before her eyes slid away. His gaze was so open and honest that for a moment she was almost tempted to bare her soul and tell him that once she had believed that there was good in everything and everyone, and that in loving Vikram she'd found her own small slice of heaven on earth. But everything was different now; the world had tilted on its axis so that life was skewed and not what she had thought.

Quickly, she pasted a professional smile on to her face.

'What I do or don't believe is immaterial. The point is that there are people who are convinced there's some kind of miraculous healing going on here, and let's be honest, Noah, that won't harm trade for you. My question is whether or not it's true?'

Noah looked saddened rather than offended by her words. 'That's a very bleak take on the world. If the swami were here she'd say you need to find peace to heal and recover from whatever happened to make you feel like that.'

Unless the ashram specialised in yogic hit men who could take Vik out with their cobra poses Priya didn't hold out much hope of finding healing here. Not that the calm and centred Noah would probably think much of such an attitude. A swift change of subject was in order.

'Hey, son!' Abruptly, Clay's foghorn tones blasted forth. 'Never mind all that Ay ... Ayur ... hippy stuff! Where are the bedrooms?'

'You're sleeping here, in the gaushalas.' Noah gestured to the long whitewashed buildings which framed three sides of the courtyard, his sleeve falling back with the movement to reveal a strong forearm, corded with sinew.

'Gaushalas?' repeated Ishani. 'Really? You make guests sleep in cowsheds?'

'Cowsheds!' Clara echoed while Clay's chin nearly hit his socked and sandalled feet. 'Ah'm not sleeping with the cows even if it does cure mah migraines! Avril never said anything about sleeping with cows.'

Several other guests nodded in agreement before Clay found his voice and began a ten-decibel diatribe about Americans expecting certain standards *even* in a Third World country. Ishani gasped at this and even the laid-back Ray looked shocked at Clay's insulting and ignorant comments, but Noah just stood perfectly still and bore the brunt of the Texans' anger. Not so much as a muscle flickered in his smooth-skinned face and Priya was impressed by his self-control. If only she could be that Zen the next time Divya and Ashwani started to needle her about being unmarried.

Maybe there was something in all this mumbo-jumbo after all?

It was only once Clay finally ran out of steam, the lack of response from Noah silencing him far more effectively than any gag, that their host finally replied, explaining slowly that people did not raise their voices at the ashram, and that sometimes days went past without anyone talking at all.

'This is a place of peace and calm,' he finished gently. 'People come here to find some quiet space and out of respect for that we try really hard not to raise our voices. Instead, we meditate and reflect on life, or at least we try to in between arguments about restricted areas and whether or not miracles really exist!'

In spite of herself Priya smiled. Okay, so it was a

gentle dig at her but she probably deserved it. It was a legacy of bloody Vikram that she no longer trusted people so readily. Perhaps she ought to try harder to get over that particular issue.

'But what about our rooms?' Clay's voice was lower now but still harsh against the stillness. 'We don't want to share with cattle. No siree!'

'Can't we sleep in those pyramids over there?' Clara added.

Noah placed a gentle hand on her pudgy shoulder. 'The pyramids are for practising meditation in. But rest assured, there are no cattle in the gaushalas. They're basic, but cool and comfortable.'

To prove a point he opened the door of one of the dormitories and let the Texans peek inside.

'It's quite pleasant,' conceded Clara.

'And not a cow in sight,' Ishani added.

'Apart from one very silly one,' Ray whispered back, causing her to giggle.

Priya gave them a stern look. 'Don't encourage him,' she told Ishani. The footage he was capturing could be really useful. The last thing she needed was to have to spend hours glued to Final Cut in order to edit out his jokes.

Traumas of accommodation over, Noah guided the group round the ashram, showing them everything from the vegetable gardens to the orchards where laden trees groaned with the weight of their fruit. Beyond the trees was a small square building which Noah proudly informed them was a school and one of the ashram's projects which helped the local Bhil tribe.

'Before Swami Attuttama took over eighteen months

ago that building was used to lock up anyone who wanted to meditate,' Noah said. 'If you thought the gaushalas were basic, then think again. It was bare earth and just bread and water in there. A bit extreme, maybe, but if anyone wants to try something similar I'm sure it can be arranged!'

He caught Priya's eye and the corners of his mouth lifted as the Texans gasped in horror.

'Aren't you glad we've moved with the times?' he added to the worried-looking Clara, who nodded vehemently.

Smart as well as handsome, Priya noted with amusement. Somehow she didn't think either Clay or Clara would be moaning about their basic accommodation or plain supper now.

'When can I meet the swami?' she asked, as they headed back to the reception area. 'She was very keen to let us film here. Can we see her now?'

'That won't be possible today, I'm afraid. The swami is on retreat out in the hills.'

Great. They'd travelled thousands of miles specifically to speak to the swami and now they'd arrived she'd gone AWOL.

'Can't you take us to visit her? We're all more than happy to hike into the hills.'

Noah spread his hands. 'I'm afraid it's not permitted to take guests into certain areas of the ashram, and the retreat falls into the restricted areas. When the swami returns I'm sure she'll be more than happy to speak to you.'

Priya hadn't worked in journalism for six years to be fobbed off that easily.

'Why are some areas restricted? What's the big secret?'

'No secret, it's just that the retreat is private and the swami's fasting,' Noah said easily, his face open and totally without guile. 'When she returns I will speak to her about meeting you and your crew.'

And with that Priya had to be satisfied because Noah refused to be drawn on the subject any further.

The afternoon passed pleasantly enough and by the time the air started to cool and the mountain tops were blushed tea-rose pink Priya had begun to feel confident she could find her way around the ashram. The restricted areas still bugged her – she always hated being kept out of things – but Noah's explanations seemed reasonable enough and she was prepared to bide her time.

Or at least she was until they were on their way back to the city and Ray played back the rushes in the car . . .

'Wait a minute!' Priya leaned forward, jabbing her finger at the small viewing screen. 'Isn't that the restricted herb garden? The one Noah made such a song and dance about?'

'Yeah, I think so.' Ray squinted at the screen. 'Let me rewind it and check.'

His huge hands fiddled with the camera and the tape buzzed backwards for a second or two before he pressed Play again, and sure enough there was the small padlocked gate to the forbidden garden, clear to see on the screen, and just beyond it the figures of three people walking amongst the plants.

'Now pause it,' said Priya. 'Can you zoom in?'

Ray pulled a face. 'Not on this camera. Maybe with

the one that never made it out of the Air India luggage hold I could have. Why? What's the problem?'

'I'm not sure,' Priya said slowly. 'But look closely, Ray. There are people in the garden, aren't there? The garden where nobody's allowed to go.'

Ray practically squashed his nose against the small screen. 'You're right! I knew I should have gone to Specsavers! You've got the eyesight of a hawk, Pri, spotting that.'

'Surely some people are allowed inside?' Ishani pointed out. 'Somebody has to tend the herbs.'

'Not these people,' Priya said slowly. A tingle of excitement started to fizz down her spine, the way it always did when her gut instinct told her she was on to a story. 'At least not if what we heard this afternoon was the truth.'

Her eyes narrowed. There was no mistaking the tall broad-shouldered figure of Noah on the screen. Not that there was a problem with his having access to the garden. Of course not. But what made her heart skip a beat was the company he was with. No stooped gardeners nor even the lean figure of Dr Marconi accompanied Noah. Instead he was flanked by the business couple, still clad in their smart suits, the man clutching his large briefcase.

What were they doing in the restricted garden? And why had Noah allowed them inside when he'd been so adamant that Priya and her crew were to go nowhere near?

Noah was definitely keeping something from her.

I t was dusk by the time Priya and Ishani returned to the city. It was a warm night, with stars stabbing the dark blue sky and a full moon rising over the rooftops, and as their taxi drew up outside the Adanis' apartment Priya yawned and had to force herself to keep her heavy eyes open. It had been a long and intense day; they'd spent hours filming in the heat as well as walking miles around the ashram, and she was exhausted.

As she dragged herself up the stairs to the apartment Priya thought she'd like nothing more than to collapse on to her bed, huddle under the cool sheets and sleep, but she had more chance of flying to the moon. Her heart sank when she heard Akhila's summons and Divya's shriller greeting. It seemed there was to be no escape from yet another interrogation at the kitchen table.

'There you are at last!' Akhila beamed at the two weary girls. 'We were starting to think you weren't coming back. You've been gone all day.'

'Of course we have. There was a lot to do.' Ishani opened the fridge, helping herself to a bottle of chilled water and passing one to Priya. 'It was fascinating, actually. I had no idea there'd be so much going on at the ashram. I thought it'd just be yoga and chanting, but there's so much more. They've got this sustainable market gardening project going on which is used to fund health care for the neighbouring tribespeople. The swami makes sure they put back in twice what they take out, you know.'

Wow, thought Priya in surprise. It sounded like Noah had a new convert.

'Do they do treatments?' Neesh asked, looking up from the important business of filing her nails. 'I could do with a mud wrap or a hot stone massage. Can you book me in?'

Priya laughed. 'You'd be more likely to have to carry the stones or shovel the mud. Their ethos is that it's hard work that brings you closer to spiritual fulfilment, not lying around being pampered.'

Neesh screwed up her nose. 'Sounds grim. Rather you than me! I'll stick to getting my fulfilment at the shops, thanks.'

'Busy day, Sanj?' Priya asked her brother-in-law-to-be, who was slumped next to Neesh and looking exhausted, no doubt from lugging the huge stack of bags piled around his fiancée.

'We went to the bazaar. It was amazing!' Neesh said, her eyes lighting up. 'They had these wicked shoes made of satin and covered in gorgeous beads. I could hardly choose which ones to buy.'

'You didn't choose, babe. You bought a pair in each colour,' Sanjeev reminded her gently, but Neesh was unrepentant.

'I'm spending to help the global economy. Gordon Brown said I should.'

'Single-handedly?' Priya teased. 'Just how much did you spend?'

'*She* didn't spend a penny. Somehow I ended up having to pay,' sighed Sanj.

'Such a generous boy,' Divya cooed. 'You're so good to my daughter, Sanjeev.'

'Too good,' he muttered darkly. 'I'll have to put in some serious overtime when I get home.'

'Priya, see how you are missing out?' Divya said sharply. 'Wouldn't you like a husband to treat you from time to time?'

Biting back a sharp retort that if she felt the need for glittery shoes (highly unlikely) she'd go and buy them herself, Priya forced herself to keep quiet. The last thing she needed this evening was a row with Divya. So instead she pretended to be entranced by miles of scarlet sari fabric and a snot-green sandal sprinkled with pink beads that Neesh insisted she couldn't live without.

Just like she couldn't live without all the other pairs of shoes and saris that crammed her closet at home.

To her surprise she suddenly saw Noah's slate-grey eyes and heard his wry, amused voice.

'We've forgotten how to take only what we need,' he'd told his guests as he'd shown them the recycling area. 'Landfill and pollution are the products of our greed and there's no saying how it'll end. Here we only eat what we grow and try our hardest to return everything back to the earth. And I do mean everything. I must show you the way we recycle the waste from the lavatories and turn it into fertiliser.'

There'd been outcries of horror at this and Clara had nearly thrown up at the thought of human waste going into the production of the lush green salad she'd consumed at lunch time. Noah had winked at Priya as he'd explained this particular ideology and she'd found herself smiling back. Clara had never thought about where her food came from, but Priya had a feeling that from now on she'd be washing her salad greens far more thoroughly.

Perhaps Noah had a point about conspicuous consumption, Priya thought, returning the shoe to the K2 sized pile of bags. After all, Neesh only had one pair of feet.

'Wouldn't you like a nice young man to spoil you?' pressed Divya, with all the subtlety of a herd of stampeding rhinos.

'Mum, I'm fine as I am,' Priya insisted. She caught Ishani's eye and had to look away when the younger girl pulled a face.

'Don't worry, Divya,' Akhila said smoothly. 'I've found the perfect occasion to introduce Priya to some of the most eligible young men in Jaipur. My dear friend Ashoor has passed away and tomorrow is his funeral. Everyone who's anyone will be attending, so she's bound to find someone who suits.'

Priya was staggered. Talk about a death penalty! She was just on the brink of telling Akhila exactly where she could stick her matchmaking when she caught a warning look from her mother. *Don't you dare insult our host!*

Biting her tongue, Priya cast her eyes down, but inside she was seething.

What was this, a bad episode of *The Jeremy Kyle Show*? Did they seriously expect her to go on the pull at a funeral?

Absolutely no way! She'd rather swim back to England!

'I'm so sorry about my mother,' Ishani apologised later on when she and Priya were alone in the courtyard garden. 'She doesn't mean to offend anyone; she's just trying to be hospitable.'

'By turning a funeral into a husband hunt? Surely that's a bit extreme?'

'Not for my mum.' Ishani raised her eyes to the purple skies where the fat moon drifted above a sprinkling of stars, and sighed. 'She's a force of nature all right, but she means well.'

'I'm sure she does, but I really don't appreciate her interfering with *my* love life! With all due respect it's none of her business.' Priya shook her head in annoyance. 'It's bad enough when my mother starts, but both of them together? That's just a nightmare.'

'I can imagine,' Ishani agreed. 'I'd hate it too.'

'How come you're not being subjected to all this? You're Akhila's daughter, after all. You should be way ahead of me in the queue to find an eligible husband.'

'Mum leaves me alone because I'm already betrothed,' Ishani explained, shredding a jasmine flower between her slender fingers. 'I've been engaged for almost four years.'

'Oh!' Priya was taken aback. She'd not linked Ishani with any of the identikit young men she'd met at the Adanis' and neither had the other girl mentioned a fiancé. She glanced at Ishani's left hand but there was no sign of an engagement ring. Priya was puzzled.

'Baadal's a physicist, not a romantic,' Ishani said, following Priya's gaze. 'He's studying in the States and when he's finished his PhD he says we can choose a ring and take things to the next level.'

How very scientific and logical and . . . cold, Priya thought. She supposed Akhila would view this as prudent and responsible behaviour but it hardly spoke of burning passion.

'How long is the PhD likely to take?' she asked.

'Three years? Maybe four? It's a lifetime away anyhow. At this rate I won't be married until I'm in my thirties, and by then we'll have been apart for so long he'll be a total stranger.' She turned wide brown eyes on Priya. 'How can I marry a total stranger?'

Priya swallowed. Maybe there were worse things than having to endure a morning of awkward embarrassment at a funeral.

'Did you know him well before he went to the States?'

'We grew up together. He's the son of an old family friend and it was always assumed we'd marry one day. Our parents agreed the contract when we were teenagers,' Ishani explained. 'When I graduated we were betrothed and I thought we'd go to the USA together.' She paused and her fine brows drew together in a frown. 'Baadal didn't want that, though. He thought I'd be a distraction from his studying.'

Priya thought Baadal sounded a right barrel of laughs. Not.

'Didn't you mind?'

Ishani shrugged her slender shoulders. 'It's not a love match, Priya, so I'm hardly heartbroken. Maybe I was a bit annoyed that he was so relaxed about putting me on hold. It wasn't because I'm madly in love with him, and he certainly doesn't love me. The word on the grapevine is that he's got an American girlfriend anyway, not that Mum has a clue. She'd freak.'

'My God,' said Priya. 'Don't you mind?'

'My pride was a bit hurt, I suppose, but then I realised that my being engaged keeps Mum off my back. I've been able to get on with my career without her matchmaking like a Jane Austen mother on speed.'

Priya laughed.

'If I were you I'd let them plot,' was Ishani's advice. 'It keeps them happy and out of your hair.'

'But letting my mother choose my husband? Surely that's my job? We're talking lifetime commitment here,' Priya pointed out. 'It's not like choosing a new handbag.'

'Maybe our mothers know best.' Ishani smiled gently. 'At least I don't have to worry about dating and being let down by guys. Everything's already taken care of.'

Priya's brow crinkled. She certainly knew all about guys letting her down. Maybe there was something to be said for accepting a mother's choice after all. If Ishani was to be believed it certainly seemed to bring some measure of calm.

Or, she wondered when a brief expression of sadness flickered across Ishani's face, maybe it wasn't calm after all? Perhaps a better description would be resignation.

Even though the evening was warm Priya shivered as fingers of moonlight stroked her bare forearms. Was she being overly romantic to dream of more from her future husband, or was resigning herself to Divya's choice the best she could hope for? Maybe she should listen to Angela and just accept that in matters of love her mother knew best.

Because, let's face it, her own choices had hardly been up to much.

11

By the following evening Priya was no longer quite so convinced that *mother knows best* was a maxim she wanted to live her life by. In fact with every minute that passed it was feeling more like a recipe for disaster than the oasis of calm and acceptance she'd hoped for.

Standing in the pouring rain, her sari plastered to her bare legs and her sandals sodden, Priya thought that at least the miserable monsoon weather matched her miserable mood. Ignoring the persistent young man on her left, whose moustache was thicker than a shag pile rug, she edged closer to Neesh's brolly and wished herself a million miles away. If only she'd stuck to her gut instinct and told Divya exactly what to do with her matchmaking she could have been at the ashram pressing on with the documentary, rather than having to watch her mother scent out the economic prospects of the chief mourner.

Maybe in her past life Divya had been a bloodhound?

From the moment that the Adanis and the Guptas had arrived at the shamshana, a sacred cremation ground close to the river, Akhila and Divya had gone into overdrive, informing every parent in the vicinity of Priya's eligibility. Even as they'd trailed after the bullock cart bearing Ashoor's white-clad corpse to the pyre Divya had been busy boasting about her daughter's well-paid job at the BBC. Mentioning Auntie was like uttering a magic word because within seconds countless excited mothers were buzzing round Priya, pinching her cheeks and sizing her up for her childbearing hips (too narrow) and her bank balance (hugely inflated by Divya and certainly not bearing any relation to reality). Since then everywhere she went Priya had been propositioned by a host of unmarried sons, all of whom thought they could knock Brad Pitt into cotton socks. Short, tall, fat, thin, hairy and bald, it didn't matter, they were all desperate to make her acquaintance and ask her about her job at the hallowed British Broadcasting Corporation. So far she'd been propositioned along the parade, teased in the temple and praised by the pyre. Worst of all, and she *prayed* that in this she was mistaken, Priya was pretty sure that as he lit the pyre the deceased's eldest son had winked at her.

No way. Could you imagine having to explain to the kids how Daddy fell in love with Mummy while he was setting Grandpa alight? That was one conversation she was so *not* going to be having!

No, the sooner this funeral was over the better. Not that anyone seemed in a hurry to go anywhere. Apparently the mourners didn't leave until the corpse had been consumed by the flames, which could be anything between one and three hours. However, as thick choking smoke had filled the air the heavens had opened again, forcing the mourners to squeeze themselves into a pavilion or shelter beneath umbrellas, and Ashoor's widow had decided that only close family should remain, leaving the others free to leave and dry off.

'Shame,' Neesh said to Priya as, huddled beneath the umbrella, they followed the sodden mourners away from the shamshana. 'You were on a roll there, sis. I nearly bet Mum a hundred quid you'd leave an engaged woman. The chief mourner didn't need a torch to light the pyre. One of those smouldering looks he was giving you would have done!'

'Stop it, you! I've never been so embarrassed in my whole life!' Priya replied, her cheeks scarlet. She hated attention at the best of times and nobody in their right mind could describe a funeral as that except perhaps for Divya and Akhila who were waiting by the car, dark heads bent together as they pored over the scribbled notes and phone numbers they'd collected.

'Why are you embarrassed? You're Jaipur's answer to Angelina Jolie,' Neesh teased.

Priya sighed. The level of interest had been ridiculous but she wasn't silly enough to believe it was actually *her* the guys were interested in. Okay, so she wasn't hideously ugly – past boyfriends had been known to like her small curvy body, unusual jade eyes and fuchsia bud lips – but she was hardly a contender for *Britain's Next Top Model*. The dull truth was that these guys were so desperate for a wife, and preferably one without two heads or a moustache, that they'd be delighted with anyone halfway human. Add to that a job at the Beeb and a British passport and bingo! Everyone wanted an introduction.

How was that flattering?

'I mean, it's not as though you're exactly fighting men off with a stick at home, is it?' continued Neesh, with about as much tact as Simon Cowell chewing out *X Factor* wannabes. 'You never know, some might be almost decent. You must have fancied one of them?'

Priya sighed. Almost decent? Was that as good as it would ever get now?

'Don't tell me now, though,' her sister continued, as they clambered into their waiting taxi. 'Save it for the restaurant, so that everyone can hear. The aunties will be gagging to hear all about the handsome bachelors.'

'So would I if there'd been any.' Priya slammed the door shut and sank into the plastic seat. Then she sat bolt upright again as her sister's words registered. 'Hold on. What did you just say about a restaurant?'

'Mum and Akhila have booked a table at the Suvarna Mahal. We're all having dinner there to celebrate the wedding. The aunties can hardly wait.'

'Great.' Priya buried her head in her hands. Just the thought of dinner with Divya, the Adanis and her pushy aunts was enough to give her indigestion.

Could today possibly get any worse?

Priya hadn't seen much of the Pink City, as the locals affectionately called Jaipur, so the drive into the city was a chance for her to admire the beautiful buildings, all turrets and elaborate domed rooftops like Brighton's Royal Pavilion on speed. Once the rain stopped, as abruptly as it had started, the setting sun blushed the ancient buildings and streaked the sky like candy cane, turning the palaces into elaborately iced cakes. Priya captured as much as she could on her mobile phone's video camera, thinking how much she'd like to send Ray out to shoot the opulence and beauty as a direct contrast to the clean lines and austerity of the ashram. She could picture silk-clad maharajas, draped in emeralds and rubies the size of chicken's eggs, reclining on velvet cushions in these palaces, eating delicacies while dark-eyed slaves fanned them silently.

Somehow she didn't think Noah would have approved of *their* consumer habits either.

She shook her head as though water was trapped in her ears and slid the phone back into her bag. Why did Noah keep popping into her thoughts with his quiet words and strong convictions?

'Maybe on your next visit?' he'd said gently, fixing her with those lustrous grey eyes. 'I think she'd like you.'

Priya had looked up into that high-cheekboned face and seen nothing there but honesty.

'Why can't I wait and see her now?'

'Why so impatient?' Noah shook his head, the long curls dancing with the movement. 'All in good time, my friend. There's no hurry.'

All in good time when they'd had time to hide all traces of whatever it was they were up to, Priya had thought with annoyance, but as her eyes locked with his the sharp retort withered on her lips and to her surprise she'd found herself agreeing that of course it would be fine to wait.

There was something so calming about Noah, she reflected, as the taxi came to a stop outside the restaurant. Or perhaps the peace of the ashram had that effect on you after a while. Maybe tomorrow she'd find Clara and Clay clad in robes whilst striking the tree pose and chanting.

She was still smiling at this thought when she joined her extended family inside the restaurant. Although restaurant was an understatement, she thought, glancing around the sumptuous interior where liveried waiters glided by like figure skaters and chandeliers the size of icebergs threw dancing diamonds on to the diners; this was more like a palace. As the maître d' showed her to her seat, spreading over her lap a napkin more snowy white than alpine peaks, Priya let the waves of classical music wash over her. The ambience was perfect, from the strains of Vivaldi to the soft alabaster lamps that threw buttery light across the room.

Surely now she could relax.

But Priya had forgotten to factor Bhavani, Chandani and Darsani into this equation. It would be easier to relax on a bed of nails than go out for a meal with them.

'Did you find any men for Priya?'

Bhavani's cry was so shrill that Priya half expected the beautifully engraved glasses to shatter. Heads swivelled to their table and Sanjeev, who was seated beside her, almost went into orbit. Ishani caught Priya's eye and pulled a sympathetic face.

'There were many suitable men all very keen to meet my daughter,' Divya said smugly. 'Priya has her pick of Jaipur's eligible bachelors.'

'Really?' Bhavani's mouth fell open, treating all the

other diners to a view of half-masticated pakora. 'Well, I suppose there aren't so many available young women these days. They all want to be working rather than concentrating on marriage and family.'

'I don't,' chipped in Neesh, sliding into the seat next to her fiancé and winding her slim arms around his waist. 'I'm more than happy not to work. Aren't I, Sanj?'

'Unfortunately so,' he sighed.

'All the young men we spoke to were very impressed by Priya's career at the BBC, weren't they, Akhila?' Divya boasted.

'Yes indeed,' confirmed her partner in crime. 'Priya was very popular and she has many lunch and dinner invitations.'

'Which I can't possibly accept because I'll be working,' said Priya, fighting rising annoyance. If she ground her teeth any more she'd have nothing left but stumps.

'Tell us all about the ashram,' said Kettan smoothly as he took the seat on her other side. 'Was it true about the miracles or just good PR?'

Priya could have hugged him for changing the subject. 'I haven't seen enough yet to judge. I'm supposed to be meeting the swami tomorrow so I guess I'll have more of a picture then.'

But nobody was really listening to what she had to say. Divya, having seen Kettan gravitate towards Priya, had lit up like the national grid, while the aunties were whispering behind plump oil-smeared hands. Priya sighed. She wouldn't even be able to sit with her ally now. Seeing her with Kettan too often would only get Divya's hopes up and put more pressure on her. What was the point of incurring even more grief when she knew it was hopeless?

Not that she cared about its being hopeless, of course. Kettan was handsome and smooth but a bit too much like Barbie's Ken for Priya's taste.

'Please go and sit somewhere else,' she whispered into his left ear. 'Mum's going to combust with excitement if you sit with me.'

Kettan looked up from the menu and pulled a face. 'Let her have some fun, Priya. It's not hurting anyone if we chat.'

'That's where you're wrong. It gets Mum's hopes up and then she'll be really disappointed when nothing comes of it. And as usual I'll get the blame because it's not as though I can tell her why you're not interested, is it?'

He sighed. 'Fair point. Okay, you win. I'll sit next to Ishani. God knows what we'll talk about, though. I'll probably die of boredom. That girl's so quiet she makes Trappist monks seem chatty!'

Priya was surprised. During their day at the ashram Ishani had chatted non-stop and matched Ray in terms of banter, which was saying something. So what made her different with Ray? Was it their shared passion for filming?

'You can't sit here,' Ishani said to Kettan when he tried to take the seat beside her. 'It's taken.'

'Who by? The invisible man?' Kettan said good-naturedly. 'Come on, cuz, I'm not that bad. I promise not to nick your starter!'

Ishani raised her chin and slammed her bag on to the plush red seat. 'I've invited a friend to join us for dinner.'

'Really?' Akhila looked surprised. 'You didn't mention it.'

'Didn't I?' Ishani's eyes slid from her mother's. 'Sorry. I must have forgotten.'

'So who's your friend then?' grinned Kettan. 'Maybe I can sit on their lap?'

'Try that, mate, and we might need to scrape yous up from the floor,' said a familiar voice. 'You're a right pretty boy but you're not my type.'

'Ray!' Ishani cried, leaping to her feet. 'You made it.'

Priya's head snapped up from her menu as though on elastic. What the bloody hell was Ray doing here?

'Course I made it. I'm bloody famished, man! And I've read up on this place. It's supposed to be the dog's b—'

Crash! Priya's side plate and glass slipped to the floor.

'Bit clumsy there, Pri,' Ray said, ruffling her hair as he passed by. Then he caught the expression on her face and said quickly, 'This place is supposed to be top banana, right?'

'Absolutely!' Behind her glasses Ishani's eyes shone like damp peat. 'Jaipur has thousands of restaurants but this one's the best. Its Dal Batti is to die for!'

'Great, bring it on!' beamed Ray, although Priya knew he hadn't the foggiest what Ishani was on about. 'Thanks for inviting me along.'

'Ray's Priya's cameraman,' Ishani was explaining to her mother while Ray shoe-horned his lanky frame into the spare seat, sending Kettan scuttling back in Priya's direction. 'We've been working on the documentary with Priya. Ray's staying at the Sheraton and I thought it might be nice for him to come out and sample authentic Rajasthani food. He's been eating in McDonald's.'

There was a collective sigh of horror from everyone around the table except Priya, who was happy for Ray to live on Big Macs for ever if it kept him away from her mother. She glowered at him but he was immersed in the menu and totally oblivious.

'The Mas Ke Sule sounds mint,' he said happily.

'You're staying in a hotel?' Akhila asked, putting her menu down and shaking her head. 'That's not acceptable when you are a friend of our family. You must stay with us. I insist!'

'I couldn't possibly expect that, m'am,' Ray said. 'You don't even know me.'

'We do. You work with Priya and you guys go back ages,' Ishani argued.

'Not that long,' said Priya hastily. 'I hardly know him.'

'You're such a card, Pri.' Ray laughed. 'Dinosaurs roamed about when we joined the Beeb together.'

'And any friend of the Guptas is a friend of the Adanis,' Akhila added firmly, in a voice that wouldn't be argued with. 'We couldn't possibly allow a family friend to stay in a hotel, it goes against our famous Rajasthani hospitality. After dinner, young man, you will pack your things, check out and come to our house. I absolutely insist on it.'

Priya was appalled. Not only would Ray now witness the total humiliation of her matchmaking hell but he'd be a loose cannon, wandering around ready to shoot his mouth off about her and Vikram. How on earth could she keep him away from Divya when they were crammed into the Adanis' apartment like sardines?

The only person possibly more upset than Priya by this new arrangement was Divya, who with pleated brow and pursed mouth glowered down at her plate. No matter how long and how hard Priya had tried to convince her that there was nothing between her and Ray except a working friendship Divya had never been convinced. As far as she was concerned Ray had designs on her single daughter and knowing her mother as she did Priya was sure that she was already planning how to warn him off. The minute she struck up a conversation Ray would be sure to blab the truth about Vik and then it was game well and truly over.

Her appetite vanishing, Priya sighed heavily and picked up the wine list.

Suddenly she really needed a drink.

12

'Top grub, Mrs A!' Ray announced at breakfast. He'd just hoovered up an enormous pile of pancakes and now was leaning back in his chair with his hands resting on a bloated stomach. 'If I keep eating like this I'll be the size of one of those psychedelic trucks yous lot seem to have everywhere.'

'Nonsense,' scoffed Akhila. 'You're far too skinny. Eat some more. I insist. Ishani! Give our guest another pancake.'

'Maybe I can squeeze another one in,' Ray said gallantly. 'Actually, Ish, make that two. I may as well fill up while I can. They don't seem to do food at the ashram. I didn't see anyone eat a bloody thing yesterday.'

'That's because they were fasting, you idiot!' Ishani laughed, dolloping a mountain of food on to his plate.

'It's supposed to help focus the mind on spiritual matters,' Priya added. 'According to Noah the swami's been away on retreat fasting.'

Or at least that's Noah's story, she added under her breath. The swami was proving to be more elusive than Lord Lucan, the Scarlet Pimpernel and Elvis all rolled into one. If she was still AWOL when the team arrived today Priya had every intention of getting stroppy. If everything really was as straightforward and open as Noah insisted then what was the swami's problem with giving interviews? Priya was no great mathematician but something didn't add up.

'The poor woman must have faded away. No wonder we still haven't seen her. And how is starving yourself supposed to improve your focus? All I'd be able to focus on would be my rumbling stomach,' Ray laughed.

'That's because you're about as spiritual as those pancakes,' Priya sighed. Then she glanced at her watch, blanching at the time. 'Hurry up, Ray, the taxi will be here any minute.'

'Leave the boy to eat in peace,' Akhila admonished. She'd taken a shine to Ray, as older women tended to, feeding him up and treating him as an honoured guest. Nothing was too much trouble for Akhila when it came to taking care of her visitors. Hospitality and generosity were of paramount importance to Indian families; to treat Ray any other way would bring shame and dishonour on the entire Adani clan. If Ray was the Guptas' friend then he was the Adanis' friend too, more's the pity, Priya reflected grimly. Ray hadn't been staying with them long but already her nerves were more frayed than his cut-off jeans as she tried frantically to make sure he didn't spill the chilli beans about her and Vikram. How she was going to keep this up for the next few weeks was anyone's guess.

'I've had a great idea about how I can repay your hospitality,' Ray said to Akhila through a mouthful of pancake.

Akhila looked horrified. 'I won't hear of you paying for anything! Absolutely not. As I've already said, any friend of the Guptas is a friend of the Adanis.'

'I wasn't thinking of money.' Ray scooped up his final mouthful and chomped thoughtfully for a minute. Then he set his fork down with a clatter, mopped his mouth with a napkin and fixed his hostess with his sweetest smile. 'I was wondering, seeing as I'm just a cameraman and everything, whether you'd like me to film the wedding and all the events that lead up to it? Then you'd have something really special to remember it by.'

Ray, who had several awards to his name, was significantly more than 'just a cameraman'. He didn't tend to offer his services either, often moaning to Priya that everyone he knew was always on at him to film their weddings and christenings for free, so this was out of character and Priya was surprised. He must really appreciate Akhila's hospitality to offer to do it. On top of the ashram documentary it would mean an awful lot of extra work.

'Ooh!' Neesh's eyes were big saucers of excitement. 'That would be wicked! Wouldn't it, Sanj?'

Sanjeev looked up from the sports pages of the *Navbharat Times*. 'Yeah, cool.'

'Will you have time, Ray?' Priya asked gently. 'There'd be a lot of editing.'

'Aye, course I will. The only thing I might struggle with is your culture. Some of the rituals will take a bit of explaining.'

'You're not alone. I'm learning all the time too,' Priya sighed. She'd not been in India long but already she was aware that her knowledge of her parents' culture had more holes than Swiss cheese. It was weird. Back in England she was always aware of her Indian heritage but here in Jaipur she felt more British than fish and chips. The rituals, the food, the big-eyed beggars who thronged the street corners, all these things made her feel lost and very foreign.

Ray scratched his head thoughtfully, as though trying to think of a solution. But Priya knew him better. Ray might look scruffy but his mind was Sabatier sharp. This was no sudden idea on his part. He'd already thought it through very carefully.

He frowned. 'Maybe Ishani could help with the culture side? She could explain everything to me, if that's not too much trouble for her?'

'Of course it isn't. I'd love to,' Ishani said.

'Wicked!' Neesh clapped her hands. 'Ray, you have to come with us when we go wedding dress shopping.'

'He will not,' barked Divya, bolt upright with outrage. 'A man filming you undressing? Chi! Chi! I won't hear of it. Never!'

'I'll film and edit those bits,' Priya said quickly.

'And I'll do the same for you one day,' promised Neesh, blowing her a kiss. 'If you ever get round to getting married.'

'Well, don't hold your breath,' Divya snapped. 'She had a wonderful man and she threw him away like a piece of trash.' And she swelled up with indignation like a sari-clad puffer fish, crossing her arms and glowering at Priya.

'Mum, please don't start,' Priya pleaded, but she

might as well have told the earth to stay still. Divya was on a roll and off she went at warp speed, giving Priya a dressing down for letting go of such a paragon as Vikram, who was right up there with Lord Krishna for virtue, it seemed. Priya buried her face in her hands as her mother washed all her dirty linen in full view of everyone in the room. Metaphorically it was all there, from the grotty grey fat day pants to the skimpy red and black set she saved for special occasions, and she wished the earth would swallow her up.

'Hang on!' interrupted Ray, holding up his hands and miraculously halting Divya in full flow. 'Who exactly are yous talking about here?'

Divya gave him a look so icy that it was a wonder Ray didn't shrivel up with frostbite. 'Priya had a wonderful boyfriend, a wonderful *Indian* boyfriend, whom she threw away without a backward glance! Poor Vikram, he didn't deserve to be treated like that. He adored Priya.'

'Vikram?' parroted Ray, only needing some colourful feathers and a cage to complete the look. 'You're talking about Vikram? The same scumbag, lying git Vikram who stitched Priya up?'

Priya was horrified. 'Ray, please don't,' she pleaded, but Ray wasn't listening. He loathed Vikram and couldn't bear to listen to Divya singing his boss's praises. In fact he looked as though the very idea was enough to bring his pancakes bouncing back.

'Aye, you're right! Vik didn't deserve to be treated the way Priya treated him. He should have been treated like the sly underhand weasel he is. He stabbed her right in the back, Mrs Gupta. What kind of man does that and thinks it's acceptable? A bloody poor excuse for one, if you ask me.'

Priya leapt to her feet and slammed her hands down on the table. 'Ray! We didn't ask you! That's enough!'

'It bloody well isn't, Pri! How can you let your mam sit here talking about Vik like he's some paragon of sainthood? You're ten times the boss he'll ever be! Stick up for yourself, for God's sake!'

The Adanis were following this exchange with mouths open so wide that their tonsils were practically on view. Neesh was shaking her head in disbelief and Ishani looked shocked. Even Akhila was lost for words.

Divya, unfortunately, was not.

'I knew it!' she screeched, rounding on Priya furiously. 'You put your career before your man! What did I say to you, my girl? No man wants a wife who prefers her career to him! Work should always be a man's domain. Poor Vikram! Jobs are for men who need to support a wife and family. You should be concentrating on finding a suitable husband. I'm sure Vikram only ever had your best interests at heart. Priya Gupta, I despair. How did I manage to raise such a daughter? What did I do wrong? I'm ashamed!'

'There's nowt wrong with Pri— Ouch!' Priya's foot connected with Ray's shin beneath the table. She was normally a pacifist but he'd said quite enough.

'Mum, I can explain everything,' she began, but Divya was having none of it, her mouth set in a tight line and her arms still crossed tightly over her chest.

'You don't have to. I think your *friend* has explained quite enough. Thank God the aunties left early to go to the bazaar. Whatever would Bhavani say? The shame!'

'Shouldn't you be sticking up for Priya, here?' Ray looked confused. 'Or is this all part of the culture thing again that I don't get?'

'Just be glad you don't have an Indian mother,' said Neesh with a grimace. 'Come on, Priya, what really happened with you and Vik? What did he do? You've been so secretive and we're all gagging to know the truth.'

'Shut up, Neesh. I'm not having this discussion now,' Priya said.

Below the apartment a car horn blasted and her eyes slid to the kitchen clock. Eight thirty. Time to go.

Thank God.

'Mum, I've got to go to work. Can we talk about this when I get back?'

Divya shrugged. 'Why bother now, Priya? What's left to talk about?'

'A great deal, I should think,' Ray spluttered. 'You don't know the half of it.'

Right, that was enough. Priya was done with providing the stunned Adanis with a live alternative to breakfast television.

'Mum, we'll talk later, okay?' she promised, but Divya refused to make eye contact, instead fixing her gaze on her teacup, every rigid line of her body speaking volumes of righteous indignation. Priya sighed. Thanks to Ray and his motormouth she was well and truly in the doghouse. What a start to the day. All she needed now was to discover that Swami Attuttama was still in hiding and things would be just perfect.

Suddenly she was desperate to escape from the tiny

kitchen and the pairs of accusing eyes trained on her face. The peace of the ashram and Noah's calm voice had never seemed so appealing.

Grabbing Ray's arm and yanking him from his seat, Priya frogmarched her cameraman through the kitchen and down the stairs, Ishani in hot pursuit. Bundling Ray into the taxi, Priya slammed the door furiously.

'Right, you've had your say, Ray!' she said, hands on hips and green eyes shimmering with anger. 'Now it's time for you to shut up and listen to me!'

13

By the time the taxi had crawled through the heavy morning traffic and was heading out into the hillside Priya had run out of steam and Ray was looking very shamefaced. She hadn't minced her words and he was in absolutely no doubt that he'd really and truly upset her, even if he still couldn't quite understand why.

Cheeks flushed and breathless she bit her lip hard and blinked back angry tears. I'm not going to cry, she told herself furiously. Ray's ruined the morning; don't let him ruin your eye makeup too!

'I'm so sorry, Priya,' he apologised for the umpteenth time. 'I really didn't mean to hurt you, pet. I'd never intentionally do that. I just couldn't bear to listen to your mam blaming you for something that wasn't your fault and I saw red.'

Priya gnawed at her thumb nail before stopping and looking at the ragged stump with disgust. God, she should have given up nail biting at about the same time she'd binned her Westlife posters. What was it about these confrontations with Divya that whizzed her back in time like something out of *Doctor Who*?

'I'm your friend, Priya,' Ray continued, leaning

across and gently taking her hand. 'I just couldn't bear listening to Divya singing Vikram's praises when we all know what a total shit he is. She needs to know the truth.'

'No she doesn't, Ray!' Priya snapped, wishing that she hadn't scooped her hair up into a short pony tail and could hide her teary eyes behind her fringe. She hated to show weakness, and tears to her meant exactly that. How could she turn up at the ashram to interview the swami with red-rimmed eyes? That would hardly be presenting the professional face of the BBC.

'You're very upset. What exactly did Vikram do to you?' Ishani asked.

Priya took a deep breath and then exhaled very slowly, willing the stress to leave her body. Maybe she'd learned something after all from filming endless yoga classes beneath the bright blue sky?

'You don't need to know, Ishani. It really doesn't matter any more.'

'Doesn't matter!' Ray spluttered. 'Of course it bloody matters! You can't just let it go!'

Priya fixed him with a steely look. 'I can and I will. And if you *ever* mention this again, if you so much as breathe it to my family, I'll pull the plug on this whole documentary and stick you on the first plane back to London. Do you understand?'

He looked down at his sandals. 'Roger that, boss. Sorry.'

'He was only trying to help,' Ishani pointed out gently. 'It's hard for Ray to understand our culture, not having grown up in it.'

'I know that,' retorted Priya. 'Why do you think I've

worked so hard to keep him away from my mother?'

Ray's head snapped up. 'I knew I wasn't imagining it! You *were* giving me the cold shoulder. That's why you didn't invite me to your housewarming and didn't want me on the same flight!'

'And now do you understand why?'

He spread his hands helplessly. 'I still can't honestly say I get it, why your mam would react like that, I mean, but I do understand why you didn't want me to bump into her and open my big gob. Especially in front of the in-laws. Don't worry. I'll apologise to everyone as soon as we get back.'

Priya sighed. 'It's not your fault. I should have warned you what things are like with Mum. It's just . . .' Her voiced faltered and for a second or two her throat clotted dangerously and she had to swallow hard before continuing. 'It's just that I like . . . I need . . . to keep work and family separate. Blurring the two only complicates things.'

But Ray just looked more puzzled, running his hands through his sandy hair in agitation, and she knew that there was absolutely no point in saying anything further. If she told him that work was the place where the earth was solid beneath her feet and she was Priya Gupta, respected documentary director, or that she didn't want any of her colleagues to see her through Divya's disappointed eyes, diminished from demanding boss to useless daughter in the blink of an eye, would he understand? Or would he be even more confused? Maybe Ishani had a point. How could anyone understand unless they'd had the same upbringing?

So maybe Divya was right after all, and she was

upsetting the natural balance of things by insisting on stepping outside the roles offered to her. Was *she* the real problem here? Vikram came from the same culture as she did. An only son, he'd been brought up by an adoring mother who'd told him practically from the minute he drew breath that the world was his for the taking. All his life he'd expected to be the best, the leader, the number one. What had he actually done but continue on his destined path? She'd been taught to step back and take second place to a man, so why hadn't she been able to do it?

Was *she* the one out of kilter?

'I really, really am sorry,' Ray was still saying sadly.

Suddenly Priya knew she was wrong to be so mad at him. How could she have possibly expected Ray to understand the complexities of her mother culture when she could barely fathom them herself?

'I know you are,' she told him softly. 'I know there's not a malicious bone in your body, Ray, and I know you meant well and were only sticking up for me. Let's just forget about it.'

'I'll never mention anything again in front of your mam,' Ray promised.

'That goes without saying,' agreed Ishani.

Forgiven, but obviously still feeling bad, Ray knew Priya well enough to give her space for the rest of the journey. Switching on his camera and settling the cans on to his ears he turned his attention to the footage shot the day before while Ishani peered over his shoulder, pointing out sections she particularly liked or that she thought needed shooting in a different light. Priya listened to them for a while and was impressed by how well they worked together. Ishani would learn a great deal from Ray, and in turn he seemed more than happy to take her opinions on board.

At least the documentary was coming together, even if her personal life was crumbling faster than the world economy.

Priya turned away from her colleagues and gazed out of the window, but try as she might to concentrate on the desert landscape all she could see instead were scenes from the past, like her own private edit suite of recollections. Ray's outburst had well and truly blown the lid open on a Pandora's box of memories, memories she'd tried hard to forget but which lurked beneath the surface of consciousness like the emotional equivalent of piranha fish.

She was still hurt by Vikram. She still smarted at his betrayal but the furious exchange with her mother cast things in a whole new light. What if this wasn't all his fault?

My God! she thought, taken aback by a sudden revelation. Vikram's as caught between cultures as I am!

Had he just been behaving in the only manner he knew? Perhaps he really hadn't been able to understand why she'd been so upset. He certainly seemed taken aback when she'd ended their relationship and even now he hadn't given up on winning her back.

As if bunches of flowers and fluffy bears could make up for the stunt he'd pulled!

She bit into her thumb nail viciously. How could he ever think they could move forward after what he'd done? No matter how many times he looked at her with those big sad eyes and reasoned with her she'd always resent him.

And resentment was no basis for a marriage, was it?

'Please, babe,' Vik had pleaded before she'd left, like a stuck record, waving roses/chocolates/teddy bears under her nose, 'this is ridiculous. I love you! We can't split up over this. It's just work stuff!'

Well, it might have been just work stuff to him, she thought as she shredded the poor nail (just as well Neesh had recently mastered the art of applying falsies) but to her work meant the world. And what made it worse was that he'd known that. All the begging and reminders of how good they'd been couldn't make up for the way he'd betrayed her.

No way.

Okay, things between them hadn't always been bad, Priya recalled wistfully. In fact a lot of the time their relationship had been fantastic. Vikram with his thin clever face, floppy raven wing hair and gym-honed body had caught her attention from the moment they'd first locked eyes across a crowded edit suite and every time they bumped into each other the air had crackled with sexual attraction.

It was all totally unnerving. Priya was used to being in control of all areas of her life, so in the end she'd reacted the only way she knew how: she'd changed teams and projects and managed to avoid him. Or avoid him until he'd finally cornered her by the photocopier and demanded to know what he'd done to upset her.

'Nothing,' Priya had insisted.

In her haste to escape his scrutiny she'd shoved in a fat wad of papers without stopping to change the settings and within seconds the copier had ground to a halt. Lights blinked and from deep within its bowels came a horrible grinding sound.

Not good.

'Here, let me have a look,' Vik said, putting a slender hand on her waist and moving her aside. That slightest touch was enough. If she hadn't been leaning against the copier she would have been a puddle of desire on the floor.

What was going on? She was an educated woman, for God's sake. Get a grip!

But Priya couldn't get a grip, no matter how hard she'd tried. While Vikram wrestled with the copier she'd admired the way his Levi's moulded to his lean muscular legs.

'There's the problem.' Vikram plucked a sheaf of ink-stained paper out of the copier's innards and beamed at Priya. Then he kicked the door shut with the toe of his biker boot and nodded with satisfaction when the machine whirred back into life. 'All sorted!'

'Thanks,' Priya said. Was her face actually on fire or did it just feel like that? 'I thought I'd broken it.'

He laughed. 'The copier's just temperamental. It always goes on strike if you give it too much work – it has serious issues. Must be a bloke, eh?'

She giggled. What? Where had that silly, girly sound come from? Priya Gupta *never* giggled. She got her head down, worked and focused on her career.

'Whatever its gender you seem to have the magic touch,' she said.

Vikram's eyes held hers like magnets.

'My magic touch doesn't stop with photocopiers,' he

said, a thread of amusement in his voice, before pulling her into his arms as his mouth found hers. For a second Priya's lips parted and she found herself returning his kiss before common sense had taken over and she'd wrenched herself free.

'Who the hell do you think you are?' she'd cried. 'We're at work, Vikram!'

'Ah, if it's the setting that's bothering you and not my kissing then how about we just change the venue?' he suggested.

There was something about his utter confidence that Priya found really sexy. Looking back she supposed that was before she'd realised it was actually his arrogant streak emerging even at that early stage. She should have known better.

But she hadn't and as she fanned her flushed face with the retrieved documents Priya found herself agreeing to meet him the next day, and had spent the rest of the afternoon driving Ray demented with her dreamy smile and shredded concentration.

Now, as the taxi sped towards the ashram, Priya wished she could turn back time and be that optimistic, happy person again. Being cynical had a way of sucking the joy out of you, that was for sure.

Why couldn't everything have remained as perfect as their first date? When Priya thought back to that magical day it made her feel like howling. How had things ended up so ugly when they'd begun so beautifully?

'Who's that beeping their bloody horn on a Saturday morning?' had grumbled a hungover Neesh, who was nursing Alka-Seltzer and looking like death after a night out clubbing with Sanjeev.

Divya had looked up from the *Mail* and glanced out of the window. 'I've no idea who he is, but it's a nice car.'

'Why do wankers always get the nice cars?' wondered Neesh, wincing with every blast of the horn. Putting down her glass she shuffled to the window and peered out blearily. 'Hey! That *is* a nice car!'

Priya peeked over her shoulder. A beautiful Jag had pulled up under the plane trees, driven by a very familiar figure. Her stomach flipped. It was Vikram.

'Who's that?' breathed Neesh, nose pressed to the glass and hangover forgotten. 'Phwoor! He's lush!'

Vikram swung his muscular legs from the car and leaned nonchalantly against the bonnet. Seeing Priya at the window he waved and smiled widely.

'Come on, Priya,' he called up. 'I can't wait to show you Cliveden.'

'Bloody hell. You've pulled!' squeaked Neesh. 'No wonder you're all dressed up.'

'She looks lovely!' said Divya, looking approvingly from the eligible Indian bachelor outside to Priya, who was dressed in a floral prom style dress and soft brown leather knee boots rather than her habitual jeans and Skechers. 'Are you going on a date?'

'Don't be silly!' Priya blushed to the roots of her hair and shrugged herself into her new cream lambswool coat. 'Vikram's a colleague. We're meeting for lunch, that's all.'

'That's all?' squeaked Neesh. 'Sis, have you any idea at all where he's taking you?'

Priya wound a scarlet scarf around her neck. 'We're

just going for lunch to talk about a new project.'

But Neesh wasn't bothered about anything so mundane as projects. 'Cliveden's one of the most luxurious hotels in the country,' she shrieked. 'It's where Steven Gerrard got married! Babes, he must be really keen!'

As Priya shut the front door she smiled to herself. She guessed you could say he was keen. They'd not been together for twenty-four hours yet but already Vikram had gone out of his way to make her feel special. When she'd arrived home a big bunch of fat pink roses had been waiting for her (thank God Neesh was still at work and her parents out visiting Bhavani) with a sweet note apologising for his impulsive behaviour by the photocopier.

She frowned and told herself sternly that Vik's enthusiasm was because he'd met a single Hindu girl rather than because he was really besotted with her. But she'd still woken up at four a.m. with a lovely knot of excitement twisting in her tummy.

Well, it was either that or an extreme reaction to her mother's chickpea curry.

'You look beautiful,' said Vikram when she reached the car. 'Here, these are for you,' he added, thrusting a stunning bouquet of freesias into her hands.

'Thanks. They're gorgeous!'

'And so are you,' he said quietly. 'Now, hop in! We've got a bit of a drive before lunch. Just relax and let me spoil you,' he said as the car pulled away from the twitching curtains. Once out of parental sight Priya settled down to the tones of Verdi's *Requiem* and gazed through the tinted windows at the blur of London's streets. Soon terraces gave way to the M40 and then the green sweep of Buckinghamshire lanes.

The car drew up outside the hotel, the tyres scrunching on the gravel as Vikram turned the wheel sharply. Liveried footmen appeared from nowhere to park for them, show them inside, take their coats, seat them – Priya almost expected to be taken to the ladies' room.

Pizza Hut this was not!

'We're eating in the Terrace Dining Room,' Vikram said, taking her arm. 'I hope you like it.'

Once they were seated and had ordered Vikram took her hand in his, stroking the palm with his forefinger and making her insides curdle with hopeful excitement. Then, maybe sensing her nerves, he released her hand and poured two glasses of wine and swirled his thoughtfully. Looking up she met his burning dark eyes and blushed. Emotional static crackled so loudly she was amazed the entire room didn't get a shock.

'Priya,' said Vikram gently, 'you're spilling wine.'

'Oh no!' In horror she grabbed the nearest napkin. Unfortunately she also snatched the tablecloth and, as she tugged it, sent the beautiful table arrangement flying. Flowers sailed merrily into the lap of a nearby diner, plates smashed at ten decibels and the bottle of Sancerre gave poor Vikram an impromptu shower. The silence in the restaurant was suddenly colder than Frosty the Snowman's gonads. Priya wanted to die. Next time she was sticking to Pizza Hut.

'Vik, I'm so sorry,' she began, but stopped mid-grovel

because he was doubled up with laughter. Tears ran down his face and he clutched his sides.

'Priya Gupta,' he gasped. 'Do you throw drinks over everyone you date?'

'Only those I really like or really hate!'

'Really?' Suddenly he was deadly serious, the laughter dying on his lips. 'And which category do I fall into?'

Her mouth dried. 'Maybe the first?'

He smiled. 'I'm glad to hear that, Priya, because I really like you. Can we see each other again? But maybe without the photocopiers and the impromptu showers?'

'I'm not sure yet,' Priya said thoughtfully, as a waiter materialised from nowhere and cleared away her mess. 'I guess that depends.'

Vikram looked crestfallen. 'Babe, what more do I need to do to show you how serious I am? I borrowed my dad's car, I booked the most gorgeous place in the world and I've said I'm sorry about my, er, loss of control yesterday. Please tell me what your decision depends on.'

Priya decided to put him out of his misery. 'It depends on how good this lunch is.'

'In that case,' beamed Vikram, 'I'm very glad I brought you to a five star restaurant!'

And as the sun slipped below the Chilterns they'd strolled across the moonlit terrace and he'd kissed her in the silvered light, softly at first and then with a growing urgency and passion.

And this time she hadn't pushed him away.

*

Priya placed her hot head against the car window, vowing that as soon as they returned to the city she'd hire a car with air con. It was hot in the morning sun and her body pressed against plastic seats felt sticky. Thinking of the good times hurt because of course it hadn't all been bad. Some of it had been bloody amazing. And almost better than the sex (which had been great, she couldn't lie) was Vik's rare talent for handling Divya in a way that left her feeling charmed and Priya feeling backed up. She certainly missed those happy days of basking in her mother's approval, a far cry from the scene at breakfast, when being part of a couple had been so easy and so safe. Even work seemed to have an extra gloss, and Priya could hardly get to Shepherd's Bush quickly enough, feeling like the luckiest girl on the planet that the two great loves of her live, Vik and work, were so intrinsically linked. It had seemed too good to be true.

Which, of course, had turned out to be the case.

She sighed again and started to attack her index finger. Vik had been trying really hard to make amends lately – she suspected this was why she'd been given the ashram commission – and he did have many good points, but could she really forgive him? As soon as she'd found out what he'd done something inside her had shrivelled up and died, and she'd not been able to feel anything for him that came close to what she'd once felt. All the desire, alongside the passion and respect, had vanished instantly like monsoon rain into the parched earth.

No, Priya decided firmly as the taxi pulled up outside the ashram and she caught sight of Noah raising a hand in greeting, there was no way she could ever take Vikram back, no matter how convenient it might be or how happy it would make Divya. Their relationship was over because what had shrivelled up and died that day when he'd made his confession hadn't been her heart.

It had been her love for him.

14

'Here at the ashram we believe that the energy of nature helps us in our pursuit of Nirvana.'

As Ray's camera rolled and Ishani's slender arms valiantly held the boom above the shining bald pate of the robed guru, Priya smothered a yawn and tried to look as captivated as the rest of his audience. Although they were in the shade of a small wooded copse it was still punishingly hot, and even dressed in shorts and a floaty top she still felt sticky and her feet were dusty and sore from trudging endlessly through the trees. Her pretty flowery flip-flops were trashed and resentment slithered through her like a snake.

'Take this neem tree for instance,' the speaker crooned, stroking the trunk tenderly with fingers as dark and wizened as the bark. 'We prize it here in India for the shade its wide canopy offers in the heat.'

Priya was glad she was wearing her Ray-Bans so nobody noticed her rolling her eyes. All the way to India for Gardeners' bloody Question Time! This was all very worthy and she was sure if you liked plants it would be riveting, but it hardly made for compelling viewing. Maybe she should ask Ray to film the grass growing instead?

'This tree is very important to our healing work here because it has great antiseptic and other medicinal properties. Many of our guests have been amazed to find their ailments cured after a short course of simple treatments.'

'There's your miracles, love,' said Maggie, digging a bony elbow into Priya's ribs. 'Didn't I tell you it was all down to simple remedies?'

'Mmm,' Priya murmured, but she still wasn't convinced. It all sounded very plausible, but the swami was still unavailable and she'd yet to catch a glimpse of the mysterious business couple or figure out why they were touring the forbidden herb garden. Maybe she was being a tad paranoid but it was almost as though she was being deliberately kept away from them.

'What are you growing in the fields beyond the ashram?' Ishani was asking, clearly sharing Priya's disenchantment with the tree lecture. 'I went for a walk yesterday and I didn't recognise any of the crops. Is it more medicine?'

Priya nodded approvingly. Ishani was sharp, that was for certain, and the more Priya worked with her the more she liked what she saw. Ishani had a natural aptitude for spotting avenues to explore, her sunny open manner drawing people to her, relaxing them and encouraging them to answer her questions honestly. She was an asset to the team and Priya longed to poach her for the BBC but, of course, Akhila would never stand for that, not when there was a betrothal in place. It was a shame but Ishani was obviously a fully paid up member of the Mother Knows Best school of thought and would never dream of upsetting her mother the way Priya seemed to constantly upset hers.

Their guide had been stumped by Ishani's question and his domed head crinkled. 'I'm not really involved in that area of our work so I can't answer your question, I'm afraid. Maybe you could ask somebody else when we return?'

'Could we go back and do that now?' wondered Priya, fanning her face with her sun hat. 'It's really hot and I'm a bit treed out.'

'Not enjoying the nature lecture?' Noah asked her, tilting back his head to gaze at the thick green canopy. Diamond patterns of light danced across his face and throat. 'Tell me, just what *do* you enjoy, Priya Gupta?'

The way he looked at her made Priya feel flushed and not just from the heat. There was something in the dark grey depths of his eyes that suggested he wasn't solely alluding to nature rambles and outdoor pursuits.

'I enjoy lots of things,' she said swiftly, hoping that her face wasn't as tomato-like as it felt. Did eating Marks & Spencer's meals for one in her knickers and vest while watching *Lost* count? Or crashing out on the sofa with a glass of Blossom Hill? Raising her chin a fraction she said, 'I do lots of stuff, actually.'

'Such as? What do you do in your spare time? Do you go out clubbing? Shop for England? Moonlight as a female mud wrestler?'

In spite of her annoyance at all the personal questions, Priya laughed. 'Damn! Who told you about the mud wrestling? I thought I'd sworn Ray to secrecy.'

'Just a lucky guess. That glowing complexion had to

come from more than the Rajasthani sun. But seriously, tell me a bit about yourself.'

She looked down at her painted toenails. 'There's nothing to tell, Noah. I'm actually so boring I make this tree lecture sound fascinating.'

She paused awkwardly and the silence was immediately filled by the voice of the guide droning on about the healing qualities of bael trees. Clay yawned loudly and Noah pulled a face at Priya, breaking the tension and making her laugh.

'Now come on,' he said sternly. 'Nothing competes with that for an insomnia cure. You're young, talented, successful and seriously attractive. There has to be more to you than work.'

She was taken aback. Seriously attractive? Had Noah just complimented her? Confused, she countered quickly, 'What about you, Noah? What do you do back in the real world?'

'Now that's cheating. I asked first.' He wagged a finger at her in mock anger. 'Answering a question with a question might work when you're interviewing people but it won't wash with me. I'll tell you something about me if you tell me something about yourself. How about that for a deal?'

'You're assuming my curiosity will get the better of me.'

'Of course,' Noah agreed. 'You're a nosy journalist! You'll have been wondering all sorts of things ever since you first arrived. Come on, just admit it. Why I'm here, how I fit in to the place, what I do in the real world. Why I went to prison . . . shall I go on?'

If her face hadn't already been resembling the

nuclear core of Sellafield, it would be now, thought Priya. All these thoughts and of course the mystery of why he was showing the business couple around the secret garden had been racing round her mind for days. Was Noah a mind-reader too?

'It's okay, don't look so embarrassed,' he said. 'It's your job to ask questions, just as it's mine I suppose to help people find answers. So how about I ask first?'

She grimaced. 'Do I have a choice here?'

'Of course, but it's between talking to me and listening to the tree lecture.'

'Some choice.'

Noah grinned. 'Just wait. Any minute now he'll be telling us how bael fruit is Nature's own laxative and the spiritual atmosphere will explode like an upset stomach! But it's up to you.'

'Gross!' Pushing her sunglasses up into her hair she cast her gaze around. There had to be a better story at the ashram than laxatives or this documentary really was in trouble. 'I don't think I can bear to listen to Clay and Clara discussing their bowels opening. You win. Ask away.'

'Right,' Noah said, his brow crinkling thoughtfully. 'How about this: when you're not being a hugely successful documentary maker and terrifying everyone at the BBC, what do you do with yourself?'

'I see my family and my friends when I can, eat too many hot curries from Brick Lane, and I love watching old black and white movies,' Priya told him. 'Oh, and I'm a bit of a gym freak too when I get the time. I love to work out; it's the best way I know of beating stress.'

'That explains the rippling biceps then,' he laughed. 'I must take care not to mess with you.'

'You'd better believe it. But what about you? What do you do in the real world?'

'Like India isn't real?'

'You know what I mean. Back in the UK where there are bills to pay and we can't stand around all day talking about trees, what do you do? Where do you live?'

'Two questions, eh?'

'Anything to take my mind off laxatives.'

'And there I was thinking you were genuinely interested. I guess that puts me in my place,' sighed Noah. 'When I'm in the UK I live in Brighton, not far from The Lanes. Do you know it?'

She shook her head. 'I've never been but my sister tells me the shopping's good.'

'Apparently so, but I tend to spend more time gardening than shopping. But Brighton's a great place to live. It's really vibrant and culturally there's always something going on. The dance scene's grown loads over the last few years, too, and I sometimes make a bit of extra money working as a DJ at some of the local clubs.'

Priya suddenly felt even more boring. Doing crunches at her local gym hardly competed with being the next Fat Boy Slim. She really had to get out more.

'Anyway, never mind that,' continued Noah, 'I've got a question in hand, haven't I? So I'd better use it wisely.' He looked thoughtful for a moment before raising those enquiring grey eyes to hers and saying softly, 'How about this. Are you seeing anyone special at the moment?'

'What?' She stared at him.

'Are you single?'

'You can't ask me that!'

'Why ever not? It's a perfectly valid question, I'd have thought, and very easy to answer. Are you single or not?'

This was way too personal for Priya. She never, ever talked about her relationships. Some things were just not up for discussion.

'Are you?' she countered, hands on hips.

'The old answering questions with questions trick again? Come on, Priya, I've already worked that one out.' Noah was smiling at her as he said this, which took the sting out of the words. 'I'll take that response as a no, shall I?'

She glowered at him. 'It's none of your business. I'm not talking about personal stuff like that and actually if it's time for personal questions then I've got one for you too. How come you went to prison? What did you do? Ask too many nosy questions and get arrested for it?'

He stared at her. 'Sorry, I've really hit a nerve, haven't I? Whoever he is he must have really hurt you.'

'Don't try to change the subject,' she snapped. Noah might have a way of getting under her skin and hooking out all the murky feelings but she had no intention of discussing Vik with him, or with anyone. Some things were too raw to be shared with virtual strangers.

However good looking they might be.

'*I'm* changing the subject?' Noah shook his dark curls. 'I'm not afraid to tell you why I went to prison, although for the record it's not something I'm particularly proud of.' He paused for a second as though to gather his thoughts. 'I went to prison for a drugs-related offence, Priya. I was young and I made a mistake. Not that I'm making excuses for myself because there aren't any, but I did the time and I learned a very hard lesson.'

'Oh.' Taken aback by this candid response, Priya felt ashamed of her own reticence. For a second she teetered on the brink of telling him something about Vikram but then Maggie appeared full of questions about the whereabouts of the swami and the moment was lost.

It was probably just as well, she decided. Noah didn't need to know the ins and outs of her love life, did he? And anyway, he wasn't really interested, he was just being polite. It was definitely time to change the subject now.

'So when do I get to meet the swami?' she asked Noah when Maggie had wandered off again. 'Surely she can't still be on retreat? She'll have forgotten how to speak by now.' If she even exists, she added under her breath.

He laughed softly. 'Fear not. We'll probably catch her at the Bhil village. We're heading there tomorrow.'

'So you keep saying!' Priya bristled, folding her arms. 'You said that yesterday, and the day before. Tomorrow and tomorrow and tomorrow! I feel like Macbeth.'

'Why so impatient? She will be back when she's ready. No one is able to tell the swami how long to meditate for. She makes her own mind up,' Noah said steadily, but something flickered in his eyes and instantly Priya's curiosity was ignited because that fleeting expression looked a lot like worry to her.

Interesting. What could possibly be worrying the usually chilled Noah?

'Well, if I can't speak to her, as usual, how about the business couple I saw when I first arrived? Where have they been hiding?'

What did he know? What was he concealing? Tilting her chin – because he was so very tall – she looked him right in the eye and was suddenly aware that his eyes were searching hers, the intensity of his gaze making her cheeks flush.

'Why are you always so angry?' he wondered, softly. 'Why so swift to think the worst, Priya Gupta? Who has hurt you so very badly?'

'Oh please! Spare me the cod psychology.' She stepped back from him. 'There's nothing wrong with me except that I get a bit suspicious when people vanish or seem to hide from me. Or,' she fixed him with a challenging look, 'lie to me!'

But Noah refused to rise to the bait and instead just shook his head sadly.

'Did I wrong you in a past life? What can I do to make you see that there's nothing to hide here?'

'Tell the truth for once? Let me speak to that business woman? I know you don't live in the real world and have run away to hide here, but some of us do have to go back to reality and have jobs to get on with!'

Noah sighed. The long gypsy curls fell across his face and he pushed them away wearily.

'I don't know why you're so adamant that life at the ashram isn't real. It seems to me I see far more of "real" life here than I ever do in Brighton. The business woman, as you call her, has been really unwell since she arrived. Remember how I told you that some people come here for their health? Well, she's one of them and the first part of her treatment is just to rest and recharge her energy. I promise there isn't any huge conspiracy.'

'So you say.'

His shoulders slumped and the light in his eyes seemed to be extinguished like sparklers plunged into icy water. For a second she felt regret as sharp as cider for her harsh words before reminding herself that she was a journalist, not another credulous ashram devotee, and that she was here to root out the truth rather than delve into her own psyche.

'I promise that the swami will speak to you,' said Noah eventually. 'I think you and she actually have a great deal in common. You're both very determined women, that's for sure!'

And with this unexpected comment he excused himself and joined Maggie, who was waving at him across the glade. Priya watched him stride away, powerful as a tiger, his simple robe billowing behind him like a sail, and her skin felt itchy with annoyance. Why did she now feel like the bad guy? She wasn't the one hiding anything. Seething, she rejoined Ray and Ishani filming Clay and Clara wandering around and wondering loudly where the miracles shop was. Although they'd swapped the migraine-inducing clothes for plain robes Clay still wore his Stetson and puffed away on endless cigars, while Clara's fat feet were bullied into leopard-print heels which tottered dangerously over the roots and undergrowth.

'They're even less impressed with this set-up than you are,' commented Ray.

'I'm not unimpressed exactly,' Priya said.

'Really?' Ishani looked surprised. 'You looked like you were just giving poor Noah a really hard time.'

So it was poor Noah now, was it? Priya felt even more annoyed. How come she was always the villain?

'I'm just getting a little tired with being fobbed off,' she said shortly. 'This swami is about as visible as the Loch Ness monster; in fact I've seen a picture of it whereas I'm starting to wonder whether she actually exists. Talking about trees is all very well, but we need a story.'

'Stick around and watch these two,' suggested Ray, pointing at Clara and Clay. 'I know we're not after comedy but they're very entertaining.'

'Honey, it's nothing like Lourdes,' Clara was complaining. 'Ah don't see why Avril was so taken with it. There's nothing to buy.'

'Say, Noah!' boomed Clay. 'Where can I buy some of those laxatives that guy was telling us about? I sure don't know what you put in the food here but I haven't been for days.'

While Clay described his bowel problems in lurid detail to Noah, Priya's phone rang. When *Mum* lit up the screen she chose to ignore it and slid the Nokia back into her pocket, where it continued to ring and buzz at regular intervals until she turned it off in irritation. What part of *I'm at work* did her mother not understand?

Seconds later Ishani's phone rang and she answered it straight away, mouthing 'sorry' to Priya, but clearly far more in awe of her formidable mother than of her new boss. Moments later she was handing the phone to Priya, saying apologetically that it was Divya on the phone.

'Your crafty old mum!' said Ray. 'She's caught you now, pet!' and everyone laughed, including Noah. Somehow his laughter infuriated Priya more than anything else and she felt like throttling him.

Noah certainly had a way of getting right to her, she thought as she returned Ishani's phone and stomped away on the pretext of setting up a shot. He asked way too many personal questions and seemed intent on trying to delve into things she'd rather not have to talk about. Well, she fumed, kicking at a tree root and wincing when she stubbed her toe, two could play at that game. There were things about the sainted Noah that she wanted answers to as well. Such as why someone who'd done time for drugs was suddenly a spiritual guide at an isolated ashram for one thing, and what exactly his dealings were with the business couple for another.

It was time to find out exactly who and what Noah was. And then see how much *he* liked being interrogated!

15

It is a truth universally acknowledged that a young woman in possession of her father's money must be in want of some serious shopping, and Neesh Gupta was determined to make the most of every second.

'*Shopping in Jaipur is an electrifying experience,*' she read from her guide book, '*and today it's renowned as the fashion centre of Rajasthan.* Great! Time for some serious retail therapy.'

After days of living with the Adanis, playing hide and seek with the swami and being subjected to endless matchmaking Priya thought she needed more than retail therapy to sort her out. More like a month in The Priory. Maybe even two months if her family became any more demanding. The so-called urgent phone call had turned out to be a summons back to the city for a wedding dress fitting that couldn't possibly be rearranged for the next day. Shaking with fury but unable to refuse Priya had had no choice but to leave the filming in Ray and Ishani's more than capable hands and take a slow hot ride back to Jaipur in the ashram bus. She was still fuming now. Twenty-seven and being ordered around by her mother. No wonder Noah had been amused.

Priya wasn't laughing, though. What was it about her work that Divya just didn't understand? Thanks to the Scarlet Pimpernelesque swami she was already behind schedule and taking this afternoon off was only going to set her back further.

Well, no way was that going to happen. If she had to work twice as hard she would, Priya decided as she took a chunk out of her tattered thumb nail. She'd do whatever it took to make this project a success, even if she had to lie in wait for the swami and ambush her when she came down the mountain track.

'You'll love the shopping, girls,' promised Akhila, turning round to beam at them from her prime seat at the front of the people carrier. 'Neeshali is very lucky to be able to purchase her trousseau here. There's so much choice she'll not know where to begin.'

'Let's start with my wedding dress! Wait until you meet the dressmaker I've found! She's amazing and she's designed for Bollywood stars like Aishwarya Rai,' Neesh said excitedly. 'I've sent her my designs and she's already made a start. She's found the most stunning pink fabric with hand-stitched crystals! I can hardly wait for my fitting.'

'Pink!' Akhila gasped. 'Never!'

'Neeshali! We never agreed on a pink dress! We decided on crimson,' exclaimed Divya.

'You might have done but crimson's, like, so lame!' Neesh scoffed. 'Everyone always wears it. Dull, dull, dull. Why shouldn't I be a bit different?'

'Because brides wear red. It's the custom, or at least

it is in India,' sniffed Akhila. Turning to Bhavani she said, 'These English girls and their modern ways! I suppose we cannot possibly expect them to understand the importance of tradition.'

'Oh, Priya and Neeshali have always done whatever they like,' Bhavani replied sadly. 'They've always been over-indulged and now they're totally westernised. My poor brother must despair.'

God, her aunt was a cow sometimes, thought Priya, fighting the impulse to sock her in the teeth – which she would have done with pleasure were she as badly brought up as Bhavani suggested. She knew her father was proud of his daughters and enjoyed the fact that they were independent thinkers. After all, he was the one who'd always encouraged them to pursue their education and follow their dreams. *Oh, let Neesh get married in pink if she wants*, she imagined him saying as Divya prised his nose out of a book for long enough to discuss the matter, *as long as she's happy!*

How Priya wished he was here right now. They could really do with a big dollop of his common sense.

'My daughters are not westernised,' Divya said coldly, stung by her sister-in-law's criticism. 'And they're certainly not indulged. They've been brought up just as well as any Indian girls.'

'Well, that's as may be, my dear, but let me assure you no Indian girl would dream of wearing a pink sari at her wedding. It's simply unheard of! Ishani certainly won't and all my other daughters had traditional weddings,' said Akhila with a patronising shrug.

Priya watched her mother's hands bunch into fists

and bit back a sigh. She'd known it was only a matter of time before the two matriarchs fell out.

'It's my wedding,' Neesh said sulkily. 'Why can't I have pink if I want? Lots of Asian brides wear pink these days.'

'But Akhila's right! It isn't traditional!' choked Bhavani. 'What will people say?'

'That I look a babe?' suggested Neesh, tossing back her extensions and applying a huge dollop of pink juicy tube to her lips. 'Come on, guys, chill. When you see what we've done you'll love it. You'll all be wanting to wear pink saris. We'll look like a Katie Price convention!'

'Humph!' sniffed Divya, crossing her arms. 'We'll see about that, my girl!'

Priya wanted to laugh. You had to hand it to Neesh: she certainly didn't lie down and take any bullshit from the matriarchs. The wedding dress fait accompli was a perfect example of her taking matters into her own hands and avoiding confrontation.

Maybe she should take a leaf out of her sister's book.

'Well, this is very disappointing,' said Akhila, looking put out. 'I had no idea you'd already organised something, Neeshali. I'd planned everything for today and I know exactly where to begin. I was going to start by showing you the bazaar. Those designers are frightfully expensive, you know. I really think, Divya, it's best you trust me with the arrangements. Unlike you, I have arranged many weddings and I know exactly how things should be done.'

Divya said nothing, but her jaw was clamped tightly shut and a muscle ticked in her cheek.

'And there's a credit crunch on,' chipped in Bhavani. 'My brother can hardly be expected to pay for designer items. Not when times are so hard. You're being very selfish, Neeshali. We will do as Akhila suggests and go to the market.'

'As if she wasn't already being selfish enough making her poor father fly all the way to India in his delicate state of health,' sighed Darsani, clucking her tongue with disapproval. 'Tell her, Divya!'

Priya could see her mother struggling to remain polite to her hostess while telling her to back off. After all, it was her daughter's wedding! *She* was the mother of the bride, not Akhila.

Neesh nudged Priya. 'Pink dress here I come!'

'You are one crafty cow,' Priya whispered back. 'Remind me to get you to teach me your manipulation skills.'

'Watch and learn,' grinned Neesh.

As the people carrier crawled through the traffic Priya distracted herself by capturing some images of the city for future shoots. Jaipur teemed with life and Priya was intrigued by the way new and old lifestyles fused, eastern and western traditions mingling to create a prosperous and vibrant metropolis. Every street was lined with vendors, their carts doing brisk business on the roadsides or at the traffic lights as they sold everything from roast corn to biryani to flowers.

'There's the food street,' said Akhila, pointing to a road on the left. 'Each night it's closed to traffic and transformed into an open air dining area. We must go tonight.'

'Never mind that!' cried Sanj, almost standing on the brakes. 'There's McDonald's!'

'And Pizza Hut!' added Neesh. 'Oh, can we? Please?'

'No we can't!' said Divya. 'Not when there are so many traditional restaurants to enjoy.'

The car stopped at the traffic lights and for a moment Priya thought Neesh was about to leap out in order to grab a pizza. Her hands and nose were pressed against the window as though she could absorb the taste just by staring hard enough. Then she jerked back as though the glass had scalded her. 'Oh. My. God!' she cried, pointing at a ragged figure at the roadside. 'What is that?'

Bhavani sighed impatiently. 'It's only a beggar, Neeshali. They're everywhere.'

Her aunt wasn't wrong, thought Priya sadly. India was a nation of beggars, lurking and loitering in every nook and cranny or roaming from one busy bazaar to another. They begged all day long, walking barefoot on the burning roads with no cover from the harsh sun, or thronging the traffic-clogged junctions, frantically trying to attract attention by stretching out their hands for alms and pleading piteously. And it wasn't just adults either. Small children, some not even four years old, offered to wash cars or sell dusty flowers for a few measly rupees. It was horrific and heartbreaking but sadly not unusual and Priya was ashamed to admit that almost a week into her stay in India she was growing used to the sight of the beggars.

Here was a documentary that could really do some good. God! If only she'd been promoted and had the autonomy to make executive decisions. Maybe she could help, even if it was only in a small way. Noah had said that if everyone played a small part the bigger task would be completed all the sooner.

It was very annoying but he seemed to have got right inside her head.

An hour later, Akhila led them through the heaving streets of the bazaar at a cracking pace, elbowing her way past shoppers and tourists alike and whizzing them in and out of shops so fast Priya's head was spinning. The brightly hued rolls of fabric piled high on the pavements were just blurs, as were the endless trays of rings and heavy gold bracelets that glittered from the tiny windows of small shops. Even the rows and rows of glittering slippers, sequins blinking like a thousand eyes in the hot sun, were ignored as Akhila frogmarched them onwards. Through the streets they trudged, past the small stalls where chapattis and pakoras sizzled in groundnut oil and filled the air with mouth-watering aromas, winding their way through the crowds of chattering women who were fluttering around the wares like busy butterflies in their jewel-bright saris. They didn't even pause to exclaim over the intricate rugs and carpets that lined the roadside or to watch the group of temple dancers who were gliding in formation, all jingling bells and flowing saffron robes, along the narrow street. Everywhere was like a meal for the senses; even the simplest of food stalls was brimming with colour and Priya longed to stop for a moment and marvel at the vitality of the local produce. Plump gourds, bruise-purple aubergines and fat red onions were piled high in wicker baskets alongside bright yellow cumin and violent crimson curry powders which filled the air with their pungent scents. It was India to the very bone, alive, vibrant and overwhelming, and all she wanted to do was pick up her camera and start to film. The last thing she felt like doing was shopping for a wedding dress with a sister she knew would be impossible to please.

Already Neesh was complaining that Akhila was taking them the long way round to the designer's shop just to make a point, but Priya was intrigued by the bazaar where yards and yards of cloth were laid out for passers-by to examine, a kaleidoscope of colours and designs that shone and sparkled like something from Aladdin's cave.

As if the bazaar weren't enough there were also numerous boutiques selling ready-made shalwar kameezes, churidar kurtas, saris, and of course bridal wear. As they wandered through the narrow lanes Priya was dazzled by the glittering displays of ever more exotic wares, everything from garments to glass bangles to gold necklaces.

She didn't know where to start.

But the rest of her party did and before long Sanj was laden down with purchases. Akhila's haggling and grasp of numbers would put a Wall Street trader to shame, and thanks to her Neesh and the aunties were able to splurge on all the shimmering shift saris and cool kaftans they desired.

So much for the credit crunch, Priya thought drily, watching Bhavani cram more bangles on to her fat arms while her sisters haggled over some cat-sick-yellow fabric. Her mother was joining in too and before long even Priya was the proud owner of the most gorgeous emerald sari, embroidered with silver thread and sparkling jade sequins. Then poor Sanjeev had to carry all their purchases back to the car like a pack mule, leaving the womenfolk to continue on foot down the narrow side alley to the studio where Neesh's dream wedding dress was waiting.

'Oh my God!' Neesh squeaked, stopping outside a small shop front and checking her list. 'We're here! This is it! Pink frock here I come.'

'She may be able to change the colour,' Akhila said hopefully.

'Or give us a refund,' suggested Bhavani.

Divya shot them both a glare. 'Leave this to me,' she said, and raising her hand she knocked on the door, striking harder when there was no answer.

'No one is home,' Akhila turned on her heel. 'Come. I know the perfect place.'

'Wait, this is definitely the right address.' Neesh's brow was wrinkled in confusion as she looked up from her directions. 'Parthavi Patel Designs, that's her. Where the hell is she?' She hammered her small fist on the door. 'Hello? Hello? Is anyone home?'

The shutters were closed and there were no lights on. It didn't look hopeful and Priya was starting to think that even if they knocked for an hour they wouldn't get very far. Slipping away from the others she gently opened the door of the small goldsmith's shop opposite and was horrified to learn that Parthavi Patel had been called away urgently to tend her sick mother.

'Is there any way we can contact her?' Priya asked, with a sinking heart. 'Only my sister's getting married next week and the dress is supposed to be completed by then. Will she be back soon?'

'Alas, no,' said the goldsmith, and the eyes set in his wizened face were brimming with regret. 'Her mother is most grievously ill. Mrs Patel left several weeks ago and I've no idea when she will return.'

'Did she leave an email address? Or a mobile phone number?' Priya was clutching straws now, knowing from bitter experience what happened when things didn't go according to plan for Neesh. Vesuvius in full pyroclastic flow would be peaceful in comparison. 'There must be a way of reaching her?'

But again all she received was another sad look and the news that Mrs Patel's mother lived in a very isolated village in the Punjab, where emails and mobiles were as common as hens' teeth.

Neesh's dream dress, it seemed, was doomed to remain exactly that and unfortunately it now seemed to be Priya's job to break the news.

Some girls just had all the luck.

And then came the tinny tones of her mobile. Fumbling in her bag she flipped it open, her heart lifting when she saw the identity of the caller.

Thank God! Sanity at last!

'Dad!' she cried, her mouth curving into a smile as she pictured him curled up in his favourite chair with an open book on his lap, light years removed from the traumas of missing wedding dresses and feminine hysterics. 'It's so good to hear from you! How are you feeling? Are you surviving without your devoted team of nurses?'

Ashwani laughed. 'My health has improved beyond

my wildest imaginings! I fear that my devoted nurses might have not been doing me quite as much good as they intended. But we won't tell them that, hmm?'

'Just be glad you're not here,' Priya said wryly. Although the market was heaving with bodies and buzzing with conversation she could still hear Neesh's wails and Bhavani's chuntering. 'It's not exactly relaxing. Did you want to talk to Mum or the aunties? Only they're a bit busy at the moment.'

Well, that wasn't a lie, was it? They were busy. Ignoring each other.

Ashwani cleared his throat awkwardly. 'Actually, sweetheart, I'd prefer it if you didn't tell them I've phoned. There's a slight problem here and you know how they panic.'

Priya's insides swooped. The last 'slight problem' her father had mentioned had left him in ITU wired to machines and struggling for breath.

'You are okay, aren't you, Dad?' she asked, her heart bouncing off her ribs like a squash ball.

'I'm fine, my love,' he reassured her. 'Fit as a fiddle, albeit a rather tatty old one. No, the problem's with my travel arrangements. There's a baggage handler's strike on at the airport and it's causing absolute havoc. My flight's going to be delayed and you know what it's like in summer season, there's going to be chaos. For God's sake don't let your mother watch *News 24*. She'll panic if she thinks I'm not going to make it in time for the wedding and Neesh will have absolute hysterics. I'm going to do my best to make alternative arrangements but I don't know how successful I'll be. It's not looking good at the moment.'

'Oh, Dad!' Priya was horrified. 'The wedding's only days away.' She glanced at her sister, quieter now and slumped against Divya in exhausted resignation. 'It'll break Neesh's heart if you can't be there.'

'I know, my love, which is why we can't say anything yet and upset her unnecessarily. It would break mine too if I had to miss my little girl's special day.'

There was a long pause and Ashwani's sadness reverberated across the network. Then he sighed. 'I'll get another flight, Priya, don't worry. Even if I have to sleep on the concourse floor for a few days in order to get in line I'll make sure I get to Neeshali's wedding.'

Priya was horrified. Ashwani had almost died of pneumonia and although on the mend he was still frail. The last place he needed to be was on a cold airport floor, lying in draughts and with no one to make sure he took his medicine. He'd be bound to contract another chest infection . . .

'Dad, you can't!'

'Darling, I must. I don't have any choice. I'm going to get a good night's sleep, pack my bag and then take a taxi over to the airport and see what I can do. I'm just telling you so that if the worst does come to the worst and I can't make it you can explain to the others what's happened. But let's not alarm them yet, hmm?'

It was all very well for her father to say that, Priya thought as he swore her to secrecy and then rang off, but what about *her* being alarmed? She was thousands of miles away and totally unable to do anything to stop her brave, foolish father risking his health in an attempt to reach his family. Why did she always have to be the one he confided in? How she wished she could just collapse into a sobbing heap like Neesh.

But unfortunately that option wasn't open to her. Now she had just under twenty-four hours to formulate a rescue plan to get Ashwani to India without a detour via A&E.

Attacking her poor thumb again Priya racked her brains and by the time they reached the car the skeleton of an idea was starting to take shape even if her cuticle was shredded. She checked her watch, and doing a quick sum worked out that it was still before noon in England. The person she really needed would be working. She'd have to call later if she was to put her plan into action and go into full grovel mode, a thought which truly set her teeth on edge.

Yes, Priya thought with a grimace, it was an idea she supposed but it didn't make her feel at all happy. It went against her every instinct to have to ask this person for a favour. But for Ashwani she'd swallow a huge slice of humble pie.

In fact she loved her father so much she'd even go back for seconds.

16

That evening Jaipur's electricity decided to give up the ghost, a common occurrence according to Akhila, and one which offered Priya the perfect chance to slip away from the press of bodies in the apartment. Neesh was in bed sleeping off her earlier hysterics, Divya and Akhila flat out with preparations for the Varalakshmi Vratam, a pooja celebrated by the women of the house in honour of the goddess Lakshmi. Meanwhile, the aunties, glued to a game of whist, afforded Priya the perfect opportunity to wander outside and make a private phone call.

She opened the French windows and pushed through the tangle of muslin, loving the silky touch of the night air on her hot face and the way the breeze stirred her thin cotton top. Invisible crickets chirped from the greenery and chatter drifted from the kitchen, where the married womenfolk were sorting out the pots and spices required for the next day's celebrations in candlelight.

Perfect, everyone was occupied. Nobody would notice that she was missing.

Once her eyes adjusted to the darkness Priya made

out white gravel paths meandering between the plants and flowers. Roses scattered waxy petals under her feet and swathes of jasmine brushed against her legs. Turning left, her flip-flops scrunching on the gravel, she followed a path through the jasmine beds. The milky flowers only opened after dusk and she trailed her hand through the petals, inhaling waves of fragrance. Noah had said jasmine had magical healing powers, nature's antidepressants, if you like. Maybe she should pick a bloody big bunch just in case Ashwani couldn't make it to the wedding. Neesh would need to mainline the stuff if she discovered that on top of losing her dream dress her beloved father might not make her special day.

It mustn't come to that!

Sinking on to a small bench in the far corner of the garden Priya glanced up at the thousands of twinkling stars, startlingly bright against the darkness of the sky. To think that each pinprick of light was a sun, maybe surrounded by its own planets, was a very humbling idea. Humanity really did seem pretty insignificant in comparison to nature, just as Noah had said earlier on when telling them how some of the trees in the sacred groves were supposedly thousands of years old.

Goodness, she thought with a mocking shake of her head, that guy certainly has a way of getting into your thoughts! Something about his chocolate mousse voice must have hypnotic properties.

As Priya mused on her mysterious guide and gazed upwards a blur of blue light streaked across the sky, so fast she almost missed it. A shooting star! Wow! The celestial firework traced its path across the heavens and then it was gone, as abruptly and as mysteriously as it appeared, but not before she'd closed her eyes and wished on it harder and with more desperation than she'd ever wished for anything in her life.

Please let Dad make it to Neesh's wedding!

Reaching into her bag she pulled out a cigarette – another secret she'd kept from her family – and inhaled gratefully. Peace at long last. As the nicotine exploded into her bloodstream Priya flipped open her mobile and before she could back out punched in the one number that she couldn't erase from her fingertips, no matter how hard she tried. It was a number she'd once loved to dial, her heart constricting with love when the man at the other end answered and sounded so happy to hear from her. The number was Vikram's, of course, and these days he was the last person she wanted to speak to, the last person she wanted to ask for a favour, and ironically the only person she trusted enough to help her now.

How bloody screwed up was that?

Miles away in London Vik's mobile shrilled, echoing through the network, and Priya found that her heart was thumping in time with each ring. It was funny to think of her call being bounced up there into the sky, past the shooting stars and cold-eyed moon, before plummeting back down to Shepherd's Bush where it was only just gone five and Vik was probably still sitting in his office admiring his reflection in his Mac Book.

Er . . . she meant working.

'Priya! Hey!' Vik said, finally picking up. 'Sorry, babe, I didn't hear the phone for a minute. I hoped you'd call. Are you missing me? Do you miss us?'

Priya bit back the sharp retort that she was no

longer his *babe* and curled her nails into the palms of her hands as she fought to remain calm. Vik's confident belief that she was bound to come to her senses about their relationship sooner or later was more annoying than a too-tight G-string.

'This isn't a social call, Vik,' she said quickly, not wanting another game of relationship chess. 'I'm not phoning to talk about us. Not that there is an us, anyway.'

He sighed. 'I think you're wrong, babe, but okay, let's talk about work then if that makes you happier. How are you coping without a sound engineer? I'm sorry, but finding someone's proving to be a lot trickier than I thought it would be. I hope it hasn't set your filming back too far.'

Priya couldn't be bothered to explain about Ishani. The shorter she kept this conversation the better as far as she was concerned. 'Don't worry. We've managed so far and the filming's going well. I'm following a few leads.' She inhaled on her cigarette in an attempt to calm her nerves. If he asked what those leads were she was stuffed, not having much more than a gut feeling that there was more going on than met the eye at the ashram. And gut feelings were hardly the stuff of hard core journalism, were they? How often did John Humphrys attack the Prime Minister on a gut instinct?

'That's good you're making progress,' Vik said. Then with a smile in his voice he added, 'Are you smoking, Ms Gupta? Vile habit! I thought you were giving up?'

Priya stubbed her cigarette out in annoyance. 'You know I only smoke when I'm stressed.'

'And are you stressed tonight?'

She took a deep breath, already missing the soothing nicotine, and taking the plunge told him about Ashwani's predicament. Priya didn't need to explain to Vik why she was so worried about her father, because they'd still been together when he was first taken ill and Vik, for all his faults, was devoted to his parents and totally understood just how much her family meant to Priya. Those shared family values had been one of the things she'd really treasured about their relationship. It was just a shame he'd lacked other equally important values . . .

'No way!' Vik was horrified by Ashwani's camping in the concourse plan. 'He'll catch his death of cold if he tries to pull a stunt like that. Listen, Priya, leave it to me. I'll sort this out, I promise. In fact, I'll make some calls now and see what I can do, okay? Then I'll drive over and have a chat with your dad. There's no way I'll let him anywhere near a concourse floor. I promise!'

Priya felt limp with relief. Vikram would keep his word, she knew. He'd call in every contact and connection in his Rolodex and if anyone could get Ashwani to India in one piece it'd be him.

Damn. Now she really owed him! Time for a big chunk of that humble pie. She could always take a Rennie later.

'Thanks so much for doing this for Dad, Vik. I really appreciate it.'

'Priya,' Vik said slowly, and even though there were thousands of miles between them she sensed the emotion in his voice, 'I'm not doing it for your dad. I'm doing it for you.'

Once he'd rung off Priya sat alone in the dark and fragrant garden, struck by a sharp pang of regret that things had ended so badly between them. She curled her legs underneath her and wrapped her arms around her slender body, allowing herself for once to recall the early days of their relationship, when everything had seemed so perfect.

Why had he gone and wrecked things? It was all such a bloody waste.

Priya was so lost in thought that she didn't notice until it was too late that she was no longer alone. There were footsteps scrunching on the gravel, the murmur of low voices, a soft giggle and then a sigh. She sat bolt upright, mortified at being cast in the role of voyeur, almost leaping into orbit when a couple rounded the corner. Closer than words they held each other, only breaking apart from a passionate kiss when the man snapped a jasmine flower from the hedge and tucked it tenderly behind his partner's ear. The moon had slipped behind a cloud and with the electricity still out the garden was inky, shielding the pair from view, but from the sighs and moans they were clearly enjoying a very romantic interlude.

Young love, thought Priya indulgently, but with a pang. Well, enjoy it while it lasts.

She smiled even though in the blackness she couldn't decipher who they were; young Adani cousins probably, catching a few private moments in the friendly darkness, away from Akhila's eagle eye. And who could blame them?

But moments later, when the clouds melted away and moonlight silvered the garden, illuminating the lovers like a searchlight, Priya cried out in surprise because this was no loved-up teenage couple.

Oh, God, if only it was. This was all she needed!

The two sprang apart guiltily, looking horrified at being caught out.

As well they might.

'Priya? Is that you, pet?' Ray called, stepping out of the shadows, his face screwed up against the gloom, while Ishani peered over his shoulder, her eyes behind her glasses wide with anxiety. Although it was dark her cheeks were even darker as a guilty blush stained them livid red.

'Jesus, Pri! You've just knocked about ten years off our lives, skulking around like that!'

'I'm not the one skulking!' Priya snapped back, goaded out of her surprise by his aggressive attitude. She glowered at him. 'And I'm not the one who needs to explain themselves, either. What the hell do you two think you're playing at? This isn't the bloody Playboy Mansion, you know. What's going on?'

Ray and Ishani didn't say anything. They didn't need to; their linked fingers and eyes said it all. Priya could have kicked herself for not seeing this coming. Was it her fault for being so wrapped up in her own problems and throwing them together at the ashram today?

'Come on, pet,' said Ray eventually, pulling Ishani tightly against him. 'Don't make us spell it out. Isn't it obvious? We're together.'

Priya had the sensation of the ground heaving beneath her feet. If Akhila found out that the young man she'd so generously taken into her house had made advances towards her betrothed daughter all hell would break loose. She'd blame the Guptas, make Sanj call the wedding off, throw them out . . . it was a disaster just waiting to happen.

'But Ishani, you're engaged! You can't possibly get involved with Ray when you're promised to Baadal.'

Ishani's chin was raised defensively and her hand was still tightly clutched in Ray's big paw. For someone who was cheating on her fiancé she didn't look very sorry.

'Please don't judge me before I've had a chance to explain,' she said in her soft, sweet voice. 'It's not as bad as it looks. Baadal and I decided a long time ago that we're not suited and we've got no intention of ever getting married. Why else do you think he's chosen to stay in the States for so long?'

'I thought he was studying and that you'll get married once he graduates?' Priya asked, feeling stupid. Had she just been spun a line?

Ishani smiled sadly. 'It suits both of us to keep our families believing that. It buys us a bit of time and space. Come on, Priya, you've seen what my mother's like. Can you imagine what my life would be like if she thought I was single?'

Priya swallowed. Akhila went about matchmaking with the thoroughness of the Spanish Inquisition pursuing heretics. Ishani's life would have been unbearable. There'd be no freedom to pursue her career or have a life of her own; every spare minute would be devoted to playing the dutiful Asian daughter as an endless line of suitors paraded through the Adanis' apartment. Did she blame her for lying?

No, of course she didn't. Of course she should be

free to find love wherever her heart led her, but with Ray of all people? Big Geordie Ray with his love of real ale and blue line in banter? Was Cupid having a laugh?

'But you guys,' she whispered. 'What can you possibly have in common? You come from totally different worlds.'

'You're wrong. We have everything in common,' Ishani cried. 'Our filming, our humour, our love of real ale!' She giggled. 'Well, I've promised to work on that one if Ray will try to work on loving my family!'

That was a tall order, thought Priya, nervously chewing her thumb nail. If Akhila got wind of this Ray would be out on his ear and back to the Sheraton before you could say *western boy* and the Adanis' wrath would make *Romeo and Juliet* look like a Mills & Boon novel.

17

'Excuse me, son, but did I hear you right? Where did you say we were going? Surely not up there?'

Shielding his eyes with a meaty paw Clay squinted up into the hillside beyond the ashram, where the burnished slopes were still swathed in early morning mist, the mountain peaks barely visible above the swirling vapours. The look of pure horror on his face would have been comical if Priya hadn't been feeling so utterly shattered herself and already dreading the steep climb to the Bhil village. It was all very well for Noah to tell them how beautiful it would be up in the hills and enthuse about the myriad spiritual qualities of the ancient temples; he hadn't been forced to spend the whole of the previous day trying frantically to keep Ray and Ishani apart.

Priya sighed and took a big swig of ice-cold Evian. It would have been easier to separate two industrial-strength magnets than her loved-up colleagues. They might think they were being subtle but the smouldering looks they'd been exchanging across the breakfast table had almost set the toast alight. Busy as Akhila was she had eyes on elastic when it came to her daughter and

Priya had spent most of the day glued to Ray's side under some pretext or another while desperately trying to convince him that he should step back. But Ray was stubborn and she might as well have had a conversation with the sacred kalasha pot for all the good it did her, and after a day of this she was mentally exhausted. And for what, exactly? All she'd achieved was to raise Divya's suspicions. Her mother was more convinced than ever that there was more than just friendship between her daughter and the gangly Geordie.

Look on the bright side, Priya said to herself as she shoved her water back into her rucksack, at least that takes the pressure off Ray and Ishani even if it makes your own life hell.

Although *hell* might be putting in mildly if Divya really got upset and decided to say something; a nuclear explosion would seem restrained in contrast.

Groaning wearily, Priya crouched down to lace up her hiking boots and listened to Noah soothing Clay about the long walk ahead.

'This area is widely believed to be one of the most spiritual in Rajasthan,' he was telling the group. 'The swami often retreats to these hills when she wishes to meditate. She's there now, in fact.'

Of course she flipping was, thought Priya acidly, hanging out with Santa and the Tooth Fairy probably. More likely she was shopping in Jaipur.

'Will she be back soon?' Maggie was asking, her eyes hopeful. 'I've really missed seeing her on this visit. Attuttama's such a wonderful woman, so wise and so spiritual.'

Priya snorted but turned it into a cough when she

sensed Noah's clear-eyed gaze light upon her. So he thought she was a cynic? Not everyone could live in la-la land like him. Let him believe his precious swami was out there for the good of her soul; more likely she was hiding from nosy journalists. She probably had a mansion up there with hot- and cold-running Jacuzzis and a garage full of sports cars all paid for by gullible suckers like Maggie and the Texans.

'Don't worry, she'll be back soon enough,' Noah assured Maggie, laying a hand on her bony shoulder. 'And she'll be refreshed after her time alone. Don't forget that the swami believes fasting and meditating up in the hills brings her closer to a higher plane of understanding.'

'It looks like we'll be on a higher plane soon if we're going up there,' Ray quipped, shielding his eyes and peering up into the hills. 'Are you sure you really need me to film this, Priya? Maybe you could just take the camcorder and Ish and I could stay here and get some more sound bites from other guests?'

'I'd rather have the proper kit up there. Some of the scenery could be really useful. Take the steadicam and the boom; we can leave the rest. Besides, we've got all the sound bites we need. I'm only waiting on the swami now.'

'Right you are, boss,' sighed Ray. He pointed at their camera kit and grimaced. 'I'll lug all this lot up a mountain for you then, shall I?'

'Here, let me help carry some of your kit. I'm used to carrying supplies up the hill.' Noah swung Ray's camera bag, easily twenty pounds, up on to his shoulder as though it was stuffed with feathers. He was dressed for walking today in frayed cut-off jeans, hiking boots and a loose white shirt, the linen bright against the taut mahogany sheen of his skin, and his curls were tied back from his face, leaving the sun to dance off those Mont Blanc cheekbones.

Goodness, but he really was beautiful. When she'd played the rushes back a few nights ago Priya hadn't been surprised by just how much the camera loved him. Why was someone with such potential wasting his life here in the back end of nowhere?

Noah caught Priya staring at him and smiled warmly, while she dragged her eyes away, furious with herself. Now he'd think she'd been looking at him – which she had, of course – but not in the way he'd think. Her interest in Noah was purely journalistic. It took more than smoky grey eyes and a body that would make Brad Pitt jealous to turn her head. Besides, after Vikram she'd had her fill of good-looking, untrustworthy men. Who was to say Noah was any different just because he worked in an ashram? He was a convicted drugs offender after all, she reminded herself sternly, something that he'd made no secret of. It seemed that there wasn't a man on the planet who wasn't a disappointment in one way or another. Feeling irritated with herself for still finding him attractive, even in a purely academic way, she took another long sip of her water and hoped that it would slow her racing pulse.

This was all Vikram's fault. She'd been settled if not totally happy before she'd spoken to him, and more than able to handle Noah. Hearing Vik's voice over the telephone had reawoken all sorts of memories and feelings, which was why she was feeling so odd this morning. Stuffing her drinking bottle back into her rucksack Priya told herself firmly that she was definitely not engaging in any heart-to-hearts with Noah today. In fact she'd do her best to not even be anywhere near him during the hike because he seemed to have an uncanny instinct for sensing her weak areas and making her examine them right then and there.

And she was so *not* in the mood for that today.

'All set?' Noah asked his group, who nodded and murmured excitedly, with the exception of Clara and Clay who still looked worried.

'I bet they don't walk much further than the fridge,' Ray whispered.

'And that probably has a remote control to bring the sodas to them,' giggled Ishani.

'We'll hike for two hours to the Bhil village,' Noah told them all. 'The swami believes that you must not cut yourself off. This is why she always asks that her guides take the guests beyond the ashram.'

Or to get us out of the way, Priya added silently. Still, the rest of the group seemed happy with this explanation and were hoiking rucksacks on to their shoulders and adjusting their shades. Even the business couple were joining them today, looking strikingly different now that they were wearing loose linen trousers and T-shirts instead of the razor sharp suits. The woman didn't look too sick to Priya either, for someone Noah had said was unwell. Her eyes sparkled, there was a cinnamon dusting of freckles across the bridge of her nose and even her tortoiseshell hair seemed to bounce with a life of its own. She was friendly too, falling into step next to Maggie and chatting about the beauty of the landscape and how wonderful the ashram was.

'She looks like a different woman,' Priya remarked to Ray. 'Do you think she was really ill? Look how fast she's walking up that slope.'

'She does seem to have made an amazing recovery,' he said. 'I reckon they've fed her up on some of those magic mushrooms they're secretly growing.'

After climbing steeply for an hour and hiking further into the tree canopy Priya could have done with some magic mushrooms herself. Her feet were hot and chafed in the heavy boots, her hair was plastered against her cheeks and her arms were scratched from pushing through the undergrowth. Although it was cooler higher up the mountainside it was still a relief when Noah suggested that they break for lunch and rest.

'This is the site of an ancient temple dedicated to Lord Shiva,' he was telling them while unpacking his giant backpack and handing out a simple meal of plain naan bread and fruit. He'd barely broken a sweat, striding ahead of them with ease, and she'd nearly ruptured herself trying to keep up. Sinking on to the grass and draining the tepid dregs of her water, Priya vowed that she really must up her gym routine when she got home.

'Once you're rested, feel free to explore. But please respect the sanctity of the place and leave your cameras outside,' Noah warned them. 'This is an ancient and very holy spot, not a tourist attraction, and that is the way the swami wishes it to remain.'

As they ate, the group fell into a contemplative silence. Priya closed her eyes for a moment and luxuriated in the peace, letting it wash over her tangled thoughts like a cool clear stream.

'Hey, wake up! It's time to explore.'

Noah's hand brushed Priya's cheek, rousing her gently from an unexpected snooze. As her eyes fluttered open she saw to her surprise that the area was empty apart from a pile of abandoned rucksacks and cameras. God, she hoped she hadn't been drooling or talking in her sleep. How embarrassing would that be?

'Sorry,' she apologised, rubbing her eyes. 'I didn't mean to nod off. Did I snore?'

Noah chuckled. 'Maybe once or twice.'

'How awful! I'm really sorry.'

'Don't apologise. Sleep was your body's natural response.'

'After the last few days I could sleep for a month,' she sighed. 'And it's so quiet here – I don't think I've ever heard such silence. It's like a balm for the soul.'

What? Where did that come from? Was she channelling Anita Roddick?

Noah looked at her thoughtfully for a moment and then held out his hand. 'I think it's time you saw the temple. It's a very special place.'

'I'm not sure,' Priya hedged. 'I'm not that bothered about religious stuff to be honest.'

'So it won't hurt for one afternoon to just suspend disbelief. Come and have a look. I promise you won't be disappointed.'

There was no use arguing. She was miles away from London, and her colleagues had abandoned work to wander off. She let Noah take her hand in his and raised her eyes to his sea-grey ones as he pulled her to her feet and guided her through the tangled undergrowth. The eerie stillness made her feel as though they were the only two people in the world, the only sound their feet scuffing the earth and the blood pounding in her ears.

Her hand still clasped in his, Priya followed Noah up the mountainside. As the path narrowed she found herself pressed tightly against him, and when the taut muscles of his bicep brushed against her breast her heart began to beat double time as delicious waves of gooseflesh shivered across her arms. She was suddenly aware that his forefinger was stroking the soft skin of her palm and this small innocent caress sent shocking shivers of longing rippling through her. Priya didn't think she'd ever been as aware of someone else's physical presence.

It's the heat and the thinning oxygen! she told herself sternly. Get a grip!

But she slipped her hand from his all the same and stepped back a little just to be certain.

'Are you okay?' Noah asked, turning round, concern etched on his face as he looked down at her, taking in the pink cheeks and her shallow breathing. 'It's steep, isn't it? Do you want to stop and catch your breath?'

She stared up at him, the sharp-planed face shaded in the dappled light and the eyes dark with some emotion she couldn't quite pinpoint, and knew that if they didn't keep going she was quite frankly in danger of never being able to catch her breath again.

'I'm just a bit hot,' she hedged. 'Give me a moment and I'll be fine.'

His hand rose to push a lock of hair away from her cheek, playing with the strands and tucking them away behind her ear. 'Take all the time you need. You're under a lot of pressure, I think, so just stop for a moment and be still. There's no need rush up here.'

There is, thought Priya. I need to get away from you before I make a total idiot of myself.

All the pent-up feelings from the days before, the worry about her father, her feelings for Vik, her worries about Ray and Ishani, seemed to be rising up inside her like bubbles in a shaken cola bottle. But what alarmed her even more was that Noah's closeness was unlocking something else in her, something she thought she'd long buried and locked away.

Desire.

Priya felt giddy and totally thrown. Suddenly all she could think about was the overwhelming need she had to reach up and touch his face, to trace the angles of his cheekbones with her forefinger before pulling his lips down to meet hers. What would it be like to kiss him? To wrap her fingers in that thick silky hair and feel those strong arms pull her closer against his hard body?

God! What was the matter with her? It must be because she was on her own with a man, the first one she'd been alone with since Vikram. This wasn't sensible or logical. In fact it was ridiculous. Taking a deep breath she told herself to get over it. None of this was real.

Noah frowned. 'Hey, you're trembling.'

'I'm fine, just unfit!'

He shook his head. 'No way. You're a gym bunny. It must be the altitude affecting you. It can do strange things to people.'

Tell me about it, thought Priya.

'Put your arms around my neck,' he continued. 'I'll carry you the rest of the way.' When she started to protest, he insisted, 'Yes, I will! No arguments for once, Priya, okay?'

And before she could so much as squeak he'd scooped her into his arms just as easily as he'd lifted all Ray's camera kit and was carrying her up the mountain path, his long strides eating the distance up in seconds. Priya could do nothing but accept his help, and she leaned her head against the warm fabric of his shirt and closed her eyes. For a second she thought she felt him press his lips to her temple but that had to have been her imagination because what felt like only moments later he set her down gently beside what looked like a pile of lichen-smothered stones, draped with vines and looped with dense foliage, and said cheerfully, 'This is where the taxi stops!'

Feeling disorientated Priya swayed on her feet for a second and Noah steadied her by placing gentle hands on her shoulders.

'Take a few deep breaths,' he advised. 'We're high up now and there's a bit of a climb into the temple. Just wait until you feel yourself.'

But Priya was feeling anything but herself. She could still feel the warmth of his hands on her bare skin, the imprints of his fingers seeming as though they were seared on to her body, and her heart was still racing from being held so close. Noah's breathing was also ragged but of course he'd just lugged her halfway up a mountain, she told herself sternly. She needed to get a grip and fast. All this thin air and searing heat were clearly having a very bad effect.

Thank God she normally lived in rainy London!

Pretending to be fascinated by the view she gradually calmed her breathing, sipped some warm water from her bottle and started to feel slightly more like her usual self. Noah was right, she decided firmly as she readjusted her rucksack, the altitude had got to her. It was nothing more sinister, or more meaningful, than that.

'Better?' he asked, smiling at her.

She nodded. 'Much, thanks! I think I was just a bit overwhelmed.'

'Don't worry, you're not the first.'

I bet I'm not, thought Priya wryly. Aloud she said, 'So, where exactly are we?'

'We're at the ancient temple.' Noah leaned forward and brushed some tangled ferns out of the way of what looked like a pile of stones. 'This is one of the lesser known entrances.'

Closer inspection revealed it to be a doorway into the temple that peeped out of the hillside like a slumbering tortoise from his shell. Noah helped Priya inside, his hands closing around her waist as he lifted her down a short flight of hidden steps. For a second she felt the heat of his hard body against her bare midriff before he set her down on the smooth stone floor and stepped backwards so that she could look around, and when she did she gasped in amazement.

Her mad moment, or altitude sickness as she preferred to call it, was totally forgotten. Noah, as good as his word, really had brought her somewhere totally magical.

18

Fingers of sunshine fell through the narrow door, illuminating the vaulted space with pallid light and picking out ancient engravings on the walls. Above their heads the ceiling rose as high and vaulted as any European cathedral, strips of blue sky blasting through the cracks and striping the worn flagstones with buttery light.

'It's amazing!' Priya gasped, spinning round as she tried to take it all in. 'It's so solemn and so peaceful.'

'And timeless,' whispered Noah, his eyes closed and his wide generous mouth curling into a smile. 'The prayers and thoughts of thousands of years are here. Can you feel them?'

'Mmm,' said Priya. 'Maybe.' She closed her eyes and let the quiet seep into her heart. What a contrast to the rush and whirl of the Adanis' world.

What a relief!

'Remember the other day,' continued Noah, his voice hushed in the stillness, 'when you said what you did about me not being in the real world? Did you mean it?'

Priya felt awkward. 'I'm sorry about that. I had no right to judge you. It was very rude of me.'

'No, it was an honest gut response. Don't feel bad. You had a point, I think.'

'It's also easy to be cynical when you've never experienced anything like this.' Priya sighed. 'Sometimes being cynical is a cop out.'

He laughed. 'And sometimes so is being spiritual. In some ways I have cut myself off by choosing to be here. I've left my career, my home and my friends behind. Perhaps I should be trying harder to bring the two parts of my life together?'

She pressed her fingers against her temples. 'Noah, believe me, I'm the last person you should ask about things like that.'

He exhaled slowly. 'But you're the expert on cutting yourself off, Priya. Maybe not in a physical sense like I have, but you certainly do it in all the other areas of your life. I've seen how you separate it all out: work, home, family . . . even,' he paused and turned to face her, so that she was staring into those wide-spaced grey eyes, 'relationships?'

Priya's stomach was a Swiss roll of emotion. His smile was there in the darkness, his mouth just inches from hers, and for a minute she thought that maybe there was more between them than conversation. Then the moment was shattered by the strident tones of Clay and Clara as they squeezed into the temple and Noah carefully stepped away from her.

'I told you this was a special place,' he said gently.

And for once she didn't doubt him.

*

Priya was still pondering Noah's question when they arrived, tired but happy, at the Bhil village. She couldn't deny she'd felt something special in the ancient temple and she hoped that the sense of peace she'd experienced wouldn't slip away with the setting sun. They'd only just sat down to some very welcome cold drinks when one of the village children, tired and dusty from walking back from school, passed Noah a folded note which he pocketed straight away without reading. His brow crumpled though and for the first time that day he looked ruffled. Instantly Priya's interest was piqued and she found herself shifting back into journalist mode. What was all that about? Was he hiding something after all? Was all that talk of spirituality just a way to throw her off the scent? If so, what exactly was he going to such extreme lengths to conceal?

Stealing a glimpse at his hawk-like profile from under her lashes she was surprised to find that she really hoped he was genuine. But she'd been wrong before and something told her that she'd be wrong again, because if she were honest she had to admit that when it came down to men she really wasn't the best judge of character.

Once the group moved off again Priya picked up speed and caught up with Noah, easier said than done when her shorter legs had to go at double pace in order to keep up with his long stride.

'So will the swami be there when we get back?' she asked, skidding over the leaf litter in her haste to keep up.

Noah nodded. 'Yes. She was returning from her retreat this afternoon.'

'So I'll finally get to meet her at last!' Priya felt like whooping with excitement. 'That's fantastic. I can't wait to talk to her.'

'You may have to wait a bit longer to do that,' he said.

'What?' It was hard to talk when you were trotting after someone like Donkey from *Shrek*, so Priya grabbed Noah's elbow and spun him to face her. 'What exactly do you mean, I might have to wait a bit longer to do that? I've been waiting ages.'

'I know, Priya.' Arctic-grey eyes troubled, Noah looked at her apologetically. 'And I realise how frustrating it must be.'

'Frustrating? You have no idea. So what's the excuse this time? Another retreat? Or maybe she just doesn't want to speak to journalists?'

'Of course she wants to speak to you. And she will when the time's right, I promise.'

Priya was practically gnashing her teeth. 'So why isn't the time right now? I'm here, she's here. What's stopping her, for God's sake?'

'She's taken a vow of silence.'

'What!' She stared at him. 'You have to be kidding.'

'No, I'm afraid not. The swami often takes a vow of silence for the few days following a retreat. She feels that it enables her chakras to—'

She held up her hands. 'Oh, please! Spare me the spiritual crap. In fact, Noah, just do me a favour and don't bother trying to think up any more pathetic excuses. I'm sick and tired of being fobbed off by you and your beloved swami!'

Simmering with rage she stormed away from him,

the effect spoiled somewhat because it wasn't easy to storm up a hill, and vented her fury on a few unfortunate tree roots. A vow of silence? How bloody convenient for the swami, and what perfect timing too, just when a documentary team was scheduled to arrive. What exactly was the woman so desperate to hide? A silly accent? Or something more sinister?

Priya was still seething when they stopped for a rest half an hour later. Ignoring Noah, who tried several times to start a conversation, she took herself away from the group and popped her iPod headphones in, hoping that this would give him a hint. Thank goodness she was over her weird altitude sickness, she thought as she set the play mode to Shuffle, otherwise things could have got really awkward. Imagine if she'd kissed him, or something ridiculous like that. Talk about a conflict of interests. She closed her eyes and for a split second she was back in the cool depths of the mountains with Noah's strong fingers clasping her hand and his body pressed against hers. Her pulse quickened at the thought.

Her libido was a crappy judge of character, Priya thought sadly. First the lying Vikram and now Noah – who was more than likely a conman as well as being a convicted drugs offender. What had she been thinking earlier? No matter how wide he opened those grey eyes and protested that everything at the ashram was just peachy something just didn't make sense. There were too many secrets and half-truths here for her liking and trying to figure them out was starting to exhaust her. What she wouldn't give to be back in her flat, curled up on the sofa with a big glass of cold white wine and some chill-out music on the stereo. The sooner the wedding was over and this documentary was in the can the better.

'Hey, maybe she really has taken a vow of silence?' said Ishani, when a still furious Priya filled her and Ray in on this latest development. 'Perhaps vows of silence are all part of her spiritual role?'

'Yeah, right,' scoffed Priya. 'And a bit convenient too, don't you think? She's hiding something, I just know it.'

'Not everyone has an agenda,' pointed out Ray.

'Yes they bloody well do! It's human nature, Ray. I've got the documentary to keep on schedule, you want to sneak off with Ishani and the swami wants to keep things hidden. Everyone here's got their own agenda!'

'You're absolutely right, Priya,' interrupted a clotted cream rich voice from behind them. 'Everyone does have an agenda.'

Priya, Ray and Ishani jumped guiltily as Noah strode towards them, his arms folded and his eyes bright with anger.

'My agenda is to ensure that your documentary doesn't intrude on the sanctity of the ashram. I'm sorry if the way we do things here is inconvenient to you and disrupts your' – he nearly spat the word – 'schedule. But there are values in life that are far more important than worldly ones. You would be wise to remember that if you want to continue to film here.'

'Mate, I'm sure Priya didn't mean to offend you,' Ray said, mortified. 'But even you must admit that it looks a bit fishy from our point of view.'

But Noah didn't appear inclined to stick around and hear about Ray's point of view, preferring to turn on his heel and stride away. His lean body was taut with anger and even his thick black curls seemed to bounce with indignation.

'Bollocks,' said Ray. 'That's buggered things up. Should we go and grovel, do you think?'

'I'd leave him to cool down,' Ishani said gently. 'We've really offended him.'

'I have, you mean,' groaned Priya.

'Yeah, you certainly seem to have a way of getting to him, pet. He's normally so chilled he makes Gandhi look stressy,' Ray agreed.

'I'm sorry if I upset him,' said Priya. She was too, but a part of her was also slightly exultant. If Noah was this upset, perhaps it was because he did have something to hide? Had her comments about the swami touched a nerve?

The final hour of their walk back was subdued. The easy atmosphere of earlier had vanished and Noah joined Maggie instead, leaving Priya to endure a booming monologue from Clay.

That was another black splat in his copybook, Priya thought darkly as she trudged into the ashram with her eardrums throbbing. Why couldn't Clay do them all a favour and take a leaf out of the swami's book? Ears still ringing, she was just heading to the refectory in search of a cool drink when to her great surprise Neesh came tearing round a corner and hurled herself into Priya's arms.

'What on earth are you doing here?' Priya

demanded. Since shopping and spa treatments were more up Neesh's street than meditation she'd not shown any interest in visiting the ashram before. Something must be really wrong to send her tearing into the hillside where there wasn't a designer label in sight.

'Oh, Pri, it's a disaster,' shrieked Neesh, bursting into floods of tears. 'Everything's ruined! The wedding is ruined!'

Oh God, thought Priya, her heart sinking like a stone, she's found out about Dad. Vik couldn't pull it off after all. Wrapping her arms around her sister she said, 'Listen, babes, I know it's terrible but it doesn't have to be the end of the wedding. Dad wouldn't want that.'

'What's Dad got to do with it?' Neesh wiped her eyes on her sleeve. 'Fat lot of help he is anyway, thousands of bloody miles away. He can't find me another wedding venue from London, can he?' Her voice rose an octave. 'No one can find me another venue! Not at this short notice! Everything's ruined!'

'The venue's fallen through?' Priya's legs went wobbly with relief. Well, either that or the hike had been tougher than she'd thought. 'Is that all?'

'Is that *all*?' Neesh wept, looking a dead ringer for Munch's *The Scream*. 'I'll never find another place now. I may as well just call the whole thing off. First my dress and now this! My wedding's cursed.'

'Babes, it isn't. We'll find somewhere, I promise!'

Priya said, patting her sister's heaving back. 'We'll sort it out.'

But Neesh was not in the mood to be soothed. Her sobs gained volume by the second and before long the peace of the ashram was well and truly shattered. Soon a small crowd had gathered to listen as Neesh sobbed out her tale of woe. Even Noah abandoned washing under the tap in the courtyard and joined them, rivulets of water running down skin the colour of warm cocoa.

Not that Priya was looking at Noah's skin or the smooth muscles of his torso. She was too busy trying to stop Neesh crying which, unless she gagged her, was becoming more unlikely by the minute.

'Please, babes,' she said desperately. 'Try to calm down. It'll be okay.'

Neesh fixed her with tragic eyes. 'How will it? Where can we find a new venue at this kind of short notice? All the hotels were booked up months ago. It's a disaster!'

Maggie handed her a tissue and Neesh blew her nose loudly before dissolving into more sobs. Priya felt close to despair. There was no stopping Neesh once she wound herself into a state like this.

'We'll work something out,' she repeated helplessly. 'There's bound to be a spare venue somewhere in Jaipur!'

'All the nice ones are booked already,' wailed Neesh. At least, Priya thought that was what she said. Neesh could have been talking Klingon for all the sense she was making now.

'You could have the wedding here,' Noah offered, clearly moved by her distress. 'It's a beautiful setting, the perfect place to celebrate a union of hearts and spirits. I could ask the swami, if you'd like?'

'If she's talking, you mean,' Priya said darkly.

Noah gave her a look. 'I haven't taken a vow of silence. She only has to nod. And I'm sure she'd be only too delighted to help out.'

'Really?' Neesh looked up at him through starry lashes. 'You mean it? I could get married here?'

'No way!' said Priya, before Noah had a chance to speak. 'This is my work place. It'd be a complete conflict of interests!'

'Why would it?' Neesh asked.

'Yes,' said Noah, folding his arms across his chest and fixing Priya with those dark eyes. 'Why?'

'Because my being here has to be kept strictly professional. If you do me a favour like that it'll compromise my integrity as a journalist.'

'Priya,' said Noah wearily, 'I wish you'd believe me when I tell you that there's absolutely nothing underhand going on here. There's nothing to say you can't have your sister's wedding here *and* make a first class documentary.'

Priya opened her mouth to make a sharp retort along the lines of some people keeping to their principles but the acute look of distress on her sister's face stopped her in her tracks and she found herself relenting.

'Come on then.' Noah held his hand out to Neesh. 'Let's go and ask the swami, shall we?'

'Run that by me again?' Priya said. 'You mean I'm finally going to meet her?'

'Aren't you pleased?' he said with a slow smile that

crinkled his eyes. 'I thought that was what you were longing for?'

'An interview is what I'm longing for,' muttered Priya, following Noah and Neesh across the courtyard to a small hut set beyond the herb garden. 'Not a session planning weddings. I wanted to find out about the miracles, not discuss hats.'

But nobody was listening to her. Neesh was too busy exclaiming about the beauty of the flower gardens and Noah, probably relieved to discover that Priya was the only crosspatch in the Gupta clan, was cheerfully pointing out the small temple where Neesh and Sanj could marry. Seeing the look of excitement on her sister's face Priya realised that she was just going to have to swallow her frustration and ask the swami for a favour. There simply wasn't any choice because she loved Neesh and would do anything to make her perfect wedding happen.

Even if it meant stomping all over her journalistic principles.

Priya hadn't quite known what to expect from the swami. Maybe a cross between the Maharishi Mahesh Yogi and a stern headmistress? Or perhaps a way-out humming caricature like something from *The Love Guru*? And if neither of these stereotypes then certainly someone shifty who was concealing something. So as she and Neesh stepped behind Noah into a small dimly lit and incense-scented room Priya was fully prepared to have all her most cynical misgivings confirmed. The swami would probably be wearing an Armani robe and counting her money, or would have mysteriously vanished into the hills again on yet another pretext. Or maybe she was tearing round to hide her Jacuzzi and flat screen?

Although . . . this low-built hut was so small it would be pretty hard to squeeze anything in. Surely the swami couldn't live in such a tiny space?

'She certainly does. These are the swami's private quarters,' Noah confirmed when Priya expressed her surprise. 'Please respect her space. I wouldn't normally bring people here but this is an exception and I know she'll want to help.'

Priya squinted into the darkness. 'But it looks empty.'

'I told you we don't subscribe to worldly values here,' Noah said gently, seeing the surprised look on her face.

As her eyes grew accustomed to the gloom Priya saw that the room was barer than any monk's cell, the only furniture to speak of a pile of plain white cushions with a mosquito net draped in gossamer folds above. Beneath this a woman was sitting in the lotus position, her eyes shut and her features composed into such an expression of serenity that for a second Priya was lost for words. She was an older woman, maybe in her fifties, but with her lined face, supple straight bearing and waist-length white hair she could have been any age at all because she simply radiated energy and benevolence.

'Forgive me, swami, for intruding when you are resting,' Noah was saying. 'But my friends here need your help.'

The swami remained motionless for what felt like

ages. Priya found that she was holding her breath and Neesh was so agog that she forgot to cry.

'Wow! You look just like Shakira Caine!' she gasped.

The swami opened her eyes at this and gave Neesh a gentle smile, which lit her dove-grey eyes and creased a face that was worn into thousands of smile lines. Then, stretching out her hands in greeting, she listened carefully while Noah explained their situation before nodding her acquiescence to his request. She had agreed to allow Neesh and Sanjeev to hold their wedding at the ashram, and as they backed out of the room Priya couldn't help being impressed by her gentleness and generosity. She hadn't seemed to want anything in return.

Could she really be genuine? Or was this all a very clever double bluff, engineered by Noah to lower Priya's guard? She put her hands to her temples, her head spinning from more than the heavy incense.

'So,' Noah said softly, 'all is well. Your sister has a venue for her wedding after all.'

'It's perfect!' Neesh was practically leaping into outer space with excitement. 'Thank you! Thank you!' And she threw her arms around Noah, who hugged her back and genuinely seemed delighted.

'It's my pleasure,' he was telling her. 'And I know that the swami is equally pleased to be able to help.'

'Well, we're really grateful, aren't we, Priya?' said Neesh, digging a bony elbow into Priya's ribcage. 'Wasn't it kind of Noah and the swami to help like this?'

'Of course, absolutely,' Priya agreed, but Noah's earlier words *everyone does have an agenda* were still ringing in her ears and grateful as she was she couldn't

194

help wondering if this picture of benevolent spirituality was only what the swami had wanted her to see. It certainly made for better PR than the convenient vows of silence, rumours of miracles and strange visits from business people.

As far as she was concerned, when it came to the swami the jury was most definitely still out.

Priya was beyond caring whether or not the swami was a fake. In fact she'd hardly had time to spare the swami a second thought in the last few days. The entire documentary was pushed into a back seat as Divya and the aunts decamped en masse to the ashram to prepare for the wedding and generally drive her crazy.

Ray and Ishani were still filming and interviewing guests but Priya had been well and truly hijacked by her nearest and dearest and all her pleas that she really had to work fell on deaf ears. As far as Divya was concerned Priya's priority was the wedding now, her job well and truly relegated to second place, which made her wake up in a cold sweat at night when she realised just how far behind she was with the filming and editing.

Steven Spielberg was very lucky he hadn't had an Indian mother.

It was only early morning, the sun just peeping above the desert hills, but Priya had already been hard at work for at least an hour. Lugging her third box of silken flowers across the courtyard she winced when she heard the strident tones of Divya and Bhavani locked into yet another very loud and very public argument. So much for respecting the peace and sanctuary of the ashram! Her family seemed intent on turning the place into a war zone; Noah would need to draft in Kofi Annan to mediate if they carried on at this rate. At least twice a day a major dispute of volcanic proportions erupted, usually caused by Divya's determination to remain in control of her own daughter's wedding at the expense of any suggestions from anyone else. The aunties were feeling excluded and in retaliation attempted to put their own stamp on everything, which incensed Divya. Yesterday Chandani's contribution had been to order red lanterns to string up in the trees, which everyone had agreed would look very pretty, only for Divya to fly off the handle because she'd already purchased white ones.

'But you didn't tell me!' Chandani wailed, chins wobbling with distress. 'I didn't know!'

'You didn't need to know!' Divya had yelled back, hands on hips, practically spitting with frustration. 'It's nothing to do with you! It's my daughter's wedding! I'm the one planning it!'

It had taken hours to calm Chandani down after this spat, hours which Priya could have spent far more fruitfully editing, and she'd thought that things had been smoothed over at least for twenty-four hours.

She should have known it was too much to hope for. With a heavy heart she put her box down and pushed her hair out of her face. She'd better go and see what the problem was this time before yet another meditation session was disrupted. Noah hadn't been impressed yesterday to have to abandon his class to referee another Gupta dingdong.

Well, Priya thought smugly, that's what he gets for sticking his nose in. If he'd thought to ask her before taking matters into his own hands she could have told him exactly what he was in for.

Divya and Bhavani were squared up to one another in the courtyard like two gunslingers in the OK Corral, only instead of guns they seemed to be brandishing leaflets. Chandani and Darsani were flanking their sister like short squat minders and as she drew closer Priya could hear them joining in the latest row, squawking like outraged chickens confronted by a bossy fox.

'How dare you!' Divya was shouting, waving her leaflet. 'I'd already booked the Moonlight Tandoori to cater for the wedding! Neesh and I sampled their menu and we were very happy with what they were providing! How dare you cancel them without asking me?'

'Their prices were extortionate!' screeched back Bhavani. 'How could you even dream of making my poor brother pay those kinds of sums? It's enough to give him a relapse! Ana Purna can supply the entire buffet for less than half the price!'

'I don't care! We don't want them! You get back on the phone right this minute and tell them there's been a mistake!'

Bhavani placed her hands on her hips. 'I will do no such thing. My sisters and I will pay for the catering as our contribution to the wedding so we will decide which company to use!'

'Don't you dare try to blackmail me like that!' Divya

was incandescent with rage. 'You're not choosing the caterers! Over my dead body, Bhavani! Knowing your tastes we'll end up eating chicken tikka masala out of a jar!'

Oh God, thought Priya in dismay, now they're moving into the realms of criticising each other's cooking. If she didn't step in soon they'd be on the brink of a family feud by lunch time.

'If you were any kind of wife and mother you'd be making the food yourself!' Bhavani hissed. 'Paying caterers is nothing short of cheating! Perhaps it's your cooking that's in question here?'

'Ashwani has always looked thin since he married you,' piped up Chandani. 'And those girls are way too skinny too!'

'How dare you,' yelled Divya, snatching her sister-in-law's leaflet, dashing it on to the floor and stamping on it in a rage. 'At least my family isn't obese!'

'What's going on?' Noah joined Priya in the courtyard, looking bemused at the sight of the two matriarchs hissing and spitting like cats. Bare-chested and wearing nothing but a pair of loose white trousers he'd come from the direction of the meditation tepees, which explained why he was looking rather spaced out. His grey eyes clouded with concern when he heard the insults flying past like verbal darts.

'Another row,' Priya sighed. 'Over the catering this time.'

'No way!' Noah raked a hand through his black curls. 'Don't they ever stop?'

'Er ... what do you reckon? Still pleased you decided to invite them to create havoc here?'

He raised his eyebrows. 'Still angry with me for not running it by you first, Ms Gupta?'

She tossed her hair. 'I think you're more than getting your comeuppance now. How's the meditation by the way? Feeling serene?'

'Strangely, serenity is passing me right by,' he sighed. 'I suppose we'd better see if we can defuse this before your mum starts throwing punches. After all, we're supposed to uphold an ethos of pacifism here.'

'Try telling *them* that,' said Priya gloomily, following him to the heart of the action. Maybe she should warn him not to get too close to Divya when she was in a rage like this.

'Good morning, ladies!' Noah called, strolling nonchalantly through the middle of the spat and not turning a hair, as though middle-aged matrons frequently had fisticuffs in the middle of the ashram. 'Isn't it a beautiful day!'

Stunned by his sunny attitude and his lean masculine beauty, Divya and Bhavani ground to a halt, their scalding words withering on their lips.

'Yes indeed,' said Divya finally, skewering Noah with a sharp look. She hated anyone interfering when she was riled and Priya knew she would be seething.

'It's far too beautiful a morning to be spoiled by angry words,' he continued, raising his sharp-cheek-boned face to the sun before folding his hands in namaste, the traditional greeting, 'especially between family on such a special day as this.'

Bhavani looked confused. 'Special day? What do you mean?'

Noah treated her to a knee-melting smile. 'But

today is Raksha Bandhan! You must celebrate Rakhi, even in England?'

Oh, he was good, thought Priya, with grudging admiration. Raksha Bandhan was a special festival which celebrated the relationship between brothers and sisters. The festival was marked by the tying of a rakhi, or holy thread, by the sister on the wrist of her brother. The brother in return offered a gift to his sister and vowed to look after her. Nowadays the ceremony was often used to celebrate the close bonds between extended Asian families and to show solidarity and kinship.

In one swift killer sentence Noah had managed to remind the squabbling women that they were all sisters bound by their love for Ashwani. The aunties looked impressed by this wise young man with his encyclopedic knowledge of Hindu festivals but Divya knew she'd been outsmarted and shot Noah a very sharp look indeed.

'Are you a Hindu then?' she said bluntly, the words *you don't look like one* hanging in the air like the trail left by a sparkler on Guy Fawkes Night.

'I'm of mixed heritage,' Noah said, not rising to her aggressive tone. 'My mother is Indian and my father is Ethiopian. In terms of faith I share my mother's beliefs, so yes, Mrs Gupta, I am a Hindu.'

'Hmm,' said Divya, as suspicious of this as she would have been if Noah had told her he sacrificed babies in his spare time. 'You may find it better to follow a more traditional path, bearing your heritage in mind. Most mothers will only allow their daughters to marry *proper* Hindus of the right caste. My daughters for example will only marry good Hindu boys like Sanjeev and Kettan.'

Priya wanted the earth to swallow her up and incinerate her in its molten core. 'Mum! That's enough!'

Why was her mother being so rude to Noah? He'd done nothing but be polite and hospitable. And the whole Kettan thing was really starting to grate. Priya knew it was all for show, or at least she hoped it was all for show, but really he was far too attentive, always sitting with her at dinner and seeking her out in the evenings. No wonder Divya was starting to get her hopes up.

But that didn't excuse her being so rude to Noah. He wasn't any kind of threat to Kettan.

Luckily Noah didn't take offence. Instead he just smiled gently at Divya.

'I can't speak for the way things are in England, Mrs Gupta, but here in India the laws relating to marriage differ by religion. Hindus of any caste, creed or sect, Sikh, Buddhists and Jains are considered as Hindus and can intermarry. You needn't fear, I think all will be well for me.'

Divya was lost for words for once, her mouth opening and shutting like a Venus fly trap, and Priya couldn't resist a wry smile. It was rare that her mother was put in her place, and very enjoyable to watch.

There was more to Noah than a pretty face and a mean line in bendy yoga moves!

Catching her eye he whispered, 'Now's your chance. I think she's forgotten the great catering calamity.'

It was true. Divya was so riled by Noah that the

leaflets lay abandoned and she was deep in conversation with the aunties, all hostilities suspended. Now and then the name *Kettan* drifted on the breeze and Priya sighed. Her mother was distracted all right but not necessarily in the right direction.

Still, she supposed it was a small price to pay for the guests to be able to concentrate on their yoga.

That afternoon Divya and the aunties went into Jaipur on yet another shopping trip, enabling Priya to seize the opportunity to do some long overdue work. While the sun was a burning gold disc in the sailor-blue sky she sat in the cool of a meditation tepee watching the rushes on her laptop and fiddling around with the establishing shots in Final Cut. She was so engrossed in her work that before she knew it the sun had started to bleed from the sky and shadows were pooling across the floor of the tent. Pulling off her earphones she yawned and stretched, wincing as the blood flow stung its way back into her fingertips, and then started when she realised she was not alone.

Someone was outside the tepee, deep in conversation.

Priya didn't like to be cast in the role of eavesdropper and was just about to replace her earphones when she realised from the honey-warm tones that Noah was one of the speakers. The other, judging by that familiar strident blast, was Clay.

'Now come on, son!' Clay boomed. 'Ah'm not saying that it needs to be a great deal of money up front, but I reckon you and me could be on to something here!'

'Clay, I'm not sure,' Noah was saying. 'It seems very risky.'

'There's no success in business without parting with a bit of cash! Gotta speculate to accumulate, boy! You've sure taken your chunk from me already, and the rest! Ah'm telling you, it's a sure-fire winner! Everyone will be queuing up for a slice of this place.'

'Maybe,' Noah paused. 'But at what cost?'

'Son! You can't put a price on miracles. Jesus H Christ, my man! Once people know what I know you'll be laughing. You know it makes sense. Even the swami agrees!'

Oh, so the swami had conveniently found her voice again, had she? Priya shook her head in disappointment but she was hardly surprised.

'The swami is still making up her mind,' Noah reminded Clay. 'Like me, she was concerned that it was too much of a risk.'

'If you want the best you pay up and take your chances,' said Clay bluntly. 'Think on it, son, but don't take too long. Lots of people are only too happy to part with their cash. Wouldn't you rather divert some of it in your direction?'

'Maybe.' Noah didn't sound convinced. 'But it would have to be the right thing to do.'

'It will be, son, trust me. You're gonna make a lot of people very happy! And make all the money you could ever need!'

There followed the sound of a beefy hand thumping down on Noah's shoulder before the voices started to retreat and the air was briefly tainted by the pungent scent of Clay's cigar.

Priya exhaled slowly. She'd been holding her breath during this exchange and her lungs were burning, but not nearly as much as her curiosity. What on earth had all that been about? She was on to something, she just knew it! God, if only she'd had the presence of mind to try to film the exchange. Then she'd have some explosive material for the documentary! That would, she thought ruefully, almost make up for the mounting evidence that Noah and the swami were charlatans, happy to take gullible people's money and peddle them fake miracles and cod philosophy. How Clay fitted in she had no idea but he certainly seemed thick as thieves with Noah.

Her brain buzzing with ideas like a swarm of hornets Priya crept to the door of the tepee and peered out into the purple dusk. Noah and Clay were long gone but their words were etched in her mind like mental graffiti and she knew she'd be trying to make sense of it all for hours.

And, which disturbed her even more, trying to make sense of her overwhelming disappointment that Noah was not the good guy he pretended to be.

21

'How do I look?' Neesh asked, spinning around in her new peacock-blue sari and almost knocking Priya flying. 'Do I look like Aishwarya Rai? Or Shilpa Shetty?'

Priya looked up from fastening her own garments, easier said than done with her sister constantly interrupting, and smiled fondly at Neesh. With her waist-length hair straightened to an ebony waterfall, slender arms jingling with gold bracelets and sapphire nose ring glittering in the setting sunlight her sister looked every inch a Bollywood Princess, which was just as well since Bollywood was the theme of this evening's engagement celebration party. Everyone was glammed up in their finest clothes, gold and jewellery had been liberated from family safes and even Priya had been coaxed out of her usual combats and into the jade sari that she'd bought in Jaipur.

'You look beautiful,' she said with a lump in her throat. 'Sanj is one lucky guy to be marrying you.'

'Aw, Priya, don't! You'll make me cry, innit!' Neesh cried, hugging her hard and making Priya wince as all the bling ground into her flesh. 'You look well fit too, babes. All the single guys'll be gagging.'

'I sincerely hope not,' said Priya, with a shudder. That was the last thing she needed. Divya would combust with joy.

'I don't know why you don't always make more effort,' Neesh sighed, pouting at her own reflection and trowelling on another layer of lip gloss. 'You actually look really good when you remember to dress like a girl. You should try it more often.'

'No thanks,' Priya said quickly. 'This is far too much hassle.'

'But worth it,' Neesh insisted, turning round and, grasping Priya's shoulders, forcing her to look in the mirror. 'Look! You're a babe.'

'Hardly,' laughed Priya, although she had to admit that she hardly recognised her reflection. The jade sari hugged the slender contours of her body, making her skin glow like warm honey and picking out the green flecks in her eyes, while the emerald pendant and earrings that Divya had lent her sparkled and glittered in the evening sunshine. For once she hadn't scraped her hair back either, choosing to wear it loose, and it was surprisingly long, waving past her shoulders now like black silk. She frowned, taken aback by the glamorous stranger in the looking glass.

'Just enjoy it,' ordered Neesh. 'You can put your grotty old combats on again tomorrow if you really have to, but tonight's my engagement party and I want us all blinged up and gorgeous. This bash must have cost Akhila a bomb so we might as well make the most of it!'

The Adanis had really gone to town by hiring the grounds of a local palace, all lush gardens, pink marble pavilions and terrace gardens falling away like the smoothest green velvet. Swathes of jasmine and hibiscus nodded in the breeze, filling the air with the sweetest perfumes. The gardens had been decorated with crimson ribbons, silken bows and Chandani's red lanterns, which were strung between the trees like swaying ruby necklaces. The plaintive tones of the latest Bollywood soundtrack trembled in the air and delicious spices drifted on the breeze while guests, dressed in their gaudy best, strolled through the orchards like colourful butterflies. As the light faded the windows of the palace shimmered with wind-driven tea lights.

Never one to go for a simple option, Neesh had spent days sourcing dancers, music and even a couple of genuine actors to make the ambience more authentic. Maybe the six peacocks were a little over the top, though: they seemed insistent on making as much din as possible and Priya winced each time they screeched. Sanjeev's Amex must have really taken a savage battering to pay for all this lot, Priya marvelled as she followed her sister on to the terrace, but from what she could see it had been worth every penny. The scene was every bit as rich and sumptuous as any of the Bollywood movies she'd devoured as a child. And Neesh, stunning in her shimmering blue sari, was every inch the star of her own production.

Down below them on the velvet-smooth lawn twelve dancers were gyrating in perfect time to throbbing Bhangra music. Unlike Neesh, Priya was no expert on the Bollywood genre, finding the melodramatic plots rather convoluted for her tastes, but even she recognised this tune as being from one of the summer's biggest hits. Neesh and her friends had been playing the soundtrack non-stop for weeks and practising their moves in the garden, and she'd even joined in herself a few times. Almost of their own accord her toes started to tap and she started to sway to the beat and hum along, feeling the weight of her worries about the ashram begin to lift.

Hey! This is fun, she found herself thinking in surprise. How long had it been since she'd actually had fun? She was enjoying her time in India, there was no doubt about that, but it was very intense and, with her growing suspicions about what was really going on at the ashram, increasingly stressful. It was high time she cut loose and enjoyed herself.

'Come and dance,' said Neesh, taking Priya's hand. 'This is the best bit of the song. The boys will sing about all the pretty girls being like balloons without strings and then invite us to join them so they can catch us! You must know it, you've heard it enough times!'

Priya laughed. 'I think I could sing it in my sleep. But you know I'm a useless dancer. You go ahead, though. I'm happy to watch.'

Neesh pulled a face. 'Sheesh, Pri, you spend far too much time watching everyone else have a good time. Still, up to you I suppose. Laters!'

Priya smiled as her sister darted down the steps towards the dancers like a bolt of peacock-blue lightning, slim arms held aloft and bangles clattering in perfect time with the music. At least one of the Gupta girls had rhythm! Priya loved to dance but she was the first to admit that she was pretty hopeless, making up for a lack of talent by being very enthusiastic – as Vikram's often bruised toes could have testified.

Watching Neesh join the dancers, picking up the intricate moves as though she'd been dancing professionally all her life, Priya couldn't help feeling a little bit envious, especially when Sanj, resplendent in scarlet dhoti, joined her with a proud smile, knowing that all eyes were on his beautiful fiancée as she swayed and gyrated like a breeze-blown cornflower. Neesh grabbed life by the throat and squeezed every inch of enjoyment out of it, that was for sure. That was what made her so much fun – and so exhausting – to be around.

Maybe I am boring, thought Priya. Perhaps that was why she was content to view life through a lens or an editing package rather than actively taking part. Perhaps she ought to get up some Dutch courage and just join in. Deciding to act on that train of thought, she accepted a glass of champagne from a passing waiter and settled down to studying the professional dancers, admiring how they made such intricate patterns: spirals, stars and diamonds shimmering and shifting in a blur of flowing white robes and citrus-hued saris. It was as though she'd walked into a film. Any minute now a villain would appear and challenge the hero for Neesh's hand, or an irate parent would snatch her away and the drama would really begin.

Actually this whole trip to India had all the ingredients of a classic Bollywood movie, she reflected wryly. There was the Ray/Ishani/Baadal love triangle, the sweet romance between Neesh and Sanj, the family tensions between the Guptas and the Adanis, and if

Akhila got so much as a whiff of what her daughter was up to there'd be irate parents to contend with as well. Quite who the villain of the piece was Priya had yet to decide, but at the moment it looked horribly like a role for Noah. For reasons she couldn't quite fathom the thought made her heart sink and she shook her head in frustration. She really didn't want to think about what might or might not be going on at the ashram right now. Anyway, the plots of Bollywood movies always involved rapid reversals of fortune. Long lost relatives arrived to save the day, convenient coincidences abounded and by the time the credits rolled all was well, if rather cheesier than a Cheddar Gorge factory. So why not in real life too? Maybe there was a perfectly innocent explanation for Noah's strange behaviour and the odd conversations she'd overheard. Perhaps the product he'd mentioned was nothing more sinister than herbal tea.

The problem was that all the evidence seemed to suggest otherwise.

She sighed heavily and drained her drink. Did this make Noah the villain of her particular movie? Was he about to appear all kohl-eyed and moustached and demand a fight for her honour? The ludicrous image made her laugh aloud.

'Hey, there you are!' Talking of handsome Bollywood heroes, here was Kettan, all dressed up in a scarlet dhoti embroidered with gold and silver thread. His dark skin glowed against the rich fabric and his eyes twinkled in the dying sunshine.

'You look amazing!' he told Priya, dropping a kiss on her cheek and treating her to a wide smile.

'Thanks. You scrub up pretty well yourself.'

His cheeks turned dusky at her compliment. That's odd, thought Priya.

'Dance with me?' Kettan asked softly.

She shook her head. 'I'm not much of a dancer, I'm afraid. You'd probably end up in Jaipur hospital having your toes plastered or something. You'd be better off asking one of the other girls.'

He took her hand, closing his manicured fingers around her rather less perfectly groomed ones. 'I don't want to dance with them, Priya. I want to dance with *you.*'

Oh no, she thought, this is one complication I can seriously do without.

His fingers tightened their grip. 'Priya, I've been thinking—'

'Me too,' Priya said swiftly, sliding her hand from his grasp. 'It's my sister's engagement party and if I don't dance tonight then when will I? So, let's dance – if you think your feet can take it!'

Kettan looked a bit taken aback by her sudden change of heart but was far too much of a gentleman to say so, and moments later they were making their way into the heart of the throbbing music and frenetic dancing.

Phew, thought Priya. That was one awkward moment avoided. For now, anyway.

Down in the garden the music was thumping to a Bhangra beat, the sun was sliding down the cloudless sky and bathing the scene in a pink glow and the air was rich with turmeric and tamarind. Joining her delighted sister Priya slipped easily into the dance formation, surprised at just how quickly the steps returned to her memory. Her feet stamped, her hands clapped and her sari flew around her in a blur of emerald silk. Weaving in and out of the male dancers and singing at the top of her voice, Priya felt the tension slide away. She was having fun and she'd only trodden on Kettan's toes once.

Okay then. Maybe twice.

Three times at a push!

Finally, breathless and flushed, she broke away from the dancing and returned to the terrace, hoping Kettan would remain with the others. He was a good dancer, agile and light on his feet, and she'd seen lots of the younger Adani females casting admiring glances in his direction.

But Kettan didn't appear inclined to stay and dance. Instead he chose to collect two glasses of champagne and joined her back at her vantage point. Priya sighed. Something told her she was in for an awkward few minutes.

'Thanks.' She accepted the glass he proffered and swirled the pale liquid thoughtfully. 'Toes intact?'

He pulled an expression of mock agony. 'Ouch! So you weren't exaggerating. But it was worth it. We had fun, didn't we?'

'If pain is your idea of fun!'

'Then I suppose it must be.' He put his glass down on the balustrade and glanced down. 'It's a great party. Neesh and Sanj look really happy.'

Priya followed the direction of his gaze to where Neesh was dancing with Sanj, her head tipped back as she laughed up at him while his face was lit up with pride.

'They're a great couple,' she said.

'They sure are,' Kettan agreed. Then he paused before saying, 'They have a lot in common, don't they?'

Did they? Priya racked her brains. Clubbing? Shopping? Sex? R&B? 'Mmm,' she hedged.

'I mean they really have a shared background, don't they?' Kettan continued, eyes narrowed thoughtfully. 'The families are alike and they both understand the culture that they're coming from. It's a real bond between them.'

Priya was listening but she was also busy searching the party for Ray. It was all very well for him and Ishani to work closely alongside each other at the ashram, but eyebrows would be raised if they were seen too much in each other's company this evening. Was that his gangly form over there by the fountain? She narrowed her eyes. And did she just see his hand graze Ishani's? Her fingers tightened on her glass and her mouth was suddenly drier than the champagne.

'So that's why,' Kettan was saying. 'It was tough, but I think it was the right thing to do, don't you?'

There was a pause as he waited for a response but, otherwise preoccupied, Priya realised with a lurch of guilt that she hadn't heard a word he'd said.

'Sorry, Kettan.' She turned to face him. Even if she watched Ray and Ishani like a hawk there was no way she could keep them apart. Perhaps if she blocked the view to the terrace nobody would notice the two reckless lovebirds. 'What were you saying?'

'That I've finished with my girlfriend,' Kettan said, fixing her with anguished eyes. 'Being here put a whole new perspective on our relationship and it made me realise that much as I adore Sally she could never be a part of a family like ours. There are just too many cultural differences. It could never work.'

Priya was staggered. 'But you love her, Kettan! You told me she was the one. How could that change so quickly?'

He shrugged. 'I thought she was, but spending time here with my family has made me realise that there are other things even more important than my own happiness. Duty and honour count too, don't they?'

'More than love?' Priya shook her head. 'I really don't know. Why can't you have both? Why does it have to be a compromise?'

'Perhaps it doesn't,' he said softly, stepping forward and touching her hand. 'Priya, I've really enjoyed getting to know you since Sanj and Neesh got engaged. Akhila thinks that you and I have a lot in common and the more I think about it the more I know she's right.'

Priya frowned at him. 'Kettan, you should make the choices that are right for you. Not the choices you think your family would approve of.'

Kettan ran a hand through his dark glossy hair. 'We're Indians, Priya, and part of our culture means respecting the views and traditions of our elders. In many ways they do know best.'

In matters of love, mother knows best.

She swallowed. No way. Divya did *not* know best.

And Akhila certainly didn't. Just ask Ishani.

'So, Priya,' Kettan said slowly, 'I was wondering if you'd consider—'

But what he wanted her to consider Priya never got to discover because at that exact moment Ray decided to take Ishani in his arms and kiss her in full view of everyone on the lower terrace. Had he lost the plot? Okay, so it was a romantic setting and the champagne was flowing, but even so! Ishani was to all intents and purposes engaged, even if she'd decided otherwise. She had to stop them before Akhila got wind of their romance and went into meltdown.

Priya's stomach went into free fall and, excusing herself swiftly, she hurtled down the stone steps towards the fountain. Her feet in their thin glittery sandals flew over the uneven stone and she bunched the fabric of her sari into her fists. Down three flights of steps she ran and was almost at the final level when her foot became tangled in a pool of green silk, launching her forward far faster than she'd intended.

No wonder she normally wore combats was Priya's last thought as her hands clutched wildly at thin air and her feet scrabbled against the smooth stone.

Just as she was certain she was about to plummet into a stone wall and become a splat of Priya jam a pair of strong arms caught hold of her and circled her waist. Barely had she registered the sensation of being held close against a strong body before she was lowered back on to her feet, her head swimming with relief and adrenaline as the same arms guided her to sit on a stone bench.

'Take a deep breath,' said a familiar treacle-warm voice. 'Maybe put your head between your legs if it helps.'

Noah? What the hell was he doing at Neesh's engagement party? Priya's head snapped up so fast that she almost gave herself whiplash. Gone was the casual-looking guy in baggy white robes, replaced by a strong lithe man clad in a midnight-black dhoti. The sight of him caused a sudden inexplicable ache inside her. He looked so different dressed this way and with his hair, steel blue in the shadows, falling in loose ringlets around his muscular shoulders. With that chiselled face and those compelling eyes he looked every inch a Bollywood star just meandered from the set. There was no escaping it: he was one beautiful man, even if he was a criminal.

22

'Too much champagne?' Noah asked when she didn't speak.

'No,' she shot back. 'I've hardly had anything to drink, not that it's any of your business. I tripped, actually.'

'Right,' said Noah doubtfully. 'Well, just sit for a second and get your breath back. You look very pale.'

Priya felt very pale. One of those ringlets had fallen across his face and she suddenly had the shocking desire to push it back. God, what was wrong with her? Maybe the champagne was stronger than she'd thought. Dragging her eyes away from his she pulled herself together quickly.

'You'd be pale if you were about to be held responsible for a massive family breakdown!' She gestured to the bottom terrace where Ray and Ishani sat in the shadows, arms twined round each other as tightly as the jasmine was twined round the balustrade. Noah followed her gaze and spread his hands.

'Why are you carrying the burden of their secret? You're not responsible for their actions.'

'I am,' she said miserably, picking a jacaranda leaf

and shredding it. 'I introduced them. Ishani's already engaged and her mother will go mental.'

'They're adults. It'll all sort itself out one way or another, with or without your interference.'

'I'm not interfering!' she flared. 'I'm trying to help! What would you know anyway? You don't know the first thing about me!'

'No, maybe not,' Noah agreed. 'But I think I'm starting to build up quite a clear picture. You're a bit of a control freak, aren't you?'

'There're worse things than being a control freak!' she snapped, stung by this. 'At least I'm not trying to rip off vulnerable people.'

'What exactly is *that* supposed to mean?'

'Exactly what I said! Don't bother to play the innocent. I overheard your conversation with Clay the other day. Got to speculate to accumulate, remember?'

'And what exactly were we speculating about?' he demanded. 'I'd love to know.'

Ah. Well, he had her there. She hadn't exactly heard that bit, had she? But it had sounded dodgy and added to all the other odd incidents it had seemed overwhelming evidence at the time.

'You don't know, do you?' Noah pressed. 'You've just jumped to the wrong conclusions without even thinking to stop and ask if it makes any sense.' He looked hurt. 'Wow, Priya. You really do have a low opinion of me. Is it because I told you about my drugs conviction? That was years ago. And it wasn't as if I was selling crack. I was stupid enough to score some cannabis for a friend whose mum had MS. It was the only thing that ever made her feel better and in my naïve way I thought I was doing the right thing.' He sighed heavily. 'As you already know the police didn't quite see it that way. I thought I'd paid the price for what I did, but I haven't, have I? People will always be suspicious of me. Just as you are. No smoke without fire, they'll think.'

His eyes met hers and she saw nothing but truthfulness there. Vikram's eyes had always been full of shadows but Noah's were as clear as summer rock pools.

'I'm sorry,' she said softly. 'But you must admit that the other stuff does look really suspicious. What was I supposed to think?'

Silence fell between them just as the sun sank below the turreted roof of the palace. She closed her eyes wearily but when she opened them his were still there holding hers, hostile now and angry.

'You're supposed to trust your instincts! Come on, you must know me a little by now. Haven't we talked enough for you to have some sense of who I am? Clay was talking about advertising the ashram, Priya. He wants to market it as a spiritual retreat when he goes back to Texas. That's what we were talking about. I wasn't sure, remember? I believe the ashram is too special to be commercialised like that.'

She stared at him. Her breathing was ragged with agitation. 'It didn't sound like that to me.'

'What did it sound like to you? Like we were plotting how to rip off vulnerable people and sting them for huge amounts of money?'

Priya swallowed. 'Maybe. You must admit, it does sound rather dodgy.'

But Noah was furious. 'Only to someone who was determined to think the worst right from the very start. Some journalist you are! You'd made your mind up about the ashram and me even before you'd got off the bus! You never even gave us a chance.'

'Maybe if you'd given me some straight answers to begin with I might have changed my mind!' she retorted. 'But no, it was all secrets and vows of silence. What was I supposed to do?'

'Trust me?' he said with equal emotion. 'Or is that too much for you to handle, Priya? Trusting a man, I mean?'

'What's that supposed to mean?'

'I've seen how you need to keep everyone and everything separate. You're so desperate to be in control that it's terrifying. Whatever happened to make you feel that compartmentalising your life is the only way to survive?'

'Don't you dare try to twist this round so it's about me! I'm not the one hiding away in an ashram. If anyone's hiding it's you! I've got everything I need in my life!'

'You don't even have a space to call your own,' he said quietly.

'I do!' Her face burned with fury. 'I've got a gorgeous flat near Brick Lane, for your information! All bought and paid for by me.'

'And I bet even there you're always busy, entertaining, phoning people, editing, working from home?' He gave a snort of exasperation. 'You don't have a pocket to yourself. That's why you try so hard to control your environment.'

Priya goggled at him. Just who the hell did he think he was, spouting all this psycho bollocks? 'You couldn't be more wrong,' she said coldly. 'Don't give up the day job, Noah – if you have one, that is. Maybe we should analyse you instead of me. I'd love to know why you're at the ashram. What have *you* run away from?'

His eyes smouldered. Ah! So she had hit a nerve, then.

'Come on, Noah!' she taunted. 'Time for some truth-telling, don't you think? What's your link to the ashram if it isn't money? And, come to think of it, how come you're here tonight? Drinking and dancing are hardly the kind of activities that'll lead you to enlightenment.'

'I'm here because Neesh invited me,' Noah grated, 'and because of the swami.'

Priya was thrown. 'The swami told you to come to a party?'

He sighed. 'She's not the bad guy you have her down as. She . . .' He paused and raised his eyes to the stars. 'She really cares about people.'

Priya said nothing. The expression on his face was hard to fathom, especially in the twilight.

'I came to the ashram because I needed some solitude,' he said eventually. 'Mental elbow room, if you like. I wanted to meditate and find some space. Then the swami suggested that I be your guide. She thought that speaking to you would help unblock me in some way.'

'Unblock you?' Priya snorted. 'What are you, a drain? And anyway, why me? What had I done to deserve the Noah experience?'

'Attuttama believed that through explaining our

beliefs to you I'd be able to consolidate my own faith,' Noah explained. His lips curved into a wry smile. 'Believe me, I wasn't exactly jumping for joy. I wanted solitude and instead I got saddled with a stroppy cynical journalist.'

'Hey, I'm not stroppy.' Priya rapped him on the arm, jumping back when she felt something jolt between them. Sari static probably, she told herself sternly. 'Well, maybe just a bit. But I've got a job to do and all you seem to have done is get in the way. Anyway, if you'd come to the ashram for peace and quiet why listen to the swami? I'd have told her no. Do you always do what you're told?'

'And do you challenge everything, even if it might be good for you?' he countered. 'Is that why you always fight your mother, just because you won't be told what to do even if she might know best?'

'Believe me my mother does not know best!' Priya said hotly. 'Not that I need to explain that to you. And I'm sorry if showing me round has been such a terrible burden. Don't waste your time in future, okay? Tell your precious swami I don't need a minder!'

And she leapt up from the seat as though scalded. Suddenly all she wanted was to escape from those searching dark eyes and the even more searching words.

'Hey,' Noah said softly, his hand reaching out to clasp her wrist. 'I didn't mean to upset you. That wasn't my intention, Priya.'

Swallowing what felt ridiculously like tears, she snatched her arm away. The places where his stronger fingers had encircled her flesh felt as though they were on fire. Leaving him in the shadows she stumbled back to the upper terrace, rubbing her arm in agitation.

Ten minutes later she was deep in conversation with a young Adani cousin, who was telling her all about his ambition to read law at Oxford, when a deafening shriek from Neesh made her almost jump out of her sandals.

'Daddy!' Neesh was screaming, racing across the grass and hurling herself at a familiar stooped figure. 'Daddy! Oh my God! You're here!'

Ashwani! Against all the odds he'd made it! Suddenly Priya's irritation with Noah and all the stress about Ray and Ishani melted away like snow in sunshine. What did all that rubbish matter now? Her dad, her wonderful, thoughtful, beloved dad was here!

The strike must have been called off, she thought, as she ran to greet him. Thank goodness she'd managed to keep the whole thing quiet so the family didn't panic unnecessarily. Maybe this was a sign that things were on the turn at last and that the run of bad luck was over? It was about time.

Divya and Neesh were smothering Ashwani with hugs and kisses, which he was returning tearfully. In the lamplight his face looked tired and there were big purple hollows under his eyes. The journey had clearly taken its toll on him, and as she hugged him Priya was shocked to feel just how thin he was.

'Oh, Dad,' she whispered, kissing his bristly cheek, 'you look exhausted. The journey was too much for you, wasn't it? Even though the strike was cancelled you shouldn't have come.'

'And miss travelling first class?' Ashwani said, his eyes twinkling. 'Not likely! That was the experience of a lifetime. And all thanks to this young man,' he added, pointing to a new arrival who was striding towards them, all floppy hair, loosened tie and easy elegance. 'He well and truly saved the day. Without him finding me a place on his friend's plane I'd still be sitting in Heathrow. This boy is a hero!'

Priya's stomach flipped and flopped, the champagne curdling unpleasantly with the blinis. No way! This wasn't supposed to happen!

'I'd never have made the wedding if it wasn't for him,' Ashwani was saying warmly. 'He must be guest of honour at the wedding, Divya. I insist!'

Priya felt cold all over. This was never part of the arrangement. Closing her eyes, she prayed she was mistaken, but when she opened them again she was in for a disappointment; even in the velvet darkness there was no mistaking that gym-honed body and sherry-warm eyes.

Vikram Amin was in Jaipur, and judging from the way he was staring at her he hadn't just come for the wedding.

23

'I can't believe you haven't got any interview footage with the swami yet,' Vikram said, a small frown pleating his brow as he looked up from the laptop. 'What's the hold-up? She's the key to this whole project, surely?'

Priya gritted her teeth – an action that had become something of a habit in the twenty-four hours since Vik had literally landed back in her life – and reminded herself that she owed him big time for bringing Ashwani safely over to them. He claimed to have travelled with her father to ensure he had a safe journey, so if the downside was having Vik sticking his aquiline nose into every area of the documentary she supposed it was a small price to pay. She just could have done without him deciding to accompany her to the ashram today. Things were already hectic enough with the Adanis and the Guptas popping up like mushrooms everywhere she went. Chucking Vikram into the mix only added to her already soaring stress levels.

'The swami went on retreat for a few days and then she took a vow of silence,' Priya explained, reaching forward and minimising Final Cut because she couldn't bear looking at a paused frame of Noah, all wide grey eyes and genuine-looking smile, 'so interviewing her hasn't exactly been straightforward. But I'm working on it.'

'Come on, Pri, you can be more resourceful than that, surely?' Vik drummed his fingers on the tabletop. 'You must realise there isn't any real interest without her. You're not supposed to be here finding enlightenment; you're supposed to be finding stories.'

'I'm looking into lots of leads!' Priya said, riled by his insinuation that she'd not been doing her job properly. 'I've already told you about the conversations I overheard between Noah and Clay, as well as the odd business couple and the fields of crops that I've not been allowed to see. There's a story here, Vik, I know it.'

'Mmm, maybe.' Steepling his fingers he regarded her thoughtfully. 'What do you reckon about those fields, then? Or the herb garden? Could all this be a front for something else?'

Now it was Priya's turn to frown. 'Such as?'

'Could they be growing something illegal in those fields? Something they'd rather you didn't know about? That could explain why the swami's playing hard to get.'

'What are you trying to say? That they're growing drugs here?'

'Sure, why not? It makes perfect sense. They could be growing marijuana or any number of other illegal drugs for so-called "medicinal" purposes. No wonder they don't want anyone snooping around the crops.'

Priya laughed out loud. 'Come on, you don't seriously think so, do you? That's crazy!'

Vikram, however, was deadly serious. 'You don't know, they could be. You've just spent the last hour telling me how suspicious you are of everything here. Like that guru guy Noah? You said he was definitely hiding something and I can tell he's really annoyed you. What if he's in on it with the swami?'

Priya felt a prickle of unease, although she couldn't pinpoint why. Vikram was her boss and she was perfectly at liberty to discuss Noah with him. So why did it feel like a betrayal?

'Come on, Vik,' she said quickly, 'I know I've been looking for a conspiracy, but drugs? That's a crazy idea. I'm more than willing to believe there's something suspicious going on here financially for the swami, but exporting drugs? I can't believe that's it.'

'Don't be too swift to dismiss my ideas,' Vik warned. 'I think you'll find I'm right.'

'If you are, it'll be the first time!' she snapped.

But Vik just grinned at her, the old familiar lazy grin that used to melt her heart but now just looked smug and more than a little oily. 'As soon as I see Ray I'm pulling him off that healing workshop bollocks and sending him and his camera up into those hills to find out exactly what the swami's growing. Then at least we'll know.'

Reassigning her cameraman was tantamount to sticking two fingers up at Priya and suddenly something inside her snapped. She was through with taking his crap. Enough was enough!

'Don't you bloody well dare!' she yelled, her hands

on her hips and her eyes green with fury. 'Back off, will you? This is my documentary! Haven't you stolen enough from me without stealing this as well? Or is that why you're really here, Vikram? To stick the boot in one final time?'

He took a step backwards, raising his hands in mock surrender. 'Hey! Hey! Chill, babe! Of course not. I came because I miss you.'

'Spare me, Vik,' Priya said wearily. 'You came because you've run out of ideas as usual and what better than to find me and steal another one? It worked before, after all, didn't it? So why not do it again? Only this time it's easier – you won't even need to break into my folders and copy my documents. You can just pull rank and demand to take over.'

Vikram stared at her open-mouthed. 'Priya, I'm sorry. How many times can I say it? It was a mistake. I never meant to—'

'So it was an accident?' She shook her head in disbelief. 'Really, Vik, how can stealing my idea for a documentary and passing it off to the Controller of Factual Programmes as your own *be a mistake*? You hacked into my bloody work area, for God's sake!'

'Well, you shouldn't have such a bloody obvious password. I mean, *Ashwani*? Come on, Priya, figuring it out wasn't rocket science.'

'So that's my fault too?' God, he really was unbelievable. 'Vikram! Stop making excuses! You stole my promotion. Just admit it! You're nothing but a cheat! A cheat who used his girlfriend to fake his promotion. Bloody hell, what sort of man does that to the woman he's meant to love?'

Vikram looked down at the desk, unable to meet her accusing glare.

'I'm sorry, Priya. I can't tell you how sorry I am and I've felt horribly guilty about it ever since but I didn't know what else to do. The interview was coming up and I had absolutely nothing to pitch. I didn't have any choice.'

'Of course you had a choice! You could have chosen to withdraw your application. Nobody made you steal mine.'

'I know, I know. It was a moment of madness, Pri. All I could think about was how let down my family would be if I didn't get the promotion. It was all my mother could talk about. The disappointment would have killed her.'

'I bet she's really proud of you now, then,' Priya said coldly. 'It must be such an honour to have a son who steals his girlfriend's ideas and sells them as his own. I bet she boasts about it to all her friends.'

'Priya,' said Vikram, fixing her with eyes of liquid sorrow, 'I'm so, so sorry. You can't possibly hate me as much as I hate myself.'

'Don't bet on it,' she muttered.

'I'd do anything to make it up to you. Haven't I tried really hard to make amends? Look how I flew your dad over. Doesn't that prove to you how every day I regret what happened?'

'It didn't just *happen*, Vikram. You made it happen. You deliberately chose to trash our relationship for your ambition.' Her throat tightened with tears and she swallowed them back, furious with herself for still feeling so raw.

'Baby, I'd do anything to put things right between us,' he said, his voice breaking with emotion. 'I know I threw away something very precious but can't we find a way back to where we were? I love you, babe; I always have and I always will. You're the one I want to spend my life with, the woman I want to have my children with. Surely that still means something to you?'

Priya's heart felt as though someone was tugging barbed wire through it. She'd loved Vik so much, had really thought that he was the one for her, and to hear him pleading his love for her was bringing back echoes of emotion that she'd thought long gone. For a minute she teetered on the brink of indecision before her common sense gave her a double whammy.

Get a grip! What kind of man behaves the way he had? Was he genuinely sorry or just sorry she wasn't so blinded by love that she'd just bleatingly hand all her ideas over? He'd certainly been taken aback at her reaction when he eventually confessed all those months ago. What was it he'd said at the time? That she was *overreacting*? Well, thought Priya, let's see how he reacted to the idea that had just occurred to her.

'If you're really sorry,' she said slowly, 'then there is something you could do.'

'Anything! You know that, babe!'

'You can pick up the phone right now, call the Director of Factual Programming and tell him exactly what happened. Then I'd know you were really genuine.'

Vikram blanched. 'I can't do that.'

'So, what? You'd do anything for love? Anything but that?' She shook her head, sad because maybe for a split second he'd sucked her in with the old Vikram charm. 'Don't look so worried, Vik, I didn't really expect you to. Let's face it, if you really felt that bad about stealing my treatment you'd have done something about putting it right ages ago.'

'But I am sorry.'

'Sure you are, but not sorry enough.' With a sigh she picked up her shades and sun hat. 'Look, Vik, let's just leave the personal stuff in the past and move on. We've got a documentary to make, remember? And you've just given me some pretty crazy theories to think about.'

'But we can't leave things like this!'

'Yes we can. And if you so much as dream of stealing Ray or interfering in my documentary, I'll be on the phone to the BBC myself. I hear they can find all kinds of evidence on hard drives these days, such as who copyrighted their files first!'

She fixed him with a steely look and Vik, knowing he was defeated, sank back on to the bench. Turning sharply on her heel she strode out of the hut, leaving him clicking his computer mouse in a fury of frustration and dragging Final Cut back on to the screen, from where Noah's wide-spaced gaze watched her leave.

Priya strode through the ashram trying to calm her ragged breathing and reminding herself that nothing had actually changed. Honestly, Vikram really was the limit. He was unable to feel guilt, he just felt bad that he hadn't got away with it by batting his eyelashes and giving her that megawatt smile. Priya had a feeling that smile was never going to work for her again, and judging from the look on Vikram's face he'd just had a similar insight. She sighed. That was one problem ticked off the mental to do list, she supposed.

Outside the cool huts the hot morning was melting into an even hotter afternoon so Priya ducked into the shade alongside the dormitories, intent on fishing Ray out and warning him not to listen to any of Vikram's crazy theories. Drugs? She laughed out loud. How far-fetched was that?

But the laugh died on her lips when she turned a corner and saw the swami deep in conversation with the business woman. Priya was genuinely shocked that the swami was actually speaking. Since when was her vow of silence a thing of the past? Why hadn't Noah thought to mention it at the party? He'd had every opportunity to say something.

Or had the vow of silence never actually been for real? Was Vikram actually closer to the truth than she'd given him credit for?

Although she was too far away to hear their conversation Priya could see that they were discussing something passionately, the swami waving her arms in the air for emphasis while the business woman nodded furiously. What were they saying? She had to find out, even if it was just to discover that they were debating the meaning of life or the benefits of meditation rather than hatching a drugs deal. Scooting behind the meditation pyramids and feeling totally ridiculous doing so, Priya gradually inched forward. Just a bit further and she'd be able to hear every word.

'Priya? What on earth are you up to skulking around here?'

Kettan popping up from behind the final pyramid, arms full of white lanterns, nearly took ten years off Priya's life. Once her skittering heartbeat returned to almost normal she saw that the swami and the business woman had moved on, still deep in conversation.

Damn it! she thought, her skin prickling with irritation. Why couldn't she just be allowed to get on with her job?

'I'm working, Kettan,' she said wearily. 'I was hoping to catch the swami and get her to give me an interview.' *But you've scuppered that*, she added silently.

'Oh, right.' He nodded. 'For the documentary?'

'Yes, that's right.'

An awkward silence fell. Priya was itching to follow the swami and wrestle her to the ground if necessary to get an interview, but Kettan had an air of agitation about him as though he needed to say something too. His smooth forehead was beaded with perspiration and a muscle ticked in his jaw. A cold hand clutched her heart. There wasn't another problem with the wedding, was there? That really would be the last straw.

'Kettan, is something wrong?'

He swallowed. 'No. In fact, everything's starting to feel as though things are beginning to fall into place at last. Does that make sense to you?'

'Er, no. Not really.'

'Sorry. I'm not expressing myself very clearly, am I?' He gave an awkward little laugh. His cheeks were flushed suddenly and his eyes glittered feverishly. The smooth city lawyer was gone and in his place was a nervous stumbling wreck. When Kettan reached forward and took her hands in his she gasped in surprise.

'Hey! What do you think you're doing?'

'Sorry.' He smiled awkwardly and released her hands. 'I'm getting ahead of myself. Priya, sometimes people's feelings change and mine have certainly changed towards you. You're a wonderful girl – woman – and over the past few weeks of getting to know you I've really come to admire you. You've become very important to me and my family. We have so much in common.' He reached out for her again but missed when she stepped back. 'And I've got the greatest affection for you, as has my entire family. Priya, it would make everyone so happy if we started seeing each other, as a couple, I mean.' He fixed her with wide expectant eyes. 'What do you think? Would you do me the honour of dating me?'

Priya was dumbstruck. In terms of romance this was right up there with *you and me, babe, how about it?* It wasn't the most flattering proposition either. Basically it was a case of Kettan feeling under pressure to find a suitable Hindu wife and herself happening to fit the bill. She certainly wasn't the love of his life.

On the other hand love hadn't turned out to be the most reliable criterion for finding a life partner.

'I'm really flattered,' she told him once her vocal cords had recovered from the shock. 'But this is a big surprise.'

'It is?' Kettan looked taken aback. 'I thought I'd made my feelings clear last night at the party.'

Priya had a vague recollection of him saying something but she'd been preoccupied with Ray and Ishani and then there'd been the horrible row with Noah before Vik had swooped in like Superman and dominated the rest of the night. A headache started to beat in her left temple. Suddenly all she wanted was to get away from all the mess that the men in her life seemed hell-bent on throwing at her.

'You're a lovely man and I'm really honoured,' Priya hedged, not wanting to hurt his feelings or indeed start a family feud, 'but seeing someone and getting involved in a relationship isn't a decision that I'd take lightly. When I do make that decision it will have to be somebody very special. Somebody that I'm in love with. I won't be choosing a partner just because he seems to fit my family's criteria.'

'Oh, right.' Kettan sounded disappointed. Perhaps he'd been expecting her to burst into noisy tears of joy. Who knew what went on in men's minds? 'So are you saying that there isn't a chance that maybe we could make a go of it?'

'Listen, Kettan, one thing I have learned since I've been here is that there's no point keeping secrets or doing things just to please everybody else. I like you a lot, but it would never work because we'd be getting together for all the wrong reasons. Besides, I think you've already found the right person, haven't you? You just need to be strong and please yourself rather than your family.'

He pulled a face. 'That's easier said than done.'

'But worth it if you really love her.' Priya glanced at her watch. 'Sorry, I don't mean to be rude but I've really got to get to work. If I don't get that interview with the swami the whole documentary will fall flat on its face and I'll be in huge trouble. Can we talk about this another time, when things are a bit less hectic?'

'Of course.' Ever the gentleman, Kettan bowed his head. 'Good luck with your interview. Hope you nail it.'

So did she, thought Priya gloomily. It was about time her luck changed.

Wasn't it?

24

Fortunately Priya's luck seemed to be on the turn. Within seconds of parting company with Kettan she caught another glimpse of the swami and the business woman still deep in discussion, sitting side by side in the shade of an old stone tower that flanked the herb garden. Her breath caught in her throat; this was an opportunity far too good to miss. Not only were they still talking but the icing on the cake was that they were directly below a narrow window. If she stole into the tower she would be able to crouch down and hear every word. It was the perfect chance to really discover what was going on.

But it's eavesdropping! said a stern little voice in her ear. *You can't eavesdrop! It's wrong.*

God, having a conscience was annoying! How could she be a proper investigative journalist if she always had to justify what she was doing to her own strict moral code? It was hugely inconvenient. Lois Lane never had that problem, Priya thought wryly, hardening her resolve and ducking into the tower, but then again Lois always had Superman on hand to get her out of scrapes whereas she was totally on her own. Maybe it was better that way. After all, she'd relied on Vikram and look where that had got her.

Inside the tower it was cool and still. A small staircase wound upwards like the inside of a shell, the steps worn smooth with the passage of many sandalled feet, and ended at a door under which a sliver of sunlight trickled invitingly. That must be the location of the window, Priya decided, beginning to climb. She'd just pause by it for a minute or two and admire the view. That way if she overheard anything it would almost be by accident. She was actually doing the swami a favour. Her conversation was more than likely to be totally innocent, and then she'd be able to tell Vikram that his drug-growing theory was totally ridiculous. Then maybe she could turn her attention back to completing the documentary!

The window, she remembered, was halfway up the tower, just a narrow slit set into the thick stone wall, and pushing open the heavy wooden door Priya crept towards it, her feet leaving tracks across the dusty floorboards. Crouching beneath the window she pushed her hair behind her ears and held her breath, desperate to catch every word. The nuances of the conversation rose and fell in the herb-scented breeze but, try as she might, Priya just couldn't hear what they were talking about. The frantic pounding of her own heart against the stillness muffled things even further and even the blood rushing through her veins conspired against her. Maybe she should risk standing on her tiptoes and leaning out the window to see if she could hear more. What were the odds of the women below looking up and seeing her? And even if they did she could just wave and say that she was exploring.

Rising on to her toes she curled her fingertips around the window ledge and pulled herself upwards, wincing as the muscles in her forearms protested. Damn! She still couldn't see. Maybe if she managed to get a footing in the rough brickwork she could balance more easily.

'Maybe this is a stupid question, but what on earth are you doing?'

The question was simple enough but the last thing Priya had been expecting was company and she practically jumped out of her baggy combats with shock. Her hands and feet flailed and plaster crumbled like stale birthday cake as she lost her hold on the wall and thudded on to the floor, dust and flakes of stone settling all around her. Brushing it out of her eyes and blinking, she made out through the dust a familiar lean-hipped loose-limbed man with folded arms and a perplexed expression on his face as he stared down at her.

'What's going on? Indoor rock climbing?'

Priya's heart flopped into her sandals and her face flamed with a potent cocktail of guilt and embarrassment.

Where was bloody Superman when she needed him?

Scrambling to her feet and feeling sick to her stomach at being caught so blatantly eavesdropping she hastily brushed herself down and tried her hardest to ignore those searching grey eyes.

'I was exploring,' she muttered. 'Is that okay with you?'

Noah inclined his dark head. 'Yeah, it's fine. Explore

away by all means. Just try not to destroy the tower in the process. It's an ancient monument and we'd really miss it.'

'Very funny,' Priya snapped. 'I've seen enough anyway.' Trying to mask her embarrassment she strode past him to the doorway, only to discover that the door wouldn't open. Furiously she rattled the handle, frantically twisting it backwards and forwards, but to no avail. The door simply wouldn't budge.

'There's no point getting cross,' Noah told her. 'It gets stuck sometimes. Violence isn't the answer.'

'It bloody is!' Priya kicked the door, yelping in pain when she stubbed her toe, and continued to pound at the handle, but still the door refused to yield. She felt like screaming, especially since all the time she struggled and cursed Noah just stood watching with his lips curved into a sardonic smile.

'You could stop looking so smug and give me a hand!'

He shrugged. 'There's no point. You won't be able to open it, Priya.'

'So we're stuck in here? Fantastic! That's all I need. Have you any idea how much work I have to do?'

'Someone will be along eventually. As for work, can't it wait? Tonight's sunset will only ever exist this once. Why don't we climb up to the top of the tower and watch it?' He indicated a spiral metal staircase leading up to a hatch in the ceiling.

Priya swallowed. Humiliation and anger were still fizzing through her bloodstream and she was frustrated beyond belief at failing to overhear the swami and the business woman, but as Noah held out an expectant hand something in her melted like ice cream in the midday sun and to her surprise she found herself reaching out and grasping his strong fingers, which closed around hers like the most perfect glove.

What was she doing? She should snatch her hand away and break the door down. That's what she *should* do.

But her feet weren't obeying her head, and heart spluttering she watched him climb the staircase, push open the hatch and disappear into a pool of satsuma-hued sunshine. This was crazy! Getting trapped in a tower with Noah was so not up there on her top ten of things to do in Jaipur! If the time they'd spent together at the party was anything to go by they'd probably be arguing until they were released. It seemed that they couldn't spend five minutes together without bickering. But then, she reminded herself as she climbed carefully in his wake, why shouldn't she argue with him? It seemed he'd been lying to her for the last two weeks. Maybe rather than being angry at this enforced incarceration she should look on it as a handy opportunity to find out some truths about the ashram, starting with the swami and her so-called vow of silence and moving swiftly on to the mysterious crops that nobody seemed willing to talk about, although she may just keep quiet about the drugs idea because no matter how convinced Vikram was it still sounded pretty far-fetched to her. She could stretch to believing that the swami might stoop to ripping off credulous tourists, but selling drugs? That was just one step too far.

She had reached the top of the stairs now and pulled herself smoothly up into a round room ringed with windows through which there was an uninterrupted view of the desert, bathed in rosy light. The land rolled away for miles and Priya gasped in astonishment when she made out the Amber Fort on the horizon and the city walls all pink and pearly.

'Worth abandoning your work for?'

She rounded on him, riled by his superior attitude. 'Yes! Okay, Noah? It must be great always being right.'

'Whoa!' He held up his hands. 'Is that what you really think of me?'

'Well, *don't* you always know best?' she accused him, her eyes flashing with anger. 'Isn't that why you've been manipulating my every move since I first got here? Hiding things from me and the crew? Keeping me from seeing certain things? Making sure I didn't meet the swami?'

Their eyes locked in a silent battle of wills. Then Noah sighed heavily and turned away, leaning his elbows on the window sill and gazing out across the rosy landscape.

'You're right,' he said slowly. 'I have been keeping things from you, but not in the way you think. I wanted you to experience the magic of this place and not get embroiled in logistics.' He turned to face her. 'I wanted you to be able to find some space like you did in the temple, a pocket of calm that was just for you in the middle of what seems like a really hectic life. When we walked to the temple it just seemed that we really connected. I could tell that the place caught at your soul the same way it always does mine. You remember how that felt, don't you?'

For a second Priya was back in the vaulted gloom

feeling the tension slide from her body like quicksilver. 'I remember,' she murmured.

'Listen, I admit I was wrong to try to protect you from the business side of the ashram. My God, even I can see how that could be construed as suspicious. You're right, you are entitled to see everything and I'm sorry if I've made things difficult. Believe me, that was never my intention.'

Priya was gobsmacked. She'd been expecting a major row, yelling, shouting and accusations, not this admission that he really had been concealing things from her. Wrong-footed, she stared at him. Who was Noah? And why was he so very concerned about her? Why did he seem to care so much?

And why was she suddenly so very glad that he did?

'I'll show you everything you want to see,' Noah promised. 'No more secrets. I'll tell you how we fund the ashram, I'll show you the accounts, I'll make sure the swami meets you and gives you an interview. Whatever you need to make your documentary work I'll do my best to make sure you get it.'

Wow. This was some turn-around. 'Thanks. I appreciate it.'

'It's the least I can do. I won't stand in your way any more. I promise.'

They smiled at one another, both feeling the pull of the cord of attraction.

'Anyway, seeing as we're here let's look at the view,' Noah said eventually. 'I think it has to be my favourite in the entire world. See over there? That's the Jal Mahal, or the Amber Palace, and that shimmering pool of water is the Mansarovar Lake. It's so beautiful when the water hyacinths bloom after the winter monsoons. I'd love you to see that.'

'It's beautiful now,' Priya breathed, joining him at the window and gazing at the lake which shimmered with the trembling rays of the dying sun. She felt as though she were standing at the top of the world, small and insignificant in the face of such an awesome landscape. As she gazed at the view she had the strangest sensation that all the stresses and worries she'd been carrying around for months were slipping away. What did any of it matter when there was such a beautiful world just waiting to be explored? Maybe it was time she stopped always striving to reach the next goal and just sat back and enjoyed what she already had.

'It's a magical place,' Noah murmured. 'You're the first person I've ever shared it with.'

It was magical, so magical that when he took her hand in his again she didn't resist. Instead they stood side by side and watched the sun slip below the horizon.

When he bowed to kiss her, it felt like the most natural thing in the world. Noah's lips brushed hers and she felt the muscles of his strong arms ripple as he pulled her close, his mouth seeking hers in a kiss that grew deeper and more questioning. Priya closed her eyes and gave herself up to the delicious sensation of those strong lips on hers. She could feel the drumming of his heart against her own, and the trembling of his hands as they traced the soft curves of her body was echoed in the trembling of her knees. As his mouth became more demanding every part of her body turned golden warm and pliable as the dying sunshine.

She'd had boyfriends. She'd been kissed. She'd had what she'd thought was some pretty good sex, but compared to Noah's kiss these things were just poor shadows of an infinitely more powerful attraction. When Noah pulled away she really would have crumpled if it hadn't been for the strong arms that held her so tightly.

My God, thought Priya in amazement, I've landed in a Mills & Boon novel!

Noah grinned and shook his head. 'That is definitely *not* what a guide's supposed to do!'

Priya reached up and brushed the dark locks back from his face. They were just as springy and silky as she'd imagined, and she *had* imagined touching them. She'd just not wanted to admit it to herself.

'Hey, it's fine by me,' she said, winding her hands into his hair and melting into him. 'I like this type of guiding!'

'But I really shouldn't be kissing you when I'm still your guide, especially since the swami specifically requested I took that role. Maybe she's testing my willpower?'

'I think you may have failed!'

He kissed her again, a long searching kiss that left her heart pounding and her body tingling from head to toe.

'I think I don't have any willpower when it comes to you,' he sighed. 'We need to get out of this tower quickly!'

She reached out and touched his lips with her fingertips. 'Far be it from me to encourage you to break your guiding code! Come on, let's go and see if we can shout loud enough to be rescued.'

'Ah,' Noah said, looking rather sheepish. 'I think it may be a little easier to escape than you think.'

Priya was puzzled. 'But the door's stuck! I tried to open it and it wouldn't budge. You said it couldn't be opened.'

'Er, I didn't actually. What I said was that *you* wouldn't be able to open it. I don't recall saying I couldn't. Come on, let me show you.'

He led her down the twisty steps back to the first room where she'd been so intent on trying to listen in to the Swami's conversation. Priya shook her head in wonder. It felt like an episode from someone else's life. Noah put his shoulder to the door and pushed with all his might. He struggled for a minute or two before there was an arthritic-sounding click and the door swung open.

Priya's jaw dropped. 'You could open it all along?'

'Sorry,' said Noah. 'When the door got stuck it just seemed like too good an opportunity to miss. How else was I going to persuade you to spend a few moments hearing me out? You're always so quick to think the worst of me. Be honest, you'd written me off weeks ago as a drug-dealing hippy drop-out, hadn't you?'

Priya hung her head. He was right. She had been judgemental and she felt bitterly ashamed.

He reached out and traced the curve of her cheek. 'I'm sorry if I misled you about the door, but I really wanted to set things straight between us. And it's selfish, but I also wanted you to myself for a minute without any camera crews or mad relatives storming over! I may be a guide but I'm still a man, so can you cut me some slack? I knew you'd just storm off otherwise. Besides, I really wanted to share that sunset with you.'

Priya's stomach was filled with a thousand fluttering butterflies.

'I'm so glad you did,' she whispered. 'I think it was exactly what I needed.'

They went down the stairs and stepped out into the twilight, not touching but still close. Priya felt as though she had a Ready Brek glow ringing her body. She wasn't sure what had just passed between them, didn't want to even try to analyse it, but she certainly felt different, all light and floaty and as though champagne bubbles were popping through her blood stream.

She was happy, Priya realised with a jolt. It had been so long she'd almost forgotten how it felt.

'There you are! For God's sake, Priya! I've been looking for you everywhere. Where the hell have you been?'

Vikram was standing at the base of the tower, hands on his hips.

'I was giving Priya a tour of the ashram,' Noah answered, coming to her defence.

'Really?' Vik's top lip curled. Priya frowned. What was the matter with him? 'All areas, was it?'

'Just the tower today,' Noah replied calmly. 'But tomorrow she can see anywhere she wishes. You too, of course, and the rest of your crew.'

'Really?' Vik raised his eyebrows. 'Well, I'll certainly look forward to that. It should be fascinating. Now if you don't mind I'd rather like my colleague back. I've got something very important to discuss with her.'

Noah and Priya exchanged glances. Noah's was

concerned but Priya's answered that things were fine so he pressed his hands together in namaste and left them alone, his footsteps fading away and taking with them the lovely sparkly magic of earlier. With a sigh Priya dragged her attention back to Vik, who was strutting ahead of her like a cockerel. Her fingers itched to slap him. How dare he be so dismissive to Noah? And who did he think he was, ordering her about like that? Vik might have his suspicions but he'd just been unbelievably rude.

'Vik! Stop right there!' She clutched his arm and spun him round. 'What the hell was that all about? You were vile to Noah. You need to find him and apologise.'

Vikram laughed. 'Me apologise to him? I don't think so, and neither will you when you see the footage I've got.'

'Footage? What footage? What are you talking about?'

Vikram smiled down at her. In the darkness his eyes glittered like jet and when he spoke his voice was a hiss of triumph.

'I'm talking about the footage I got earlier that proves your precious Noah and his saintly swami are nothing but low-life drug dealers! Just wait until you see it. They're nothing but con artists!'

Priya's blood turned to ice water. Her lips, still tingling from Noah's kisses, trembled, and her vision blurred dangerously. 'I don't understand,' she whispered.

'While you were *missing*,' Vik sneered, reaching forward and wiping a smear of lipstick from the corner of her mouth, 'Ray filmed the swami having a very enlightening conversation with a business associate. No wonder Noah's tried so hard to keep you two apart. He must have been terrified you'd overhear and then their game would be up. But you're smarter than that, aren't you, babe? You knew exactly what he was up to. Didn't you?'

Priya felt sick to the stomach. So much for her great journalist instincts; Noah it seemed had played her for a perfect fool. And, what was worse, for a few perfect minutes she'd actually allowed herself to believe in him, to believe in something *more*.

What a bloody idiot. She really should have known better.

There wasn't a man alive who wasn't a total disappointment.

'**R**ight.' Vik stopped the hire car outside the Adanis' apartment and killed the engine. 'We're safe here; nobody can overhear us or interfere. It's time you saw this, Priya. Then you can tell me if you still think it's innocent.'

Priya swallowed. Her head was still spinning from the speed of events. One moment she'd been kissing Noah, her heart blooming with unexpected joy, the next she was being dragged into the car and zooming away from the ashram as though the hounds of hell were on their heels. Her hands were still shaking, though with anger or shock she wasn't certain.

Actually she wasn't feeling certain of anything. It was like the ground had turned to quicksand beneath her feet.

'Play the tape back, Ray,' Vikram ordered.

Ray glanced at Priya. 'Are you sure you want to see this tonight? It might complicate things a bit for tomorrow.'

Priya's guts were doing macramé. Neesh's wedding was the following day. All the preparations were completed and even now Neesh was out celebrating with Sanjeev and her parents, dizzy with excitement about getting married at the ashram. Blowing the lid on a drugs-growing operation at the wedding venue would do a bit more than *complicate things*.

Her sister's special day would be ruined.

She passed a hand over eyes that felt like golf balls dipped in grit. On the other hand, if Vikram was right and there really was something criminal going on at the ashram, then it was their responsibility to do something about it. Wasn't that the whole point of investigative journalism? Righting wrongs and bringing the bad guys to justice?

An image of Noah, his eyes bright with emotion as he stroked her cheek, flickered across her vision and a lump filled her throat. Was he the bad guy after all? Had he distracted her with the kiss to deliberately prevent her from overhearing what the swami was saying? She shook her head in anguish. She had to know the truth.

'Play the tape, Ray,' she said wearily. 'I think my parents would want to know if they're about to hold their daughter's wedding in some kind of drugs factory.'

Shrugging his bony shoulders Ray flipped open the view screen of the Steadicam and passed the camera across to Priya. Ishani squeezed her arm. 'It's not totally conclusive,' she said kindly.

Vik snorted. 'It's as good as. Without a written confession I think you'll find this is as conclusive as these things get. But don't take my word for it, Priya. Press Play. What are you waiting for?'

There was a pain in her chest, which she realised came from holding her breath. Vik's face was lit with a gloating excitement. He's finally got his big break, she thought bitterly, and once again I handed it to him on a plate. Still, professional rivalry seemed the least of her problems now, and with a trembling finger she pressed Play.

Late afternoon. Sunset. Ext. Tower at the ashram. Two women sitting talking. Zoom in to the women. CU on the speaker.

The swami was looking agitated. Gone was the serene figure of Priya's memory and in her place was a tired-looking woman with a frown creasing the soft flesh between her brows.

'I'm not sure it can be done in time,' she was saying. 'That's a great deal of product to be moved in a short space of time.'

'It's possible,' the business woman replied. 'It could be done very easily and with minimum disruption. The amounts of the product could be divided up into smaller weights. Maybe just a few ounces each? It would be less difficult to transport that way, too.'

'The product damages too easily,' the swami replied. 'It needs time to be prepared properly too. It's delicate.'

'But you have some already prepared?'

'Yes indeed, but not in the quantities you require.' The swami shook her grey head. 'I'm not sure we can help.'

'But we need it! Yours is the best!' The business woman looked almost distraught. 'Just name the price you want for the stuff and I promise we'll pay it. We'll pay double if need be.'

At this point the swami was talking numbers but annoyingly the sound dipped and her words were lost. Priya exhaled shakily before pressing the Pause button. She'd heard enough.

'The business woman's husband turned up at this point,' Ray explained. 'I had to dive into the undergrowth and it's a bit muffled, I'm afraid. But you get the gist of it, I think. All three of them spend ages now talking about shifting weights of "product", whatever that product is.'

'I think it's pretty obvious,' said Vik. 'Hash? Opium?'

'Not necessarily.' Ishani's eyes narrowed behind her glasses. Priya had the distinct impression that her newest recruit was far from impressed by Vikram. Possibly Ray had been telling tales out of school; she wouldn't put it past him. 'We don't know what the product is, do we? It could be anything. Flowers? Herbs? We're jumping to conclusions here.'

'Maybe,' said Priya doubtfully. The trouble was, though, that the evidence was pretty damning and she had an extra piece of the puzzle that they didn't know about. Sick as it made her feel to admit it, it seemed pretty obvious that Noah had only lured her away to kiss her in order to prevent her from overhearing this incriminating conversation. The swami had probably ordered him to do it; they were as thick as thieves, those two.

He was up to his neck in it. That was clear. But how was she going to prove it?

'I think Ishani's right,' Ray was saying. 'This is all very interesting but it's totally circumstantial evidence.

We need to actually find something tangible if we're going to prove they're growing drugs.'

'So that's what we'll do,' said Vikram firmly. 'Tomorrow we'll head up into those fields they're so secretive about and see exactly what's what.'

'But it's the wedding!' Priya and Ishani chorused.

'Exactly.' Vik nodded. 'Everyone will be far too busy to notice a couple of us slipping off. It's perfect.'

But it didn't feel perfect. In fact, as Priya followed her colleagues into the apartment she thought that things were probably as far from perfect as they could possibly get. Neesh's wedding hung in the balance, the ashram was more than likely a front for some international drug smuggling operation and as usual she'd made a major error of judgement about a man.

Pleading a headache she left the others deep in conversation and, still holding the camera, trudged wearily up the stairs to her room. Thank goodness Neesh and Divya were out celebrating, she thought, sinking on to the bed and burying her face in her hands. One look at her and they'd know that something was up.

She sat cross-legged on her bed and played the tape again, pausing bits and rewinding them over and over again, but the more she watched the more confused she became. There was only one thing she was certain of and that was that Noah had seen her coming. He must have laughed out loud when he realised just how easy it would be to distract her. One flutter of those long eyelashes and one knicker-melting kiss and she'd been lost like the stupid idiot she was. All men were liars; why on earth had she thought Noah was any different? Had she learned nothing?

She thumped her pillow. First Vikram with his lies, then Kettan who was lying to himself when it was blatantly obvious he was still in love with his English girlfriend, and now Noah who was proving to be the biggest liar of them all, and a criminal to boot.

But he'd seemed so plausible, and his kisses had felt real too. Her hand stole to her lips. Was it crazy to think that she could still feel the hard touch of his mouth against hers? Even the memory made her pulse flutter.

How could such a kiss be nothing but a lie? And how could she have been so stupid? Of course Noah wasn't really interested in her. Why would he be, a stunning man like that? He probably had his pick of the ashram's female visitors. All she'd been was an irritation that he needed to deal with and he'd certainly managed that all right. One kiss from him and all thoughts of her story had melted away, along with her dignity. Some journalist she was. He and the swami were probably having a right old laugh about it now as they weighed up their drugs, or whatever it was that dealers did in their spare time.

Round and round went Priya's thoughts like a masochistic merry-go-round. No matter what angle she examined it from there was only one answer: Noah had used her.

Finally, head pounding and tears slipping silently down her cheeks, she pulled the hateful tape out of the camera and buried her face in the pillow. Her heart was thudding frantically against her ribcage and in spite of the heat she was drenched in icy cold sweat. She was clutching the mini dv tape so tightly that her palms were scarred with crescent moons.

There was no way she was letting that tape out of her sight. It was the only means she had of showing Noah that no one, however gorgeous, messed with Priya Gupta and got away with it.

Letting a man make a fool of her wasn't a mistake she intended to make twice.

26

Neesh raked her fingers through her extensions and scowled at her reflection in the mirror. The sari she was wearing was vivid crimson, elegant and traditional, and the soft silky fabric of the highest quality. A present from Akhila, along with a mountain of heavy gold jewellery, it was everything that a demure young Hindu bride was supposed to dream of.

If that bride wasn't Neeshali Gupta, of course.

'I hate it,' Neesh wailed, her eyes filling with tears. 'I look horrible. Like a giant tampon.' Her hennaed hands started to pluck at the fabric, unravelling the yards and yards of silk which Priya and Divya had been patiently winding and folding for hours, as she frantically tried to escape. 'I'm not wearing it! I'd rather get married in my jeans!'

'You'll do no such thing, my girl!' snapped Divya, grabbing fistfuls of crimson fabric and frantically stuffing them back. 'You look beautiful and I won't hear another word otherwise.'

'I am so not wearing this! Tell her, Priya!' Neesh spun round like a scarlet whirlwind. 'If I can't get married in one of my own saris then the wedding's off!'

Priya closed her eyes wearily. It was late afternoon and she'd been up since sunrise preparing for the wedding and trying her hardest to join in all the rituals with a smile on her face; easier said than done when it felt as though somebody had driven a monster truck over her heart. She'd hardly slept the night before, tossing and turning in her narrow bed as images from the previous afternoon flashed through her mind's eye like a video nasty, and when she had finally drifted into a fitful slumber her dreams had been filled with images of Noah's sexy mouth inches from her own. All she wanted to do was find a cool quiet spot to sit for a few moments and gather her thoughts, but thrust into the mayhem of the wedding she had more chance of flying to the moon, especially now that Neesh had taken such exception to a wedding dress she'd loved at breakfast time.

'You look beautiful,' she sighed. 'Honestly, Neesh. You really do.'

But Neesh wasn't listening. Instead she was busy ripping off her gold bangles and tugging at her necklaces, muttering furiously that she wasn't getting married like this, she'd rather get married naked/ in jeans/in a sack. Divya was frantically trying to reason with her – which after living with Neesh for twenty-four years she ought to have realised was a pointless exercise – but Priya simply didn't have the energy. Besides, she wasn't certain whether Neesh and Sanjeev would be able to get married at all. Ray and Vikram had left at lunch time on the pretext of shooting wedding footage but in reality to explore the mysterious crops outside the ashram. If they found evidence of anything illegal then all hell would break loose.

There was no way that Priya could allow a drug dealer to host her sister's wedding.

The whole thing was a nightmare.

'We don't have time for this, Neeshali!' Divya barked, driven to the end of her patience. 'We're supposed to be leaving in an hour. It's almost dark and they'll be lighting the sacred fires any minute and the men will already be there getting ready for the procession. Sanjeev will be waiting. You can't get hysterical and let him down. Now come on, dry your eyes and let Priya redo your makeup.'

'Priya needs to sort her own makeup out,' snapped Neesh, stress making her cruel. 'She's got bigger bags than Louis Vuitton. Do you want some Touche Éclat, Pri?'

Personally Priya felt she could live in a vat of Touche Éclat for a week and still look like death. Neesh might be amazed to know that there were some things in life that couldn't be cured by a makeover or a new frock. Unfortunately.

'You do look tired, darling,' Divya agreed, a concerned frown wrinkling her forehead. 'You work far too hard. Maybe you should have a nap before we leave?'

'I'm fine, it's just a headache,' Priya fibbed. 'Come on, Neesh, how about I do your hair again and then we see how you feel?'

'Even if Nicky Clarke turned up I'd still hate this bloody sari,' grumbled her sister, but she sat back at the dressing table and passed Priya a comb. Divya and

Priya exchanged a glance in the mirror. The tantrum had passed for now but it was only a matter of time before something else set the highly strung bride off again. Priya just crossed her fingers that it wouldn't be discovering that her wedding was going to be called off thanks to a drugs bust prompted by her journalist sister.

She could seriously do without that.

'Knock! Knock!' called Bhavani, barging in with her sisters hot on her heels. 'We have a surprise for you, Neeshali!'

'Great,' Neesh whispered to Priya. 'What now? If they've changed anything else without asking Mum she'll freak, man!'

'Family trait, babe,' Priya murmured in her ear. All day long Divya had been doing battle with the aunties and Akhila, sending them off on countless errands as she fought desperately to maintain control. Priya recognised some of her own personal qualities in her mother and it didn't make for a happy comparison. Was this her in twenty years? Set in her ways and never satisfied unless everyone danced to her tune? She swallowed nervously; she really hoped not. Noah might have turned out to be the biggest liar since Pinocchio but some of his observations had been rather near the knuckle.

Not that she was going to let herself think about *him* just now.

Clad in their wedding finery of green, yellow and blue respectively the aunties looked like a collection of snooker balls being potted into the room. Divya sighed loudly and raised her eyes to the ceiling. She'd been relieved when they'd vanished around lunch time amid whispers of surprises and presents, and now as they crowded the room, pinching Neesh's cheeks and getting all sentimental, Priya could almost see her mother's blood pressure soaring.

'What a beautiful bride you make!' Darsani cooed, wedging herself next to Neesh at the dressing table.

'I look like shit,' Neesh grumbled. 'This bloody dress makes me look like a hippo.'

A tiny size eight, Neesh had never looked fat in her life, but because she was the bride and allowed to be stressed the aunties just shook their oiled heads and told her she looked lovely.

'Now, Neeshali,' Bhavani was saying, 'we have a present for you. A very special one which we have made ourselves, indeed it has taken us three days of hard work.'

Chandani, who was clutching a big glittery parcel proudly to her wobbly chest, beamed widely. 'We wanted to do something for the wedding and this seemed like the perfect idea.'

'I must say,' chipped in Darsani, 'it isn't the most traditional idea and it was only your father who was able to finally persuade us that we were doing the right thing. Ashwani always knows best and of course we defer to his judgement at all times.'

Neesh's eyes were like saucers. She loved presents. John Lewis was practically her second home and her wedding list could easily be her *Mastermind* specialist topic.

'What is it?' she asked.

'Open it and see!' they chorused and within seconds Neesh's false nails were ripping the paper into confetti.

Moments later a cascade of sheer pink fabric glittering with embroidery and sequins pooled on to her lap.

It was a shimmering pink sari.

'Oh! My! God!' Neesh squealed. 'I don't believe it!' She leapt to her feet and held the sari against her body, twirling round and round like a Disney princess and sobbing with joy. 'You made me a pink sari? After all you said about how awful they are?'

Bhavani blushed. 'Maybe we were a bit hasty. It is your wedding after all. Besides, we wanted to do something special for you, Neeshali. We can all see how much your dress means to you, even if we don't understand why. When your father said he didn't mind what colour you got married in this seemed like the best gift we could find.'

'It is! It is!' Neesh sobbed, throwing her arms around her aunt and hugging her. 'I love it!'

The aunties must have been sewing day and night, thought Priya, as she admired their handiwork. This was no tacky pink affair but a work of art, meticulously cut and beautifully stitched and fashioned from the most delicate blush pink and palest old gold silks and chiffons, the exact hues of the rosy sunset she'd watched with Noah. The edges twinkled with thousands of gold sequins which must have taken hours to sew on. It was a true labour of love and Neesh was going to look stunning. Even Divya was smiling and thanking them, although this was probably because they'd prevented the mother of all strops rather than genuine delight with the pink sari.

Neesh ripped off the red sari, wound herself into the new one like the Tasmanian Devil and seconds later was waltzing around the bedroom in all her pink glory. With her sparkling eyes, coral-hued cheeks and tumbling raven hair she looked every inch the radiant bride. Then Chandani produced a headdress decorated with diamonds and pale pink pearls with a teardrop-shaped pendant which rested on Neesh's forehead. Chattering like starlings, the aunties loaded her up with her wedding dowry, the outward show of Ashwani's success and her value as a prize that Sanjeev had been lucky enough to win. A diamond and gold choker was wrapped around her neck and bell-shaped diamond earrings dangled from her ears. Excitedly she crammed her fingers full of rings and pushed the gold bangles back on to her slender arms.

'What about the nath?' Bhavani asked, holding out the nose ring with punky style chain to hook into the hair. 'It's traditional.'

'I think it's a bit late to worry about tradition now,' Divya pointed out as Neesh pulled a face.

'No way, man!' Neesh said. 'Gold snot dripping from my nose? Gross. I've got a much better idea. Look what I got Sanj to buy me when we went shopping yesterday,' and reaching under the bed she pulled out a Swarovski bag. Moments later a twirly armband circled her bicep and a crystal anklet ringed her slim ankle.

'Ta-da!' crowed Neesh, beaming at her reflection. 'Me in all my blinging bridal glory! Well, what are you waiting for?' she added, spinning round to fix Priya with a determined look. 'I need my hair and makeup done, sis, like now. We've got a wedding to go to!'

She flicked her iPod on and instantly the room was filled with a thumping Bhangra beat. Swaying to it, the sari flying out behind her like a silken sail, she shimmied around the room with a hundred-watt grin etched across her face.

'I'm getting married! I'm really getting married!'

'Thank God for that,' Divya exhaled, a hand over her heart. 'I thought you were going to call it off for one awful moment.'

Neesh looked at her mother as though she were mad. 'Call off my wedding? Like duh!' She glanced at the alarm clock and her face broke into a huge smile. 'No way am I calling it off! I can't wait to be Mrs Adani! This is going to be a wedding to remember, right, Priya?'

'Right,' Priya agreed, feeling queasy. Picking up the brush and attacking Neesh's extensions she prayed they'd remember this wedding for all the *right* reasons.

She didn't think her family would ever forgive her otherwise.

27

Once at the ashram Priya didn't have a second to think about anything other than the wedding; her worries about what Vikram might have discovered, her anger at Noah's betrayal and her reservations about whether or not the swami should be allowed to marry Neesh and Sanjeev were swept away when all her worlds collided at once. From the moment the Guptas stepped out of the car they were plunged into the wedding celebrations, family and work boundaries blurring so rapidly that Priya felt dizzy.

'Oh my God! It looks amazing!' breathed Neesh, gazing around in delight and twirling with excitement like a pink butterfly.

Neesh and Sanj were getting married in the ashram's small temple but that hadn't stopped the gardens from being lavishly decorated too. The whole place looked like something out of a fairy tale. The weather was fine and warm, the sun slipping into a picture perfect sunset, and already the horizon was deep scarlet. A sprinkling of stars freckled the sky and a white balloon moon was rising. Twinkling across the gardens were long ropes of fairy lights shimmering in the breeze and the trees were festooned with Divya's white lanterns. An archway of jasmine and gardenia led towards the temple and the lawns were covered with bouquets of herbs and flowers, filling the air with a rich heady scent that mingled with the delicious aromas from the two barbecues that had been set up and were being tended by the Ana Purna chefs dressed in plumed emerald turbans. Jewel-hued cushions were scattered across the ground for guests to sit on and tea lights in coloured jars were dotted among them, their flickering flames sprinkling rainbows into the darkness.

Guests strolled across the grounds chattering excitedly, a band was knocking out the latest Bollywood tunes and flares had been stuck at intervals, throwing leaping shadows. Because all Hindu weddings are essentially a Vedic Yajna, or fire sacrifice, the torches were a major feature and spluttered phoenix-bright sparks into the darkness, marking out the boundary of the ashram in a circle of leaping flame. What was beyond that dancing light, wondered Priya, shivering in her thin gold sari. Just the herbs that Noah claimed or something far more sinister? He had a history of drug dealing – he'd never hidden that. How could she have been so stupid as to have been taken in by him?

How could she have allowed her sister to hold her wedding at this place?

But Neesh, of course, had no such concerns. Throwing her arms around Priya she cried, 'Oh, babes! It's just the most amazing setting! Thank you so much for letting me have the wedding here! I just know everything's going to be perfect.'

Priya gulped as she hugged her sister back. So far

she'd not caught sight of Vik or Ray and nobody had texted her to say there was anything more to report. Crossing her fingers, eyes and anything else crossable she hoped desperately that Neesh was right.

The male members of the wedding party were waiting on the far side of the ashram for their procession to the temple. The female contingent was already half an hour late – Akhila had gone into meltdown when she'd seen the pink sari – but Neesh was in no hurry to put Sanjeev out of his misery. Instead she insisted on having a glass of champagne and a quick stroll around the grounds, followed naturally by the wedding photographer who was busy taking endless shots of her in full Bollywood starlet mode. Neesh had been planning this day practically from the minute she popped out of the womb and Priya couldn't help smiling as she sank on to a cushion and watched the impromptu photo shoot. After two years of dating her sister, Sanj would have probably keeled over with shock if she'd been on time.

'Can I join you?' Noah slipped out of the darkness beside her. He was dressed in a simple white robe that clung to his powerful shoulders, his hair was caught back at the nape of his neck with a leather band with just a few loose curls brushing his cheeks, and his grey eyes were crinkled in an expectant smile.

For a second Priya was speechless. The gall of him!

Taking her silence as acquiescence Noah sat down next to her on the cushion. As his warm body brushed against her arm goosebumps of longing Mexican-waved across her body and in spite of her fury with him she couldn't help but steal a glimpse of that strong hawk-like profile and curling mouth. How frustrating that he was still one of the most beautiful men she'd ever seen, even though he'd turned out to be such a con artist.

'So,' Noah said softly, 'how are you? All ready for the wedding?'

His long lean thigh leaned against hers and Priya flinched, drawing her legs up under her chin and winding her arms around them defensively. Deliberately she shifted away from him. Her heart was pounding against her ribcage, from anger of course, and her mouth was dry. Annoyingly all the cutting comments she'd dreamed up in the silent watches of the night vanished and to her horror she realised she was dangerously close to tears.

With a shock Priya realised that their kiss had meant even more to her than she'd thought. It had been more than physical; in getting to know Noah she'd bared her soul in a way that she never had before, had told him things and let him see the vulnerable side of her that she usually kept private. When he'd talked about her need for space and islands of serenity to keep a grip on her life it had been as though someone had opened a door into her soul, seen what was there and accepted it; liked it even. To discover that it had been nothing but a cynical ploy hurt beyond imagination.

'I'm fine, thanks,' she said, hoping her voice was colder than the freezer section in Iceland. 'I was just having a few quiet moments before the ceremony, actually.'

'Oh.' He inclined his head slowly. 'I understand. It's an important rite of passage, a family wedding. I guess it makes you think about all kinds of things.'

'Hmm.' Priya looked stonily ahead. She was so not having this conversation.

'It's made me think too,' Noah continued, looking towards where Neesh was posing. 'Cutting yourself off isn't always the right thing to do. Sometimes it's braver and better to take a risk.'

He'd taken one sitting here, she thought, her hands balling into fists. As soon as she had control of her temper she was going to tell Noah exactly what she thought of his particular brand of risk taking.

'I didn't like leaving you last night,' Noah continued. 'Your boss seemed really agitated. Was it okay?'

He tried to take her hand but she snatched it away, her temper rising like lava. 'Don't touch me!'

'Are you angry I didn't stay? Believe me, I've never wanted anything so much in my life, but I thought I was doing the right thing by giving you some space. I guess I messed up there, did I?'

Oh, he was too much. Watch out Jack Nicholson, this man was truly Oscar-worthy! Galvanised by fury she leapt to her feet and glowered at him, her hands on her hips and her eyes bright with hurt.

'Oh come on, Noah, you can drop the lover act now. You got what you wanted from me, just as you've been plotting all along.'

His dark brows drew together in a frown. 'What?'

'The sunset? The locked door? All the romantic crap you spun me?' She laughed harshly. 'Oh, you're good, I'll give you that all right. You almost had me believing it for a moment there.'

'Why wouldn't you believe it?' He didn't raise his

voice but sat still, staring up at her with liquid velvet eyes.

'You know why, we both do. But hey, why waste another minute lying? You got what you wanted.'

Noah exhaled slowly. He looked calm but a muscle ticked in his cheek. Well, he could do all the bloody yogic breathing he liked, Priya decided, but if he thought he could talk her round he was wrong. She'd seen right through him.

'Is this about the door? Look, I explained that and I'm not ashamed to admit I wanted to kiss you. I've wanted to kiss you from the minute you clambered out of that bus all dusty and cross and unbelievably gorgeous. Is that a crime? I'm not a monk, Priya; I'm just an ordinary guy trying to figure things out. I don't have all the answers either. Is that what's upset you? You feel I haven't been the guide I should have been?'

'Oh, I think you've been *exactly* the guide you were asked to be!'

'And what's that supposed to mean?'

'It means I know why you kissed me so don't go kidding yourself it means anything or that I'm stupid enough to volunteer for a repeat performance. I might have fallen for all your clever lines once, but it's not going to happen again.'

'I kissed you because I wanted to. Because I couldn't *not* kiss you!'

'Crap!' she hissed. 'You're a liar!'

They glowered at each other. Then a voice shrilled, 'Priya! There you are! Chi! Chi! This is no time to chat!' Divya, totally oblivious of the atmosphere, swooped down on them like a sari-clad hawk. 'It's time to get the bride into the temple before poor Sanjeev thinks he's been jilted.'

Priya's hands were shaking and she tucked them into the folds of her sari, hoping that she didn't look as ruffled as she felt. Noah, damn him, was just looking confused and hurt as though he was the one who'd been wronged.

'I'll be needed in the temple to light the sacred fires,' he said coolly. 'Maybe we can catch up later?'

'Whatever,' Priya said, staring down at her French-manicured toes, anything rather than meet those soft wounded eyes. They seemed to grab her just in the heart region, which was most inconvenient seeing as he was a lying manipulative conman.

Noah sighed and seconds later was just a blur of robes as he strode across the grass towards the temple. Priya followed him with narrowed eyes, noting the set of his shoulders and the fierce pace. If she didn't know better she'd have said he looked upset, but then, if he thought his game had been rumbled, he was bound to be upset. It certainly wasn't down to any genuine feeling for her, she already knew that much.

She swallowed back her misery. This was supposed to be a happy occasion. There would be plenty of time later to mull over her car crash of a love life.

As she made her way towards the temple Priya was so lost in thought that when someone tapped her on the shoulder she almost went into orbit.

'Sorry!' Vikram said, grinning at her like a Halloween lantern. 'I didn't mean to make you jump. Can I have a word?'

She wiggled her shoulder so that his hand slipped

off her bare flesh. 'Look, Vik, I know we have a lot to talk about, as usual, but can it please wait until after Neesh and Sanjeev have got married?'

He shook his head. 'Not really. Anyway, for once this isn't about us, Priya. It's about the story.'

'You want to talk about work now? My only sister's about to get married any minute! Work's the least of my priorities.'

'It won't be once you hear this,' Vik insisted, taking her elbow and guiding her away from the stream of excited chattering guests flowing towards the temple.

Angrily she shook him off. God! He was unbelievable. Her sister was getting married any second and Vik thought it was an appropriate time to talk shop. What was the matter with the guy?

'Babe, I've been doing some investigating into what's really going on here.' He lowered his voice and she had to strain her ears to hear above the beat of the music. 'We needed something tangible so I've got us a sample of those plants from the locked herb garden. The one Noah's been so bloody touchy about.'

She stared at him. 'You've stolen some of those herbs?'

'Not stolen, exactly. More like borrowed them.'

Priya could hardly believe her ears. She was used to Vikram bending the truth but this was something else.

'I sent them to my uncle for analysis,' he continued, eyes bright with excitement. 'He's a chemist in Jaipur and believe me if there's anything dodgy about what they've been growing he's the man to spot it. We'll have the evidence we need. Just imagine if they really are shipping drugs to the USA! What a scoop! And there's another thing I've discovered: our friend Noah has a history in drug related crime. He's even been in prison for it. Now listen. What I reckon we should do is—'

But Priya didn't want to know any more about what Vik thought; she'd heard more than enough. She held up her hands. 'Whatever else you want to tell me is going to have to wait. My sister's about to get married and nothing, absolutely nothing, is going to get in the way of that.'

'But this is potentially a massive story,' Vikram protested. 'I've already told Ray to scoot about with his camera while everyone is preoccupied with the wedding. Who knows what he might see?'

'Ray's supposed to be filming the wedding! He promised ages ago that he would and you have absolutely no right to make him do something else. Bloody well go and tell him to come back right now!'

'But Priya! The story!'

She glared at him. 'For once, Vik, I actually don't give a toss about the sodding story. This is my sister's wedding and that comes first. Don't you dare spoil it. Nothing else matters, do you understand? Nothing!'

And spinning round on her heel she stormed off, even her skirts swirling in outrage, leaving Vik staring after her open-mouthed and in absolutely no doubt that she meant every word.

28

Neesh and Sanjeev were getting married beneath a mandap canopy which had been set up just outside the temple, carpeted with rich rugs and filled with wicker chairs. Most important, it contained the sacred fire, which was burning brightly in its copper dish. Music was playing softly in the background and the seated guests whispered excitedly amongst themselves as they waited for the arrival of the groom's party. Priya, who was acting as the flower girl, checked that everyone was in place, picked up the garland of fragrant jasmine blooms that the bride would give the groom and finally joined her sister and Ashwani who were waiting out of sight.

The wedding hadn't even started and already she was bone weary. Rounding up relatives, making certain all the props were in place for the ceremony, and feeling constantly on edge that Vik was about to do something mad, was exhausting. Add to that the raw pain of Noah's betrayal and all the emotion of seeing her baby sister undergo such an important rite of passage and she felt close to collapsing on to the floor in a heap.

Once this was over maybe she'd treat herself to a real holiday with no relatives in sight, and certainly no romantic entanglements.

A convent ought to do it.

'Did you see Sanj?' demanded Neesh, finally starting to look rather nervous beneath her thick layer of Chanel foundation. 'Is he ready to begin the groom's procession? Did the horse arrive? Is Mum ready?'

'Babes, you've been keeping him waiting, remember? And yes, the horse is here, and rather Sanj than me having to sit on that thing!' Priya smiled at the memory of her soon to be brother-in-law clinging for dear life to the mane of a rolling-eyed steed. 'The poor guy's terrified. What were you thinking, making him sit on a horse?'

'It's traditional for the groom to ride to the ceremony,' pointed out Neesh. 'He should count himself lucky the elephant was already booked!'

There wasn't a lot Priya could say to that, but she exchanged a wry look with her father. Neesh certainly wasn't doing anything by halves, as Ashwani's bank balance could testify.

'Is everyone inside now? Are their shoes off?' worried Ashwani. 'They do know they have to take their sandals off?'

'Chillax, Dad! Of course they do!' said Neesh. 'That's the easy bit. Sanj had better remember his garland or I'll kill him.'

'The older relatives have been seated now.' Peeping into the mandap, Priya could see the elderly Adani relatives take their places. 'That means Mum will be escorting the groom's party over any minute now.'

'Are you sure you wouldn't rather do that, Dad?' Neesh looked worried. 'Traditionally that should be your job and an uncle should bring me in. What a pain that the aunties bumped our uncles off so early! Although the uncles were probably well relieved.'

Ashwani kissed her cheek. 'Neeshali Gupta, I couldn't be prouder than I am at this moment. Never mind tradition, I'd far rather be with you. I'm the proudest father in the world.'

Priya's eyes filled at the tenderness in his voice. Her father still looked tired and drawn but there was a glow about him today that came from pure undiluted happiness. A lump rose into her throat. She was very happy for Neesh but at the same time she couldn't help wondering whether she would ever be able to make him as proud of her too.

At that moment the singing and clapping from the mandap announced the arrival of the groom. Cricking her neck to peep, Priya watched as a pale-faced Sanj slithered from the snorting horse. Even the feathers on his turban looked seasick.

The things people did for love!

From then on, after Sanjeev's trembling feet touched the earth, the ceremony was under way and Priya was catapulted into the heart of the ancient rituals. Once Sanj had been greeted by Divya and had presented her with the traditional gift of a coconut, it was time for the bride to make her entrance.

'This is it!' Neesh said, eyes sparkling with excitement. 'Wish me luck!'

Priya kissed her smooth cheek. 'You don't need it. I know you'll both be really happy. Enjoy every moment.'

If she hadn't already been welling up, Priya thought, as she followed her father and sister into the tent, she would be now from the look on Sanjeev's face as he caught sight of his bride. He looked like a man who couldn't believe his luck – as well he might, because Neesh was so stunning that there was a collective gasp from the guests when she entered.

Well, either that or they were totally outraged by the pink sari.

Sanj and Neesh had chosen a simple variation on what could be a long and sometimes tedious ceremony. There were the traditional readings in Sanskrit and invocations of Lord Ganesha as well as singing by the chorus and readings from the bride's and groom's parents. The young couple were seated facing one another for most of the ceremony and could hardly contain their delight, grinning at each other like naughty children up to mischief. Squashed in between Bhavani and Chandani, both of whom wept loudly and trumpeted into the vast stacks of Kleenex they'd purchased specially, Priya found herself blinking back tears too, especially when the swami spoke of the sacred nature of marriage and love.

'We should be able to live a graceful life that's full of mutual love and warmth,' she said, in her low musical voice. 'Our sentiments should be auspicious and we should be able to see for a hundred years, live a healthy life of a hundred years and listen to the music of spring for a hundred years if we have love in our hearts.'

Personally Priya felt she had more hope of visiting Mars than of finding love. Kettan had never really been interested in her, only in what she represented, and as for Vikram, well, the less said about him the better. She still had to find a way of convincing him it was over, easier said than done since Vik still thought his honeyed tongue could talk her round. Divya adored both guys and if mother really did know best Priya could pick either one and keep the family happy.

But she didn't love either of them and what was marriage without love? Even Vik's kisses had never made her melt inside like baked Alaska. Unlike Noah's . . .

Looking up she caught sight of Noah. He was staring back at her. Something crackled in the air before she ripped her eyes away. She mustn't let sentimentality cloud her judgement. The swami might sound genuine – and at least she was talking now – but Vikram's evidence was still pretty damning and Noah was still a liar. What was love anyway? Just a cliché peddled by the media to sell everything from knickers to washing powder. She was much better off focusing on her career.

The ceremony over, everyone trekked outside into the balmy evening where waiters in silken robes circulated with plates of delicious food and foaming glasses of champagne. After kissing Neesh and her new brother-in-law, who could scarcely take his eyes off the new Mrs Adani, Priya accepted a glass of champagne and slipped into the shadows. Her head was whirling from a mixture of incense and emotion and it was nice just to stand for a moment and watch the scene unfold. The ashram thronged with guests keen to dance and party. Some friends of Sanj's had rigged up a makeshift set of decks and the thrum of R&B beat like a pulse to which young partygoers gyrated until they clutched stitches or had to go and get their breath back. When Neesh came and drew her into the dancing Priya didn't resist but stamped her feet, twirled and clapped her hands with the best of them. Finally, gasping for breath, she broke from the press of bodies and made her way to the buffet, where she gulped ice-cold lemonade and waited for her pulse to return to a less alarming rhythm.

I must be getting old, she thought as she sagged against the table. I used to be able to party all night. Maybe she'd just sit the next few out and get her breath back. It was certainly nice to grab a few moments to herself. Her thoughts were still whirling like the dancers.

Her peace didn't last for long, though, because Vikram soon joined her, looking dark and handsome in a crimson shirt and black Paul Smith suit. His teeth gleamed white in his swarthy face and she found herself wondering if he'd had veneers fitted since she'd broken up with him. Come to think of it his forehead was looking very smooth too . . .

Catching her staring he grinned and clinked his glass against hers.

'Well done, babe. That went well, I thought, all things considered.'

'Like you panicking me into thinking we're in the middle of some drugs ring, you mean?' She shook her head. 'Yeah, thanks for that, Vikram. It was exactly what I needed just before the wedding.'

'Listen, just because I haven't managed to identify the product yet doesn't mean I'm wrong. We're on to something, I can feel it.'

'Maybe,' Priya said wearily. Her head was aching from thinking about it all. Perhaps she ought to forget about work and just enjoy the reception. The problem was it was becoming increasingly difficult to keep the two areas of her life separate.

'Anyway, never mind that right now,' Vik said, reading her mind in the uncanny way he sometimes did. 'This is supposed to be a celebration, after all. Look at the newlyweds. Doesn't it make you think? Isn't that what it's all about? Love, I mean?'

Priya looked over to Sanj and Neesh who were feeding each other wedding cake while their relatives looked on fondly.

'That could be us,' Vik said softly, placing his glass down. 'Baby, we could still be good together. You know I still love you – that's why I flew all the way over here. Can't you please forgive me for being such an idiot? I swear to God I'd make it up to you every day for the rest of your life.'

She gulped. In the flickering light he was so handsome and so familiar that it was tempting. Nothing would make Divya happier either and there was a lot to be said for that. Vikram was offering her the safe path to a settled life; marriage, children and a shared culture. What could be more straightforward? It was all she'd ever dreamed of once.

'Can you forgive me?' he whispered, his breath fluting against her cheeks. 'Can you?'

And suddenly Priya realised that actually, yes, she could forgive him. She was still angry at what he'd done but it no longer seemed to matter the way that it used to. She'd have other ideas, better ones even, and she'd be promoted eventually. *Besides*, said a small and honest part of herself, *maybe you could have helped Vik a little bit more?* She'd known how stressed he'd been about the promotion. He'd been up until all hours working on treatments, and she'd known too the terrible pressure that his family had put him under to succeed. But instead of giving him some ideas and encouraging the man who'd been her partner she'd compartmentalised the personal and the professional again, focusing on her own treatment and leaving Vik to become more desperate by the day.

She wasn't excusing what he'd done but she was beginning to understand it.

She sighed. 'I'm still hurt, Vik, but yes, I forgive you.'

'Fantastic!' Vik's beaming smile could have lit Jaipur for a month. 'Oh, baby, thank you! That's brilliant! I'll never let you down again, I swear to God. I'll be the best husband on the planet.'

'Whoa!' Priya cried, holding up her hands. 'I said I forgive you. I didn't say anything about us getting back together again.'

But, as usual, Vik wasn't listening to her. He was too busy waving at Ray who, camera slung over his shoulder, was still filming the party.

'Babes, I've got to catch Ray a minute. I really need to know what he's found out. There's bound to be something more about the drugs operation. He might have the evidence we need.'

'Please, just go,' Priya said wearily.

'We'll talk later. We've got so much to say to one another,' Vik promised.

'Bloody right we have,' she muttered. 'Starting with a very comprehensive explanation of the word "no".'

Vik strode away, in his haste pushing rudely through the dancers and calling for Ray at the top of his voice. Priya wished the lawn would open up and swallow him. This was her sister's wedding, for heaven's sake! Did he have to commandeer everything?

Then she laughed. Of course he did. He was Vikram after all, the man so selfish the word *me* ran through him like seaside rock. He wasn't going to change now. Thank God he'd gone, though, because here was her mother, pink-cheeked from excitement and slightly too much champagne, and no doubt hell-bent on striking while the iron was hot and arranging a marriage for Priya.

'Aha! There she is!' Divya exclaimed, bustling up to Priya and pinching her cheek. 'My other beautiful daughter! The sister of the bride! When will it be her turn, hmm?'

'Ouch! Don't, Mum!' Priya swatted her away. That cheek-pinching thing really hurt.

'Oh, I've just missed Vikram.' Divya looked disappointed. 'Such a lovely boy. He was talking to your father earlier.'

'So?' Priya fixed her heavy hair back up on to the crown of her head, loving the feeling of the cool night breeze against the nape of her neck. 'He talks to Dad all the time. They've always got on.'

Her gaze drifted across the wedding guests until she picked out the one person she'd been constantly searching for all evening. When she caught sight of Noah standing alone beneath a banyan tree, a glass of champagne held loosely in those strong slender hands and his long curls lifting softly in the warm evening breeze, her pulse quickened. How had he managed to slip into her every thought and haunt her dreams? It didn't seem to matter that she knew he was rotten to the core and had just been using her. Every time she laid eyes on him her heart twisted with longing.

More proof, as if she needed it, that she was a useless judge of men.

'No, I mean really *talking*,' Divya was continuing, her gleeful tone plucking Priya back from her gloomy thoughts. 'They were talking about your future – and about marriage! Oh, Priya! Vikram still wants to marry you; even though you've been so harsh to him he still loves you! You haven't lost your chance after all! Isn't it wonderful?'

29

Priya ripped her eyes away from Noah and stared at her mother.

'You and Dad have been discussing my getting married? To Vikram?'

'But of course! We are your parents. Who else would he talk to?'

For a second Priya felt as though she couldn't breathe. It was as though she'd been placed in a box and the lid was slowly but surely being shut on her. Why was nobody listening to a word she said?

Well, no more Mrs Nice Priya! Unless she made a stand now things were only going to get more complicated.

'I'm so glad that you finally saw sense and chose the right man,' Divya ploughed on. 'He's perfect. You couldn't have chosen a more suitable boy.'

Priya's mouth fell open. Was her mother for real? She drew breath to say her piece but Divya was in full flow now, whipping out a small notebook and pencil from her beaded bag and beginning to make notes.

'So, when are you going to make it official? We need to let people know. We can start tonight by announcing the engagement. Won't that be a wonderful end to such a special day?'

Priya shook her head, incredulous. Akhila's influence had been worse than she'd suspected.

'Mum, for heaven's sake!' she exclaimed, exaspera-ted. 'I'm not going to marry Vikram. Absolutely no way! I've told him I've forgiven him and we can still be friends and colleagues but in true Vikram style he's decided that means we're back together and everything's wonderful. That's just typical!'

'You're not back together?'

'No we're not bloody well back together!'

Divya's face fell. 'Oh, Priya, why not? I really don't understand you sometimes. You should be jumping for joy to receive such a good proposal, and from someone who was your own choice. Vikram's such a lovely young man and he has so much to offer you!'

Priya pulled a face. 'Believe me, with Vik it's more a case of what he gets out of something. He doesn't really love me. He only loves himself.'

'Love? Love?' Divya's voice rose an octave at this. 'What's love got to do with marriage? There's more at stake here than *love*, you silly girl! It's not every man who'd want to take on a woman in her late twenties, you know, or would be prepared to put up with her working until the children came along, but Vikram will. You must reconsider, Priya. He may be the best chance of marriage you ever get!'

'But I don't love him!' Priya shouted back, her hands clenched into fists. 'And I'm sorry if that disappoints you but I can't and I won't marry someone just to keep you happy! I'd rather spend the rest of my life alone than be with the wrong person. Two people should be together because they can't bear to be apart, not just because it makes a suitable match!'

Divya swelled visibly with indignation. 'There's nothing more important than a suitable match! You need to get all this foolish romantic nonsense out of your mind and do the right thing by your family. Ai! Akhila was right – I have allowed my girls to become far too westernised in their thinking. I've failed as a mother.'

Oh, great. Here came the good old guilt card. But this time Priya wasn't going to let it get to her. Besides, if Akhila knew about Ray and Ishani she'd be dismounting from her high horse very quickly indeed.

'If two people want to be together then that's all that matters,' she told her mother firmly. 'It doesn't matter how suitable or' – her eyes strayed back to Noah's lonely figure at the edge of the gathering – 'unsuitable they are. If they love each other that's all that counts. They shouldn't be afraid or ashamed to say how they feel. In fact they should be proud.'

Divya's mouth opened and shut like a goldfish's as Priya stormed on, 'So I'm really sorry if I've disappointed you, Mum, and if Dad feels let down, but you need to understand that I won't be marrying Vikram. Ever. *If* I do get married one day it'll be to a man *I* choose. A man who makes my heart sing, a man who wants the very best for me and who loves me for who I am not for what I can do for him. And if I can't find a man like that then I'd rather be single.'

Mother and daughter stared at each other, both taken aback by the heated exchange. In twenty-seven years Priya could never recall standing up to Divya and to do so now came as something of a shock. But at least her mother could no longer be under any illusions about her marrying Vikram.

Divya's eyes were bright with emotion. 'So disrespectful! Where did I go wrong with you?'

Priya's throat tightened with tears. She really didn't think she could bear another second of this, especially now Akhila was making a beeline towards them and gearing up to add her own two pennies' worth.

'I thought I heard raised voices. Is everything all right?' she asked, those boot button eyes bright with delighted curiosity.

'No it isn't,' wailed Divya. 'Priya's had an offer of marriage from a wonderful man but she's intent on turning him down. The best chance of marriage she'll ever have! Oh, Akhila, what have I done to deserve such an ungrateful child?'

'Listen to your mother, Priya,' Akhila said. 'She knows what is best for you even if you don't. You should take things further with this boy.'

'I've no intention of taking things any further, thanks! Vikram lies and cheats to get his own way, and when he's not doing that he's sneaking behind my back. Mum, how could you possibly want me to marry a man like that? Do you really think so little of me?'

'Your mother only wants the best for you. Just as I do for my Ishani.'

Priya bit her tongue hard at this. In her opinion Ishani couldn't do any better than Ray who was kind, hardworking and clearly adored her with every cell in his being. She just hoped they would be strong enough as a couple to weather the storm of Akhila's displeasure when and if they decided to go public.

'She wants to be in a love match,' Divya was explaining to Akhila, and the two women pulled faces and tutted.

'It's not just about being in love. I need to be with a man who understands me and expands my horizons,' Priya attempted to explain, 'not one who wants to keep me in a box and limit me. I want someone who's proud of what I achieve, not threatened by it! And while we're on the subject of men, I can't be with someone like Kettan either, before you both offer him as the next best solution. Kettan doesn't want *me*, he just wants to please his family. Any Hindu girl would do.'

'How dare you!' Akhila swelled up like a puffer fish. 'Kettan's a real man!'

'Oh come on! A real man doesn't spend his whole time trying to please his aunt and doing as he's told. A real man is loyal and true to himself. And a real man wouldn't change his feelings in an instant just because it makes life easier!'

'You see what I have to put up with?' wailed Divya, hand held over her heart. 'There's no telling her!'

'Kettan's a catch indeed and a good family boy but that's obviously not a quality you are concerned about, Priya Gupta,' Akhila said nastily. 'That nice young Vikram whom you are so harsh about, his uncle is a very prominent local chemist with a thriving business. He was just telling me they've spent a lot of time together this week, which is most generous of Vikram seeing as he's so busy with this documentary. Not all young people can be bothered to respect their elders, let alone spend time with them. I heard that his uncle is thinking of leaving him the business, so whoever marries him will be a very wealthy woman. Yes indeed. You may live to regret being so choosy.'

She looked so jubilant after making these spiteful comments that Priya almost laughed out loud. Akhila had unwittingly just hammered the final nail into Vik's coffin. Greedy and opportunistic to the last, no wonder he'd flown out so willingly! And now it made perfect sense why he'd been so keen to find evidence of drugs at the ashram. If his uncle was worried about opposition from the swami's clinic then Vik would also have been alarmed, especially if money was involved.

'I suppose it's a modern world now,' Akhila was pontificating, all swelled up with her own importance. 'I must say I am most fortunate in my own children, all of whom have never been anything but obedient and dutiful. They have the highest respect for our culture and traditions. See my Ishani over there with Ray? She's a good hardworking girl.' She waved a plump hand at Ishani and Ray who waved back and headed over. 'I hope she has been helpful to you, Priya?'

'She's been fantastic,' Priya said.

'She's such a good girl,' boasted Akhila. 'Baadal will have a wonderful wife in her. There you are, Ishani!' She tweaked her daughter's cheek. 'I was just saying to Divya how fortunate Baadal is to have a fiancée like you.'

'Right,' said Ishani, not quite able to look her mother in the eye.

'Good filming?' Priya asked Ray, who was just a step behind Ishani. 'See anything interesting?'

He rolled his eyes. 'Our boss Vik's lost it this time, Pri. I think he's the one on drugs!'

'Vik?' Akhila's ears pricked up at this. 'Is that the same Vik whose marriage proposal Priya just turned down? He's your boss? What are you thinking, turning your boss down? Ishani, maybe I need to marry you to Baadal fast before you get ideas too.'

Ishani's smile froze on her lips. 'Do we have to talk about Baadal right now?'

'It's a wedding. What better time? Actually, today has got me thinking that it's high time we started to put the arrangements together for your wedding. Baadal must have finished his degree by now. His PhD can wait.' Akhila's beady eyes narrowed thoughtfully. 'I think I will call his father first thing tomorrow.'

Ishani paled. 'Please don't!'

'Why ever not? It's time you were married. This engagement has been far too long already and like Priya here you're not getting any younger.'

Poor Ishani looked like a rabbit dazzled by the head-lights of a four-by-four. And I thought I had problems, thought Priya, her heart going out to the younger girl. Akhila's iron will was like a force of nature.

'Anyway,' continued Akhila, 'why wait any longer?'

Ishani struggled for a reason, or at least one she could give without causing World War Three to break out. 'Because . . . because . . .'

Then, slowly and deliberately, Ray's large hand fell on to Ishani's slim shoulder, and rested there in a gentle but powerful gesture.

'Because *we're* together,' he said quietly. 'Ishani and I are a couple, Mrs A, and that's why you can't arrange her marriage to another man. I love her, she loves me and the bottom line is that we want to be together.'

Now it was Akhila's turn to do a goldfish impression.

'I'm really sorry to upset you,' Ray added, but in a tone that wouldn't be argued with, 'and I know this comes as a shock, but there's no way Ishani will be marrying Baadal now, however awkward it might be to call the betrothal off.' His hand slipped from Ishani's shoulder to her waist as he drew her protectively against him. 'The only person I hope she'll marry is me. If she'll have me, that is.'

Ishani gasped. 'Oh my God! Seriously? Do you really mean it?'

He laughed, smiling tenderly down into her upturned and shining-eyed face.

'Course I bloody do, pet! Now I've found you I'm not going to be stupid enough to let you get away. You're the best thing that's ever happened to me and I love you to bits. Do you want me to get down on my knees and prove it?'

Ishani pulled his head down towards her, covering his face in kisses. 'No, that won't be necessary. I'll marry you! Oh my God! Of course I will!'

This display of emotion was the catalyst that enabled Akhila to find her tongue again.

'You'll do no such thing!' she thundered, purple with indignation. 'You're already engaged, young lady, and I have absolutely no intention of breaking my word and destroying our family's good name. You'll do as you're told and marry Baadal!'

'I won't! Besides, Baadal's already got a girlfriend in the States,' said Ishani blithely. 'He'll be over the moon to get shot of me, so chillax, Mum, as Neesh would say! He's never had any real intention of marrying me and I've certainly never wanted to marry him. I'm going to marry Ray so you'll just have to get used to the idea. He's *my* choice and I love him.'

There was no arguing with that. It seemed Ishani could be as determined as her mother, and as she and Ray slipped away into the velvet night, whispering and exchanging soft kisses, Akhila was left huffing and puffing in outrage. Finally she waddled away complaining loudly, leaving Divya staggered.

'Well,' she said slowly, giving Priya a rueful smile, 'maybe I'm not the only parent who hasn't got things right.'

Priya slipped her arm into her mother's. 'It's like I said, when two people really love one another culture and suitability and all that other stuff really don't matter any more. Ray and Ishani are soulmates; from the moment they met they were meant to be together. It was obvious.'

'Hmm.' Divya wasn't quite ready to concede this point but she kissed Priya and smiled. 'I understand what you're saying, but don't overspice the masala. Now, all this drama has given me quite a thirst. I can see Chandani and Bhavani over by the bar. I think I'll go and get a cool drink.'

Priya laughed, knowing that Divya could hardly wait to spread this exciting new piece of gossip with the aunties. Still, ever since they'd arrived Akhila's boasting about her family had known no bounds so she didn't blame her mother one bit for enjoying the sense of Schadenfreude.

And on a purely selfish note the heat was now well and truly off her and Vikram.

Priya suddenly felt as though a ton of concrete had been lifted from her shoulders. She'd been right not to try again with Vik. He wasn't the one for her. She couldn't be with someone who always had an agenda.

She needed someone whose motives were altogether purer . . .

Leaving Divya to her gossiping she crossed the soft lawn, picking her way through the chatting groups and skirting round the edge of the herb garden. The moon had risen now and was floating high in the darkening sapphire-blue sky, silvering the gardens and sprinkling magic across the sleeping world. The dance music had slipped into a slow ballad and couples swayed together to the gentle rhythm, smiling into each other's eyes and holding each other close in the lamp light. Priya sighed wistfully. If only things had been different with Noah. How would it feel to dance with him beneath the silvery moon?

Wonderful. That's how it would have felt, but now she'd never know for sure.

Then someone cleared their throat and abruptly she was aware she was no longer alone because a slender figure had materialised from the shadows and was standing next to her. A warm calloused hand touched her elbow and two dark grey eyes sought hers.

The swami. At last.

'I'm so sorry to interrupt when you are so deep in thought,' Attuttama said, her voice soft as silk but with an underlying edge of steel that brooked no argument, 'but I think, Priya, it's about time you and I had a little talk, isn't it?'

'You're troubled.' The swami stated this as a fact. Her voice, so low and musical, was as soothing as a cool summer's breeze and her gentle face wore an expression of what looked like genuine concern. Priya had the sudden sensation that she could tell this woman anything and not be judged or found lacking. Then she brought herself up short because that was exactly the feeling she'd had with Noah and look where that had ended up. They were probably both consummate con artists and the empathy routine key to softening up their next victim. Priya raised her chin defiantly; it wasn't going to be her.

'I'm fine,' she said sharply. 'A bit concerned about some of the strange things I've seen here, which I guess is what you want to talk to me about. You're wondering what conclusions I may have come to about what really goes on here, aren't you? Just like I'm wondering about the secret crops and the vows of silence.'

Attuttama inclined her head, her silver hair sweeping her cheeks, and smiled sadly. 'No, Priya, my dear, that wasn't why I wanted to speak to you. I was actually hoping to apologise if you've felt deliberately excluded from areas of our life here. That was certainly never my intention and I'm truly sorry if it's made your job difficult or caused you to be distressed. I had no idea Noah had chosen to keep you away from certain elements of our work at the ashram. Please believe that he alone made that decision. It certainly wasn't sanctioned by me.'

'You've been talking to Noah about me?' Priya rounded on the swami, furious at this idea. 'And what exactly did he have to say?'

'He admitted that he hadn't been honest with you and he's truly sorry for that,' the swami told her. 'But his intentions are pure, Priya, even if the outcome has clouded your impressions of us a little. Noah deliberately kept you away from the business side of the ashram because he wanted you to see only the magic and spiritual healing. He felt these things were what you needed.'

'Oh.' Priya was taken aback because this was almost word for word what Noah had told her. Maybe that bit was true?

'Rest assured he certainly wasn't acting on my instructions and he's been chastised for that,' the swami continued, sinking gracefully on to a scarlet cushion and folding her supple body into the lotus position. Patting the cushion beside her in invitation she added, 'Tomorrow you will see everything because we truly have nothing to hide here. I'll personally show you every area of the ashram and explain exactly how we work. You may of course film everything. We have no secrets.'

Joining Attuttama on the ground, and feeling

ashamed that although she must be at least thirty years younger she was about as bendy as a plank, Priya felt rather confused. After casting the swami as the villain of the piece it was confusing to have to do a sudden U-turn. None of it made any sense, either. Why would Noah deliberately go against the swami's instructions and try to protect her from the reality of the ashram? What was in it for him?

'You and Noah are far more alike than you think, my dear,' smiled the swami when Priya voiced these thoughts. 'Both of you work very hard to control people's perceptions and to keep areas of your lives apart.' Her full lips curled into an indulgent smile as though she knew a secret far too important to share, but which delighted her none the less. 'Noah has spoken about you to me a great deal. He understands you better than you know.'

'He does not!' Priya flared. 'He's been playing me for a fool and using me.'

The swami fixed her with eyes as calm and deep as mill pools.

'That does not sound at all like Noah,' she said quietly. 'Besides, it doesn't make sense.'

'It does if there's something big to hide. For instance, are you growing illegal drugs here? Is the ashram just a cover for other less worthy activities?'

Priya half expected Attuttama to be horrendously insulted or to deny it strenuously in *the lady doth protest too much* style. Maybe she'd even start yelling and have Noah throw the entire wedding party off her land, who knew? But she hadn't anticipated that the swami would merely throw back her head and laugh.

No. She hadn't seen that coming.

'Oh my!' Attuttama gasped, wiping her eyes and shaking her head. 'Is that what you've been thinking? That we're growing opium or something? And that's why Noah didn't show you the books or the furthest crop fields? Oh, my poor dear Priya! When you put it like that even I must admit it looks pretty incriminating!'

'What about the "product" that you were discussing yesterday with the business couple?' Priya demanded, not inclined to be fooled by the swami's compassionate approach. Ray's video tape was still their strongest evidence so far. How would Attuttama explain *that* away? 'You were talking about shipping it and weighing it. That hardly sounds innocent to me!'

'Ah yes,' nodded the swami. 'Your friend was filming us, wasn't he?' She glanced across the ashram to where Ray and Ishani were deep in conversation with Akhila, the gangly Ray gesticulating wildly like a dancing daddy-long-legs. 'He's a lovely boy but hardly inconspicuous. He was crawling in the flower beds; dear of him! I did chuckle.'

There went Ray's career as an undercover cameraman, thought Priya.

'The business lady as you call her, Laura Chase, is a chronic asthmatic,' Attuttama explained. 'She's a top lawyer and lives in LA where it's horribly polluted and the only way she keeps well is through using steroids, which thin her skin and bones and have dreadful long term effects on her health. She's been in despair until she read that we've been growing a plant called Ephedra, or Amsania in Hindi, which we use to treat bronchial asthma. Laura has had some amazing results and understandably she's very keen to continue with the treatment when she goes home. The problem is, though, that the product we make is very delicate, being light and heat sensitive, and I just don't know if it would travel well. There are also legal implications of shipping herbs into the United States. Poor Laura may have to wait a while but it's very hard for her when she feels that there's a way to get her life back.'

'Oh.' Priya felt foolish. That would explain why she hadn't said much on the bus then. The poor woman hadn't been able to breathe.

'I'm afraid all the so-called "miracles" that you've read about are actually rather mundane,' said the swami with an apologetic shrug. 'I treat conditions like diabetes, high blood pressure and arthritis with herbs that we grow in the hills. It's homoeopathy Indian style, nothing more and nothing less. I'll show you our crops tomorrow and I'll make sure that Noah explains and points out every plant.'

But Priya wasn't about to let Noah off the hook so easily. After all, where did he fit in? And what about the peculiar conversation she'd heard him having with Texan Clay?

'So how come Noah knows all about the plants if he's just here on retreat too?' Priya challenged. 'He's up to something, admit it. I overheard him talking to the Texan man, Clay, about advertising and speculating to accumulate.'

Attuttama raised an arched silver brow. 'Come, now. Noah never said that.'

'No, Clay did. But Noah was in on it. Be honest with

me, Swami Attuttama, he's more than just an ashram guide, isn't he? He's not who he seems to be.'

The swami exhaled slowly. 'Noah is exactly the man you see, Priya. He is honest, and loyal and trustworthy. You should have no doubt of his sincerity.'

That was easy for her to say, thought Priya darkly. *She* hadn't been seduced as a ploy to stop her overhearing conversations.

'But you are right when you say that he is hiding something,' Attuttama agreed, closing her eyes and exhaling again. 'Like you, Noah needs to compartmentalise his life. Yes, he is a dearly beloved disciple and guide at the ashram but he's only here for short periods. When he's away working Noah is an agricultural scientist, and a highly respected one. He's recently spent a great deal of time in Ethiopia working on developing grain that needs very little water and teaching in a village school there in his spare time.'

'He said his father was Ethiopian,' Priya recalled.

Attuttama looked surprised. 'He's mentioned his father?'

She nodded. 'Please, go on.'

The swami collected herself visibly. 'Using his knowledge of crop growth and my knowledge of homoeopathy Noah and I are hoping to build a clinic here where we can treat people effectively and holistically. The spirit and the body treated together, if you will, and healed through the power of nature and prayer.'

'Wow. It certainly beats Boots,' said Priya.

The swami laughed. 'We won't be selling makeup, that's for sure. Noah's already concerned that we're in danger of becoming too commercialised. He wants to keep the project under wraps until it's more established. Clay though sees a business opportunity and wants to invest in us and advertise what we do in the USA, which in some ways would be a blessing, but Noah fears if we become too successful it will destroy the peace of the ashram for ever. He feels passionately that the spirituality of the ancient shrines and the landscape have as much to do with the healing as the herbs.'

Priya recalled the ancient temple where Noah had taken her just to be and allow the serenity of the place to fill her soul. It made sense that he would feel antipathy to losing that sense of isolation and peace. In fact, everything that Attuttama was saying made perfect sense.

Did that mean that maybe Noah hadn't been using her after all? Her heart rose like a helium balloon at the thought.

'There's more that you need to know,' the swami said, reaching out a nut-brown wrinkled hand to touch Priya's arm. 'It's about Noah. He isn't just a guide here, he's—'

But what the swami was about to disclose Priya didn't get to discover because at that exact moment there was a major commotion, shouting and singing and chanting, as a large group of people holding torches melted from the tree line and descended into the ashram. Their faces dancing in the flames, they began to form a queue, moving swiftly towards the low-rise buildings like a procession of soldier ants. A cold sweat broke out between Priya's shoulder blades. Were they under attack or something?

Attuttama though didn't seem at all fazed, springing to her feet with feline grace as her face creased into a warm smile of welcome.

'The Bhil villagers! My goodness, I hadn't expected them already!'

For a small and elderly woman she could certainly walk fast and Priya scuttled in her wake, bunching her sari into her fists in her haste to keep up. As she got closer to the throng of people she saw that they were dressed in brightly hued robes and bearing wooden bowls. Moments later the swami was swallowed up in their midst, her slight form vanishing as hands clutched at her robes and people clamoured for her blessing.

Priya was riveted. Whatever was going on now?

'My God!' cried Vikram, materialising at her side and brandishing a camera. 'This is it, Priya! This is the coup we've been after!'

Confused, she looked from the joyful singing Bhil back to the jubilant man at her side. 'What on earth are you on about?'

'I've been talking to some of the villagers,' he panted, peering through the viewfinder and zooming in on the crowd. 'They said they've come for the miracles; I've recorded every word. Just wait, Priya. The swami's going to start doling out the drugs. Just you wait and see. And we'll have it all on film!'

He'd finally flipped, thought Priya; all the stress and crazy ambition had finally got to him. Aloud, she said, 'I think you're making a big mistake, Vikram. There are no drugs here, honestly. You've got it all wrong. The swami's just explained everything. They're growing herbs for homoeopathic treatments, not class A narcotics.'

Vik snorted rudely. 'God, it didn't take long for her to sucker you in, did it? I thought you had a bit more intelligence. Ten minutes with Guru Ganja and you're spouting more crap than the Jaipur sewers.'

'She's telling the truth!' Priya cried. 'And if you weren't so desperate to prove your crazy drug theory right you'd see it!'

'Follow me and we'll soon see who's right, and I guarantee it won't be you!' Vikram bragged, brandishing his camera and charging off into the throng like a deranged rhino. With a huge sigh Priya followed, cringing when she heard him demanding to know where the drugs were and how often the Bhil came down to score. Priya didn't know much about drug taking but she was fairly certain that anyone who wanted to buy them was usually a little more subtle about it than turning up with their entire village in tow.

Something told her Vik was about to make a total idiot of himself.

'What's going on?' Priya asked one of the ashram guides who was scuttling along carrying a huge basket of coarse bread. 'Why are the Bhil people here?'

The guide paused, heaving the basket on to her hip. 'They've come for the wedding, of course! It's a tradition here when there's a marriage that the villagers come and celebrate too. Listen, they're singing blessings to the newly married couple. In return Attuttama will feed them and give them gifts of clothing and medicine. She's even arranged for one of the guests who's a doctor to look at their children too. See? No wonder they revere her so!'

Priya narrowed her eyes against the torch glare and sure enough in the dancing shadows the ashram guides were busy giving out food and clothing to the villagers. She glimpsed Noah, his smile wide and bright in the darkness, with a small child clasped in his arms, striding towards the business woman's husband. If he was her husband, of course; she'd just assumed that as she'd assumed everything else, jumping to conclusions because it was easier than sitting down and facing the facts.

The man was holding out his arms for the child and round his neck was a stethoscope. His briefcase was open beside him and it was full of medicines.

Priya's hands flew to her mouth. Of course! He was Laura Chase's *doctor*. Not her husband.

'The villagers love the swami,' the guide explained proudly. 'Even in the short time she's been in charge here Attuttama has done so much to improve their lives. She's even arranged inoculations for all the children and paid for a new bore hole. They haven't had a case of dysentery in the village now for almost eighteen months.'

'But what about the miracles?' Priya wanted to know. 'My colleague said that the villagers were adamant they were here for miracles. What did they mean by that?'

The guide laughed. 'Just look around. These people are poor and needy. They live in poverty and sickness but tonight they have food, and clothes and medicine. For each and every one of them those things alone are miraculous, don't you agree?'

'Yes,' said Priya slowly. 'I do. I really do.'

Happiness started to whirl round and round inside her heart like a giant Catherine wheel. She felt like singing and dancing with the Bhil, and throwing her arms around the swami. Vik might have a face like thunder and no story – at least not the bad news one he'd so wanted – but as far as Priya was concerned everything in the world was perfect. The swami had been telling the truth all along. She really was genuine.

And if Attuttama was genuine, then, of course, Noah was too.

31

Even at midnight Neesh and Sanjeev's wedding reception showed no sign of winding down. Although the Bhil villagers had long since returned to their mountainside homes the ashram still thronged with guests keen to dance and party into the small hours. Everyone was having a fantastic time, except maybe Akhila whose expression could have soured milk at a hundred paces. Vik too was in a huff after realising there really wasn't a drugs ring at the ashram, but the guests were having the time of their lives. Yet there was one person missing. One person to whom she really owed an enormous apology. Priya's gaze drifted across the wedding guests until she picked out the lone figure she'd been constantly searching for all evening.

Noah.

She'd seen him in passing, carrying medicine to the Bhil and distributing food, but they hadn't yet had a chance to speak. Every time she recalled how swift she'd been to dismiss him as a conman Priya felt weak with shame. He'd come looking for her at the start of the wedding, his eyes wide with honesty and hope, and what had he got in return but sarcasm and rejection?

She hoped that he would give her a chance to explain and apologise even if their friendship was over.

There he was, standing by a banyan tree. As though sensing Priya was close he turned his head and she felt his gaze upon her like the most gentle of kisses, and remembering again how it had felt to kiss him she knew a flush was rising to her cheeks. Then he was walking towards her, those long powerful legs eating up the distance between them in seconds, until they were so close that they were almost touching. It wasn't cold but suddenly her skin rippled with goosebumps.

'Hey,' said Noah softly.

'Hey,' she murmured back, and as their eyes locked her heart spluttered with longing. It was time to be brave, to blur the private and personal once and for all, and explain that she understood exactly why he'd tried to protect her.

'I'm sorry,' she said. 'I thought—'

Noah stopped her words by laying a gentle forefinger across her lips. 'Shh. I know already and I understand.' His eyes were dark but molasses warm as he smiled down at her and Priya felt a jolt of attraction so sharp that she inhaled sharply. It's now or never, she thought. Time to take a risk and time to take a break from being predictable and anal and organised.

'Will you hold me?' she whispered.

He stepped closer, so close that his lips almost brushed hers, and as though under a spell she slipped her arms around his neck, loving the feeling of those taut muscles moving and swelling as his arms in turn pulled her close.

Being held beneath the moon by Noah was even

better than she'd imagined. It was heaven.

Then his lips were touching hers and suddenly nothing else mattered any more. Even when Ray and Ishani approached with their Steadicam Priya and Noah just held each other all the closer, answering kiss after kiss with a hungry passion while the cameras rolled and all the areas of Priya's life blurred into one. Nothing existed except this kaleidoscope of perfect sensations and being held in Noah's arms. Why had she ever believed anything else was important?

Finally they broke apart and stood smiling at one another in delighted surprise.

'I think we've just stopped the party,' said Noah. 'And by the look of her, your mother wants to stab me.'

Sure enough Divya was glowering at them. Vik and Kettan didn't look too impressed either. Priya supposed at least now they both had their answer.

She touched Noah's cheek, loving the feeling of his smooth honey-warm skin. 'Never mind her, or the rest of them. None of that matters.'

'About bloody time, you guys!' said Ray, zooming in on them while Ishani brandished the boom mike. 'Me and Ish were almost ready to lock you in a room and tell you to sort it out. Weren't we, babe?'

'Too right!' Ishani agreed. 'And on a purely selfish note you've totally taken the heat off us. My mum and yours can bitch away all night long now they're equals!'

'Let them,' said Priya happily. 'I really don't care what anyone else thinks!'

Now family, friends and everyone at the ashram knew just how she felt about Noah, but what was even better than that was that she finally knew too. As for

Noah, somehow he'd always known. Was it possible to think that he'd known her before they'd even met, or had she been immersed in Hindu mysticism for too long?

Oh, whatever! He was here right now and that was all that mattered.

'I'm sorry I leapt to conclusions,' she told Noah as with fingers laced together they strolled away from the beaming Ray and Ishani. 'I was too hasty to think the worst of this place and of you.'

He shook his dark head. 'There's nothing to apologise for. The swami was right: if I'd been more open with you then there'd never have been any confusion in the first place, would there? I kept secrets.'

'To keep me happy,' she reminded him. 'Not to hurt me.'

'Never to hurt you,' he said adamantly. 'I saw you were in pain and I wanted this place to work its magic on you.'

'Oh, believe me, it has. It really has!'

They paused to kiss again, a butter-soft kiss this time, and Noah traced her face wonderingly with his fingertips.

'Is this real?' he breathed. 'Or are you a dream?'

She laughed. 'I think you'll probably soon find I'm more of a nightmare. At least that's what my mother's probably thinking right this second.'

They both glanced over at Divya, who was a perfect study in outrage, while Akhila looked on gloatingly. Suddenly Ishani's behaviour didn't seem quite so awful.

'Attuttama's beckoning us,' Noah said, squeezing her

hand. 'Shall we join her? I know she'll be really pleased that we've settled our differences. She really likes you.'

'She does?' Priya felt absurdly pleased. 'Well, I like her too. A lot, actually.'

He pulled her close, dropping a kiss on the crown of her head. 'I'm glad about that. She's a special person, and so wise. The swami always knows best, although it's taken me a long time to come round to the idea. She knew how I felt about you before I'd even admitted it to myself.'

'It sounds like you've had better guidance than me,' Priya said as they meandered towards Attuttama. 'I met a psychic a few months ago at my friend's hen night.'

He raised a dark eyebrow. 'A psychic, eh? And what did she tell you? That you'd bump into a tall dark stranger?'

'God! If she had I'd be well impressed. But no, she was way off the mark as it happened. She told me that *in matters of love, mother knows best*. She'd obviously never met my mother.'

But Noah didn't laugh. Instead he looked thoughtful. 'In matters of love, mother knows best? I wonder . . .'

'Noah! Priya!' Leaping to her feet Attuttama reached out and grasped their hands. Her lined face was wreathed in smiles and she kissed them both warmly. 'I'm so glad you've made up your quarrel!'

Priya blushed. That was one way of putting it. Her lips still tingled from kissing Noah and her hair was probably all over the place. Sensible, thoughtful, well-planned Priya Gupta seemed to have vanished into the ether, which was probably a good thing seeing as she'd been pretty miserable a lot of the time.

'From the first time Noah mentioned you, Priya, I knew there was going to be something special between you,' continued Attuttama with a satisfied nod. 'When he planned a hike into the hills to share the temple with you, I thought to myself, This one's different!'

Now it was Noah's turn to blush beneath his Caramac-smooth skin. 'In matters of love, mother knows best,' he sighed, squeezing Priya's hand. 'I told you, she's never wrong.'

'Sorry?' She looked from the swami to Noah and then back again, feeling bemused. 'What did you say?'

Attuttama wagged her finger at Noah. 'You haven't told her yet? Is it really that embarrassing?'

'I'm thirty-two, a bit old to still find you embarrassing, although your matchmaking over the last few weeks has almost been enough to make me change my mind!' Noah laughed. Then he took Priya's hand and squeezed it gently. 'Priya Gupta, I'd like to make an introduction, one that's maybe a little overdue. As well as being my swami, Attuttama lays another claim to me. She's also my mother.'

Priya gasped. Of course! It was suddenly so glaringly obvious. Attuttama and Noah both had the same wide-spaced grey eyes, liquid grace and an innate gentleness of spirit. How ever had she missed it? Maybe it was time she packed in being a journalist.

'The swami's your mother?'

Noah fixed his mother with a beady look. 'I have a feeling my mother has been rather more involved in your spiritual guidance than she lets on. I've never known her take a vow of silence before.'

Kissing him Attuttama said, 'Well, I'd never heard

you so captivated by someone before. What else was a mother supposed to do? It was strange, you know, but when I came back from my retreat I just felt a sudden *need* to take a vow of silence, seeing as he was doing such a good job of being your guide. But then I started to think I was losing my edge because all you two seemed to do was squabble. For two such intelligent young people you were incredibly slow to realise how perfect you are for one another! And you know I'm right! As you've already said, in matters of love, mother knows best!'

Noah turned to Priya, his lips curling upwards with amusement. 'Maybe there was something in that prophecy of yours after all?'

She smiled back at him. 'Well, who are we to argue with Fate?'

Noah cupped her face in his hands and then he was kissing her again with such tenderness that her heart shimmered with pure joy as she wound her fingers into his long curls and kissed him back, while Ray and Ishani and Neesh and Sanjeev cheered their approval and the swami clapped her hands in delight.

And in an instant Priya Gupta, who hadn't believed in Fate or destiny or soulmates, knew beyond all doubt that she did now.

How could she not? The proof was right here in her arms.

little black dress

brings you fantastic new books like these
every month - find out more at
www.littleblackdressbooks.com

Why not link up with other devoted Little Black
Dress fans on our Facebook group? Simply type
Little Black Dress Books into Facebook to join up.

And if you want to be the first
to hear the latest news on all things
Little Black Dress, just send the details below to
littleblackdressmarketing@headline.co.uk
and we'll sign you up to our lovely email
newsletter (and we promise that we won't share
your information with anybody else!).*

Name: _____

Email Address: _____

Date of Birth: _____

Region/Country: _____

What's your favourite Little Black Dress book?

_____

How many Little Black Dress books have you read?_____

*You can be removed from the mailing list at any time

Pick up a *little black dress* – it's a girl thing.

978 0 7553 4715 5

THE FARMER NEEDS A WIFE
Janet Gover
PBO £5.99

Rural romances become all the rage when editor Helen Woodley starts a new magazine column profiling Australia's lovelorn farmers. But a lot of people (and Helen herself) are about to find out that the course of true love ain't ever smooth . . .

It's not all haystacks and pitchforks, ladies – get ready for a scorching outback read!

HIDE YOUR EYES
Alison Gaylin
PBO £5.99

Samantha Leiffer's in big trouble: the chest she saw a sinister man dumping into the Hudson river contained a dead body, meaning she's now a witness in a murder case. It's just as well hot, hard-line detective John Krull is by her side . . .

'Alison Gaylin is my new must-read' Harlen Coben

978 0 7553 4802 2

You can buy any of these other
Little Black Dress titles from your
bookshop or *direct from the publisher*.

FREE P&P AND UK DELIVERY
(Overseas and Ireland £3.50 per book)

TO ORDER SIMPLY CALL THIS NUMBER

01235 400 414

or visit our website: www.headline.co.uk

Prices and availability subject to change without notice.